THE
POSTMASTER'S
DAUGHTER

Louis Tracy

1st WORLD
LIBRARY
Literary Society

The Postmaster's Daughter

Louis Tracy

© 1st World Library – Literary Society, 2005
PO Box 2211
Fairfield, IA 52556
www.1stworldlibrary.org
First Edition

LCCN: 2004195646

Softcover ISBN: 1-4218-0468-9
Hardcover ISBN: 1-4218-0368-2
eBook ISBN: 1-4218-0568-5

Purchase *"The Postmaster's Daughter"*
as a traditional bound book at:
www.1stWorldLibrary.org/purchase.asp?ISBN=1-4218-0468-9

1st World Library Literary Society is a nonprofit organization dedicated to promoting literacy by:

- Creating a free internet library accessible from any computer worldwide.
- Hosting writing competitions and offering book publishing scholarships.

Readers interested in supporting literacy through sponsorship, donations or membership please contact:
literacy@1stworldlibrary.org
Check us out at: www.1stworldlibrary.ORG
and start downloading free ebooks today.

The Postmaster's Daughter
contributed by Tim, Ed & Rodney
in support of
1st World Library Literary Society

CONTENTS

CHAPTER I

THE FACE AT THE WINDOW

John Menzies Grant, having breakfasted, filled his pipe, lit it, and strolled out bare-headed into the garden. The month was June, that glorious rose-month which gladdened England before war-clouds darkened the summer sky. As the hour was nine o'clock, it is highly probable that many thousands of men were then strolling out into many thousands of gardens in precisely similar conditions; but, given youth, good health, leisure, and a fair amount of money, it is even more probable that few among the smaller number thus roundly favored by fortune looked so perplexed as Grant.

Moreover, his actions were eloquent as words. A spacious French window had been cut bodily out of the wall of an old-fashioned room, and was now thrown wide to admit the flower-scented breeze. Between this window and the right-hand angle of the room was a smaller window, square-paned, high above the ground level, and deeply recessed - in fact just the sort of window which one might expect to find in a farm-house built two centuries ago, when light and air were rigorously excluded from interiors. The two windows told the history of The Hollies at a glance. The little one had served the needs of a "best" room for several generations of Sussex yeomen. Then had come some iconoclast who hewed a big rectangle through the solid stone-work, converted the oak-panelled apartment into a most comfortable dining-room, built a new wing with a gable, changed a farm-yard into a flower-bordered lawn, and generally played havoc with Georgian utility while carrying out a determined scheme of landscape gardening.

Happily, the wrecker was content to let well enough alone after enlarging the house, laying turf, and planting shrubs and flowers. He found The Hollies a ramshackle place, and left it even more so, but with a new note of artistry and several unexpectedly charming vistas. Thus, the big double window opened straight into an irregular garden which merged insensibly into a sloping lawn bounded by a river-pool. The bank on the other side of the stream rose sharply and was well wooded. Above the crest showed the thatched roofs or red tiles of Steynholme, which was a village in the time of William the Conqueror, and has remained a village ever since. Frame this picture in flowering shrubs, evergreens, a few choice firs, a copper beech, and some sturdy oaks shadowing the lawn, and the prospect on a June morning might well have led out into the open any young man with a pipe.

But John Menzies Grant seemed to have no eye for a scene that would have delighted a painter. He turned to the light, scrutinized so closely a strip of turf which ran close to the wall that he might have been searching for a lost diamond, and then peered through the lowermost left-hand pane of the small window into the room he had just quitted.

The result of this peeping was remarkable in more

Louis Tracy

ways than one.

A stout, elderly, red-faced woman, who had entered the room soon after she heard Grant's chair being moved, caught sight of the intent face. She screamed loudly, and dropped a cup and saucer with a clatter on to a Japanese tray.

Grant hurried back to the French window. In his haste he did not notice a long shoot of a Dorothy Perkins rose which trailed across his path, and it struck him smartly on the cheek.

"I'm afraid I startled you, Mrs. Bates," he said, smiling so pleasantly that no woman or child could fail to put trust in him.

"You did that, sir," agreed Mrs. Bates, collapsing into the chair Grant had just vacated.

Like most red-faced people, Mrs. Bates turned a bluish purple when alarmed, and her aspect was so distressing now that Grant's smile was banished by a look of real concern.

"I'm very sorry," he said contritely. "I had no notion you were in the room. Shall I call Minnie?"

Minnie, it may be explained, was Mrs. Bates's daughter and assistant, the two, plus a whiskered Bates, gardener and groom, forming the domestic establishment presided over by Grant.

"Nun-no, sir," stuttered the housekeeper. "It's stupid of me. But I'm not so young as I was, an' me heart jumps at little things."

Grant saw that she was recovering, though slowly. He thought it best not to make too much of the incident; but asked solicitously if he might give her some brandy.

Mrs. Bates remarked that she was "not so bad as that," rose valiantly, and went on with her work. Her employer, who had gone into the garden again, saw out of the tail of his eye that she vanished with a half-laden tray. In a couple of minutes the daughter appeared, and finished the slight task of clearing the table; meanwhile, Grant kept away from the small window. Being a young man who cultivated the habit of observation, he noticed that Minnie, too, cast scared glances at the window. When the girl had finally quitted the room, he laughed in a puzzled way.

"Am I dreaming, or are there visions about?" he murmured.

Urged, seemingly, by a sort of curiosity, he surveyed the room a second time through the same pane of glass. Being tall, he had to stoop slightly. Within, on the opposite side of the ledge, he saw the tiny brass candlestick with its inch of candle which he had used over-night while searching for a volume of Scott in the book-case lining the neighboring wall. Somehow, this simplest of domestic objects brought a thrill of recollection.

"Oh, dash it all!" he growled good-humoredly, "I'm getting nervy. I must chuck this bad habit of working late, and use the blessed hours of daylight."

Yet, as he sauntered down the lawn toward the stream, he knew well that he would do nothing of the sort. He loved that time of peace between ten at night and one in the morning. His thoughts ran vagrom then. Fantasies took shape under his pen which, in the cold light of morning, looked unreal and nebulous, though he had the good sense to restrain criticism within strict limits, and corrected style rather than matter. He was a writer, an essayist with no slight leaven of the poet, and had learnt early that the everyday world held naught in common with the brooding of the soul.

But he was no long-haired dreamer of impossible things. Erect and square-shouldered, he had passed through Sandhurst into the army, a profession abandoned because of its humdrum nature, when an unexpectedly "fat" legacy rendered him independent. He looked exactly what he was, a healthy, clean-minded young Englishman, with a physique that led to occasional bouts of fox-hunting and Alpine climbing, and a taste in literature that brought about the consumption of midnight oil. This latter is not a mere trope. Steynholme is far removed from such modern "conveniences" as gas and electricity.

At present he had no more definite object in life than to watch the trout rising in the pool. He held the fishing rights over half a mile of a noted river, but, by force of the law of hospitality, as it were, the stretch of water bordering the lawn was a finny sanctuary. Once, he halted, and looked fixedly at a dormer window in a cottage just visible above the trees on the opposite slope. Such a highly presentable young man might well expect to find a dainty feminine form appearing just in that place, and eke return the greeting of a waved hand. But the window remained blank - windows refused to yield any information that morning - and he passed on.

The lawn dipped gently to the water's edge, until the close-clipped turf gave way to pebbles and sand. In that spot the river widened and deepened until its current was hardly perceptible in fine weather. When the sun was in the west the trees and roofs of Steynholme were so clearly reflected in the mirror of the pool that a photograph of the scene needed close scrutiny ere one could determine whether or not it was being held upside down. But the sun shone directly on the water now, so the shelving bottom was visible, and Grant's quick eye was drawn to a rope trailing into the depths, and fastened to an iron staple driven firmly into the shingle.

He was so surprised that he spoke aloud.

"What in the world is that?" he almost gasped; a premonition of evil was so strong in him that he actually gazed in stupefaction at a blob of water and a quick-spreading ring where a fat trout rose lazily in midstream.

Somehow, too, he resisted the first impulse of the active side of his temperament, and did not instantly tug at the rope.

Instead, he shouted: -

"Hi, Bates!"

An answering hail came from behind a screen of laurels on the right of the house. There lay the stables, and Bates would surely be grooming the cob which supplied a connecting link between The Hollies and the railway for the neighboring market-town.

Bates came, a sturdy block of a man who might have been hewn out of a Sussex oak. His face, hands, and arms were the color of oak, and he moved with a stiffness that suggested wooden joints.

Evidently, he expected an order for the dogcart, and stood stock still when he reached the lawn. But Grant, who had gathered his wits, summoned him with crooked forefinger, and Bates jerked slowly on.

"What hev' ye done to yer face, sir?" he inquired.

Grant was surprised. He expected no such question.

"So far as I know, I've not been making any great alteration in it," he said.

"But it's all covered wi' blood," came the disturbing statement.

A handkerchief soon gave evidence that Bates was not exaggerating. Miss - or is it Madam? - Dorothy Perkins can scratch as well as look sweet, and a thorn had opened a small vein in Grant's cheek which bled to a surprising extent.

"Oh, it is nothing," he said. "I remember now - a rose shoot caught me as I went back into the dining-room a moment ago. I shouted for you to come and see *this*."

Soon the two were examining the rope and the staple.

"Now who put *that* there?" said Bates, not asking a question but rather stating a thesis.

"It was not here yesterday," commented his master,

accepting all that Bates's words implied.

"No, sir, that it wasn't. I was a-cuttin' the lawn till nigh bed-time, an' it wasn't there then."

Grant was himself again. He stooped and grabbed the rope.

"Suppose we solve the mystery," he said.

"No need to dirty your hands, sir," put in Bates. "Let I haul 'un in."

In a few seconds the oaken tint in his face grew many shades lighter.

"Good Gawd!" he wheezed. At the end of the rope was the body of a woman.

There are few more distressing objects than a drowned corpse. On that bright June morning a dreadful apparition lost little of its grim repulsiveness because the body was that of a young and good-looking woman.

If one searched England it would be difficult to find two men of differing temperaments less likely to yield to the stress of even the most trying circumstance than Grant and Bates, yet, during some agonized moments the one, of tried courage and fine mettle, was equally horrified and shaken as the other, a gnarled and hard-grained rustic. It was he from whom speech might least be expected who first found his tongue. Bates, who had stooped, straightened himself slowly.

"By gum!" he said, "this be a bad business, Mr. Grant.

Who is she? She's none of our Steynholme lasses."

Still Grant uttered no word. He just looked in horror at the poor husk of a woman who in life had undoubtedly been beautiful. She was well but quietly dressed, and her clothing showed no signs of violence. The all-night soaking in the river revealed some pitiful little feminine secrets, such as a touch of make-up on lips and cheeks, and the dark roots of abundant hair which had been treated chemically to lighten its color. The eyes were closed, and for that Grant was conscious of a deep thankfulness. Had those sightless eyes stared at him he felt he would have cried aloud in terror. The firm, well-molded lips were open, as though uttering a last protest against an untimely fate. Of course, both men were convinced that murder had been done. Not only were arms and body bound in a manner that was impossible of accomplishment by the dead woman herself, but an ugly wound on the smooth forehead seemed to indicate that she had been stunned or killed outright before being flung into the river.

And then, the rope and the staple suggested an outlandish, maniacal disposal of the victim. Here was no effort at concealment, but rather a making sure, in most brutal and callous fashion, that early discovery must be unavoidable.

The bucolic mind works in well-scored grooves. Receiving no assistance from his master, Bates pulled the body a little farther up on the strip of gravel so that it lay clear of the water.

"I mum fetch t' polis," he said.

The phrase , with its vivid significance , seemed to

galvanize Grant into a species of comprehension.

"Yes," he agreed, speaking slowly, as though striving to measure the effect of each word. "Yes, go for the police, Bates. This foul crime must be inquired into, no matter who suffers. Go now. But first bring a rug from the stable. You understand? Your wife, or Minnie, must not be told till later. They must not see. Mrs. Bates is not so well to-day."

"Not so well! Her ate a rare good breakfast for a sick 'un!"

Bates was recovering from the shock, and prepared once more to take an interest in the minor features of existence. Among these he counted ability to eat as a sure sign of continued well-being in man or beast.

Grant, too, was slowly regaining poise.

"I hardly know what I am saying," he muttered. "At any rate, bring a rug. I'll mount guard till you return with the policeman. There can be no doubt, I suppose, that this poor creature is dead."

"Dead as a stone," said Bates with conviction. "Why, her's bin in there hours," and he nodded toward the water. "Besides, if I knows anythink of a crack on t'head, her wur outed before she went into t'river.... But who i' t'world can she be?"

"If you don't fetch that rug I'll go for it myself," said Grant, whereupon Bates made off.

He was soon back again with a carriage rug, which Grant helped him to spread over the dripping body.

Then he hastened to the village, taking a path that avoided the house.

The lawn and river bank of The Hollies could only be overlooked from the steep wooded cliff opposite, and none but an adventurous boy would ever think of climbing down that almost impassable rampart of rock, brushwood, and tree-roots. At any rate, when left alone with the ghastly evidence of a tragedy, Grant troubled only to satisfy himself that no one was watching from the house. Assured on that point, he lifted a corner of the rug, and, apparently, forced himself to scrutinize the dead woman's face. He seemed to search therein for some reassuring token, but found none, because he shook his head, dropped the rug, and walked a few paces dejectedly.

Then, hardly knowing what he was about, he relighted his pipe, but had hardly put it in his mouth before he knocked out the tobacco.

Clearly, he was thinking hard, mapping out some line of conduct, and the outlook must have been dark indeed, judging by his somber and undecided aspect.

More than once he looked up at the attic window of the cottage which had drawn his eyes before tragedy had come so swiftly to his very feet. But, if he hoped to see anyone, he was disappointed, though, in the event, it proved that his real fear was lest the person he half expected to see should look out.

He was not disturbed in that way, however. Fish rose in the river; birds sang in the trees; a water-wagtail skipped nimbly from rock to rock in the shallows; honey-laden bees hummed past to the many hives in the postmaster's garden. These were the normal sights and sounds of a June morning - that which was abnormal and almost grotesque in its horror lay hidden beneath the carriage rug.

To and fro he walked in that trying vigil, carrying the empty pipe in one hand while, with the other, he dabbed the handkerchief at the cut on his face. He was aware of some singular change in the quality of the sunlight pouring down on lawn and river and trees. Five minutes earlier it had spread over the landscape a golden bloom of the tint of champagne; now it was sharp and cold, a clear, penetrating radiance in which colors were vivid and shadows black. He was in no mood to analyze emotions, or he might have under-stood that the fierce throbbing of his heart had literally thinned the blood in his veins and thus affected even his sight. He only knew that in this crystal atmosphere the major issues of life presented themselves with a new and crude force. At any rate, he made up his mind that the course suggested by truth and honor was the only one to follow, and that, in itself, was something gained.

By the time Bates returned, accompanied by the village policeman, and two other men carrying a stretcher, Grant was calmer, more self-contained, than he had been since that hapless body was dragged from the depths. He was not irresponsive, therefore, to the aura of official importance which enveloped the policeman; he sensed a certain uneasiness in Bates; he even noted that the stretcher was part of the stock in trade of Hobbs, the local butcher, and ordinarily bore the carcase of a well-fed pig.

These details were helpful. Naturally , Bates had

explained his errand, and the law, in the person of the policeman, was prepared for all eventualities.

"This is a bad business, Mr. Grant," began the policeman, producing a note-book, and moistening the tip of a lead pencil with his tongue. Being a Sussex man, he used the same phrase as Bates. In fact, Grant was greeted by it a score of times that day.

"Yes," agreed Grant. "I had better tell you that I have recognized the poor lady. Her name is Adelaide Melhuish. Her residence is in the Regent's Park district of London."

Robinson, the policeman, permitted himself to look surprised. He was, in fact, rather annoyed. Bates's story had prepared him for a first-rate detective mystery. It was irritating to have one of its leading features cleared up so promptly.

"Oh," he said, drawing a line under the last entry in the note-book, and writing the date and hour in heavy characters beneath. "Married or single?"

"Married, but separated from her husband when last I had news of her."

"And when was that, sir?"

"Nearly three years ago."

"And you have not seen her since?"

"No."

"You didn't see her last night?"

Grant positively started, but he looked at the policeman squarely.

"It is strange you should ask me that," he said. "Last night, while searching for a book, I saw a face at the window. It was that window," and four pairs of eyes followed his pointing finger. "The face, I now believe, was that of the dead woman. At the moment, as it vanished instantly, I persuaded myself that I was the victim of some trick of the imagination. Still, I opened the other window, looked out and listened, but heard or saw nothing or no one. As I say, I fancied I had imagined that which was not. Now I know I was wrong."

"About what o'clock would this be, Mr. Grant?"

"Shortly before eleven. I came in at a quarter past ten, and began to work. After writing steadily for a little more than half an hour, I wanted to consult a book, and lighted a candle which I keep for that purpose. I found the book, and was about to blow out the candle when I saw the face."

Robinson wrote in his note-book: -

"Called to The Hollies to investigate case of supposed murder. Body of woman found in river. Mr. Grant, occupying The Hollies, says that woman's name is Adelaide Melhuish" - at this point he paused to ascertain the spelling - "and he saw her face at a window of the house at 10.45 P.M., last night."

"Well, sir, and what next?" he went on.

" It seems to me that the next thing is to have the

unfortunate lady removed to some more suitable place than the river bank," said Grant, rather impatiently. "My story can wait, and so can Bates's. He knows all that I know, and has probably told you already how we came to discover the body. You can see for yourself that she must have been murdered. It is an extraordinary, I may even say a phenomenal crime, which certainly cannot be investigated here and now. I advise you to have the body taken to the village mortuary, or such other place as serves local needs in that respect, and summon a doctor. Then, if you and an inspector will call here, I'll give you all the information I possess, which is very little, I may add."

Robinson began solemnly to jot down a summary of Grant's words, and thereby stirred the owner of The Hollies to a fury which was repressed with difficulty. Realizing, however, the absolute folly of expressing any resentment, Grant turned, and, without meaning it, looked again in the direction of the cottage on the crest of the opposite bank. This time a girl was leaning out of the dormer window. She had shaded her eyes with a hand, because the sun was streaming into her face, but when she saw that Grant was looking her way she waved a handkerchief.

He fluttered his own blood-stained handkerchief in brief acknowledgment, and wheeled about, only to find P. C. Robinson watching him furtively, having suspended his note-taking for the purpose.

CHAPTER II

P.C. ROBINSON "TAKES A LINE"

"It will help me a lot, sir," he said, "if you tell me now what you know about this matter. If, as seems more than likely, murder has been done, I don't want to lose a minute in starting my inquiries. In a case of this sort I find it best to take a line, and stick to it."

His tone was respectful but firm. Evidently, P.C. Robinson was not one to be trifled with. Moreover, for a sleuth whose maximum achievement hitherto had been the successful prosecution of a poultry thief, it was significant that the unconscious irony of "a case of this sort" should have been lost on him.

"Do you really insist on conducting your investigation while the body is lying here?" demanded Grant, deliberately turning his back on the girl in the distant cottage.

"Not that, sir - not altogether - but I must really ask you to clear up one or two points now."

"For goodness' sake, what are they?"

"Well, sir, in the first place, how did you come to find the body?"

Louis Tracy

"I walked out into the garden after finishing breakfast a few minutes ago, and noticed the rope attached to the staple, just as you see it now."

"Did you walk straight here?"

"No. Not exactly. I was - er - curious about the face I saw, or thought I saw, last night, and looked into the room through the same window. By doing so I scared Mrs. Bates, who was clearing the table, and she screamed -"

"Her would, too," put in Bates. "Her'd take 'ee for Owd Ben's ghost."

"You shut up, Bates," said the policeman. "Don't interrupt Mr. Grant."

Grant was conscious of an undercurrent of suspicion in the constable's manner. He was wroth with the man, but recognized that he had to deal with narrow-minded self-importance, so contrived again to curb his temper.

"I am not acquainted with old Ben or his ghost," he said quietly. "I can only tell you that I went inside to reassure Mrs. Bates, and then strolled slowly to this very spot. Naturally, I could not miss the rope and the staple. To my mind, it was not intended that I or anyone else should miss them. I regarded them as so peculiar that I shouted for Bates. He came at once, and drew the body out of the water."

"And you recognized the dead woman as the one you saw last night?"

"Yes."

"At about ten minutes to eleven?"

"Yes."

"Is it likely, sir, that any other person saw her in these grounds a bit earlier?"

"What do you mean?"

"Well, sir, I can't put it much plainer. Could anybody else have seen her here, say about 10.15?"

Grant met the policeman's inquiring glance squarely before he answered.

"It is possible, of course," he said, "but most unlikely."

"Were you alone here at that hour?"

Again Grant sought and held that inquisitive gaze, held it until Robinson affected to consult his notes. There was a moment of tense silence. Then the reply came with an icy stubbornness that was not to be denied.

"I decline absolutely to be cross-examined about my movements. If you are unable or unwilling to order the removal of the body, I'll telegraph to the chief of police at Knolesworth, and ask him to act. Further, I shall request Dr. Foxton to examine the poor lady's injuries. It strikes me as a monstrous proceeding that you should attempt to record my evidence at this moment, and I refuse to become a party to it."

"Now, then, Robinson, stop yer Sherlock Holmes work, an' help me to lift this poor woman on to the stretcher," said Bates gruffly.

The policeman's red face grew a shade deeper with annoyance, but he had the sense to avoid a scene. He was not popular in the village, and was well aware that the two rustics pressed into service as stretcher-bearers would joyfully retail the fact that he had been "set down a peg or two by Mr. Grant."

"I'll do all that's necessary in that way, sir," he said stiffly. "I suppose you have no objection to my askin' if you noticed any strange footprints on the ground hereabouts?"

"That was the first thing I looked for, both here and outside the window - the latter, of course, for another reason. I found none. These stones would show no signs. The ground is so dry that even the five men now present leave no traces, but I remember seeing in the bed of the stream certain marks which, unfortunately, were obliterated when Bates hauled the body ashore. They were valueless, however - shapeless indentations in the mud and sand."

"Were they wide apart or close together, sir?"

"Quite irregular. No one could judge by the length of the stride whether they were made by the feet of a man or a woman, if that is what you have in mind ... but, really -"

Grant's impatient motion was not to be misunderstood. Robinson stooped, removed the rug, and unfastened the rope, after noting carefully how it was tied, a point which he called on the others to observe as well. Then he and the villagers went away with their sad burden, the rug being requisitioned once more to hide that wan face from the vivid sunshine.

Bates had a trick of grasping a handful of his short whiskers when puzzled; he did so now; it seemed to be an unconscious effort to pull his jaws apart in order to emit speech.

"I've a sort of idee, sir," he said slowly, "that Robinson saw Doris Martin on the lawn with 'ee last night."

Grant turned on his henchman in a sudden heat of anger.

"Miss Martin's name must be kept out of this matter," he growled.

But Sussex is not easily browbeaten when it thinks itself in the right.

"All very well a-sayin' that, sir, but a-doin' of it is a bird of another color," argued Bates firmly.

"How did you know that Miss Martin was here?"

"Bless your heart, sir, how comes it that us Steynholme folk know everythink about other folk's business? Sometimes we know more'n they knows themselves. You've not walked a yard wi' Doris that the women's tittle-tattle hasn't made it into a mile."

No man, even the wisest, likes to be told an unpalatable truth. For a few seconds, Grant was seriously annoyed with this village Solon, and nearly blurted out an angry command that he should hold his tongue. Luckily, since Bates was only trying to be helpful, he was content to say sarcastically:

"Of course, if you are so well posted in my movements

last night, you can assure the coroner and the Police that I did not strangle some strange woman, tie a rope around her, and throw her in the river."

"Me an' my missis couldn't help seein' you an' Doris a-lookin' at the stars through a spyglass when us were goin' to bed," persisted Bates. "We heerd your voices quite plain. Once 'ee fixed the glass low down, an' said, 'That's serious. It's late to-night.' An' I tell 'ee straight, sir, I said to the missis: - 'It will be serious, an' all, if Doris's father catches her gallivantin' in our garden wi' Mr. Grant nigh on ten o'clock.' Soon after that 'ee took Doris as far as the bridge. The window was open, an' I heerd your footsteps on the road. You kem' in, closed the window, an' drew a chair up to the table. After that, I fell asleep."

Perturbed and anxious though he was, Grant could hardly fail to see that Bates meant well by him. The mental effort needed for such a long speech said as much. The allusion to Sirius, amusing at any other time, was now most valuable, because an astronomical almanac would give the hour at which that brilliant star became visible. Other considerations yielded at once, however, to the fear lest Robinson and his note-book were already busy at the post office. Without another word, he hurried away by the side-path through the evergreens, leaving Bates staring after him, and, with more whisker-pulling, examining the rope and staple, which, by the policeman's order, were not to be disturbed.

Grant reached the highroad just as Robinson and the men with the stretcher were crossing a stone bridge spanning the river about a hundred yards below The Hollies. A slight, youthful, and eminently attractive female figure, walking swiftly in the opposite direction, came in sight at the same time, and Grant almost groaned aloud when the newcomer stood stock still and looked at the mournful procession. He, be it remembered, was somewhat of an idealist and a poet; it grieved his spirit that those two women, the quick and the dead, should meet on the bridge. He took it as a portent, almost a menace, he knew not of what. He might have foreseen that unhappy eventuality, and prevented it, but his brain refused to work clearly that morning. A terrible and bizarre crime had bemused his faculties. He seemed to be in a state of waking nightmare.

He was stung into impetuous action by seeing the policeman halt and exchange some words with the girl. He began to run, with the quite definite if equally mad intent of punching Robinson into reasonable behavior. He was saved from an act of unmitigated folly by the girl herself. She caught sight of him, apparently broke off her talk with the policeman abruptly, and, in her turn, took to her heels.

Thus, on that strip of sun-baked road, with its easy gradient to the crown of the bridge, there was the curious spectacle offered by two men jogging along with a corpse on a stretcher, a young man and a young woman running towards each other, and a discomfited representative of the law, looking now one way and now the other, and evidently undecided whether to go on or return. Ultimately, it would seem, Robinson went with the stretcher-bearers, because Grant and the girl saw no more of him for the time.

Grant had received several shocks since rising from the breakfast-table, but it was left for Doris Martin, the postmaster's daughter, to administer not the least surprising one.

Though almost breathless, and wide-eyed with horror, her opening words were very much to the point.

"How awful!" she cried. "Why should any-one in Steynholme want to kill a great actress like Adelaide Melhuish?"

Now, the name of the dead woman was literally the last thing Grant expected to hear from this girl's lips, and the astounding fact momentarily banished all other worries.

"You knew her?" he gasped.

"No, not exactly. But I couldn't avoid recognizing her when she asked for her letters, and sent a telegram."

"But -"

"Oh, Robinson told me she was dead. I see now what is puzzling you."

"It is not quite that. I mean, why didn't you tell me she was in Steynholme? Has she been staying here any length of time?"

The girl's pretty face crimsoned, and then grew pale.

"I - had no idea - she was - a friend of yours, Mr. Grant," she stammered.

"She used to be a friend, but I have not set eyes on her during the past three years - until last night."

"Last night!"

"After you had gone home. I was doing some work, and, having occasion to consult a book, lighted a candle, and put it in the small window near the bookcase. Then I fancied I saw a woman's face, *her* face, peering in, and was so obsessed by the notion that I went outside, but everything was so still that I persuaded myself I was mistaken."

"Oh, is that what it was?"

Grant threw out his hands in a gesture that was eloquent of some feeling distinctly akin to despair.

"You don't usually speak in enigmas, Doris," he said. "What in the world do you mean by saying: - 'Oh, is that what it was?'"

The girl - she was only nineteen, and never before had aught of tragic mystery entered her sheltered life - seemed to recover her self-possession with a quickness and decision that were admirable.

"There is no enigma," she said calmly. "My room overlooks your lawn. Before retiring for the night I went to the window, just to have another peep at Sirius and its changing lights, so I could not help seeing you fling open the French windows, stand a little while on the step, and go in again."

"Ah, you saw that? Then I have one witness who will help to dispel that stupid policeman's notion that I killed Miss Melhuish, and hid her body in the river at the foot of the lawn, hid it with such care that the first passerby must find it."

Every human being has three distinct personalities. Firstly, there is the man or woman as he or she really is; secondly, there is the much superior individual as assessed personally; thirdly, and perhaps the most important in the general scheme of things, there is the same individuality as viewed by others. For an instant, the somewhat idealized figure which John Menzies Grant offered to a pretty and intelligent but inexperienced girl was in danger of losing its impressiveness. But, since Grant was not only a good fellow but a gentleman, his next thought restored him to the pedestal from which, all unknowing, he had nearly been dethroned.

"That is a nice thing to say," he cried, with a short laugh of sheer vexation. "Here am I regarding you as a first-rate witness in my behalf, whereas my chief worry is to keep you out of this ugly business altogether. Forgive me, Doris! Never before have I been so bothered. Honestly, I imagined I hadn't an enemy in the world, yet someone has tried deliberately to saddle me with suspicion in this affair. Not that I would give real heed to that consideration if it were not for the unhappy probability that, strive as I may, your name will crop up in connection with it. What sort of fellow is this police constable? Do you think he would keep his mouth shut if I paid him well?"

Grant was certainly far from being in his normal state of mind, or he would have caught the tender gleam which lighted the girl's eyes when she understood that his concern was for her, not for himself. As it was, several things had escaped him during that brief talk on the sunlit road.

On her part, Doris Martin was now in full control of

her emotions, and she undoubtedly took a saner view of a difficult situation.

"Robinson is a vain man," she said thoughtfully. "He will not let go the chance of notoriety given him by the murder of a well-known actress. Was she really murdered? Robinson said so when I met him on the bridge."

"I'm afraid he is justified in that belief, at any rate."

"Well, Mr. Grant, what have we to conceal? I was in your garden at a rather late hour, I admit, but one cannot watch the stars by day, and a big telescope with its tripod is not easily carried about. Of course, father will be vexed, because, as it happens, I did not tell him I was coming out. But that cannot be helped. As it happens, I can fix the time you opened your window almost to a minute, because the church clock had chimed the quarter just before you appeared."

Grant, however, was not to be soothed by this matter-of-fact reasoning.

"I am vexed at the mere notion of your name, and possibly your portrait, appearing in the newspapers," he protested. "Miss Melhuish was a celebrated actress. The press will make a rare commotion about her death. Look at the obvious questions that will be raised. What was she doing here? Why was she found in the river bordering the grounds of my house? Don't you see? I had to decide pretty quickly whether or not I would admit any previous knowledge of her. I suppose I acted rightly?"

"Why hide anything, Mr. Grant? Surely it is always

best to tell the truth!"

He looked into those candid blue eyes, and drew from their limpid depths an element of strength and fortitude.

"By Jove, Doris, small wonder if a jaded man of the world, such as I was when I came to Steynholme, found new faith and inspiration in friendship with you," he said gratefully. "But I am wool-gathering all the time this morning, it would seem. Won't you come into the house? If we have to discuss a tragedy we may as well sit down to it."

"No," she said, with the promptitude of one who had anticipated the invitation. "I must hurry home. There are accounts to be made up. And Robinson and others will be telegraphing to Knoleworth and London. I must attend to all that, because dad gets flustered if several messages are handed in at the same time."

"Come and have tea, then, about four o'clock. The ravens will have fled by then."

"The ravens?"

"The police, you dear child, and the reporters, and the photographers - the flock of weird fowl which gathers from all points of the compass when the press gets hold of what is called 'a first-rate story,' By midday I shall be in the thick of it. But, thank goodness, they will know nothing to draw them your way until the inquest takes place, and not even then if *I* can manage it."

" Don't mind me , Mr. Grant. You must not keep

anything back on my account. I'll try and come at four. But I may be very busy in the office. By the way, you ought to know. Miss Melhuish came here on Sunday evening. She arrived by the train from London. I - happened to notice her as she passed in the Hare and Hounds 'bus. She took a room there, at the inn, I mean, and came to the post office twice yesterday. When I heard her name I recognized her at once from her photographs. And - one more thing - I guessed there was something wrong when I saw you, and Robinson, and Bates, and the other men standing near a body lying close to the river. That is why I came out. Now I really must go. Good-by!"

She hastened away. Grant stood in the road and looked after her. Apparently she was conscious that he had not stirred, because, when she reached the bridge, she turned and waved a hand to him. She was exceedingly graceful in all her movements. She wore a simple white linen blouse and short white skirt that morning, with brown shoes and stockings which harmonized with the deeper tints of her Titian red hair. As she paused on the bridge for a second or two, silhouetted against the sky, she suggested to Grant's troubled mind the Spirit of Summer.

Returning to the house by way of the main gate, which gave on to the highway, he bethought him of Mrs. Bates and Minnie. They must be enlightened, and warned as to the certain influx of visitors. He resolved now to tackle a displeasing task boldly. Realizing that the worst possible policy lay in denying himself to the representatives of the press, who would simply ascertain the facts from other sources, and unconsciously adopt a critical vein with regard to himself, he determined to go to the other extreme, and receive all comers.

Of course, there would be reservations in his story. That is what every man decides who faces a legal inquiry as a novice. It is a decision too often regretted in the light of after events.

Meanwhile, P. C. Robinson was hard at work. In his own phrase, he "took a line," and the trend of his thoughts was clearly demonstrated when a superintendent motored over from Kncleworth in response to a telegram. He told how the body had been found, and then went into details gathered in the interim.

"Miss Melhuish hadn't been in the village five minutes," he said, "before she asked Mr. Tomlin, landlord of the Hare and Hounds, where The Hollies was, and how long Mr. Grant had lived in the village. She went for a walk in the direction of his house almost at once. Tomlin watched her until she crossed the bridge. That was on Sunday evening."

Superintendent Fowler allowed his placid features to show a flicker of surprise. In that rural district an actual, downright murder was almost unknown. Even a case of manslaughter, arising out of a drunken quarrel between laborers at fair-time, did not occur once in five years.

"Oh, she came here on Sunday, did she?" he asked.

"Yes, sir. Yesterday, too, she spoke of Mr. Grant to Hobbs, the butcher, and Siddle, the chemist."

The two were closeted in the sitting-room of Robinson's cottage, which was situated on the main road near the bridge. It faced the short, steep hill overhanging the river. A triangular strip of turf formed the village green, and the houses of Steynholme clustered around this and a side road climbing the hill. From door and windows nearly every shop and residence in the village proper could be seen. In front of the Hare and Hounds had gathered a group of men, and it was easy to guess the topic they were discussing. The superintendent, who did not know any of them, had no difficulty in identifying Hobbs, who looked a butcher and was dressed like one, or Tomlin, who was either born an innkeeper or had been coached in the part by a stage expert. A thin, sharp-looking person, pallid and black-haired, wearing a morning coat and striped trousers, must surely be Siddle, while a fourth, the youngest there, and of rather sporting guise, was apparently a farmer of a horse-breeding turn.

"Who is that fellow in the leggings?" inquired the superintendent irrelevantly. He was looking through the window, and Robinson considered that the question showed a lack of interest in his statement, though he dared not hint at such a thing.

"He's a Mr. Elkin, sir," he said. "As I was saying -"

"How does Mr. Elkin make a living?" broke in the other.

"He breeds hacks and polo ponies," said Robinson, rather shortly.

"Ah, I thought so. Well, go on with your story."

Robinson was irritated, and justly so. His superior had put him off his "line." He took it up again sharply, leaving out of court for the moment the various rills of evidence which, in his opinion, united into a swift-moving stream.

"The fact is, sir," he blurted out, "there is an uncommonly strong case against Mr. John Menzies Grant."

"Phew!" whistled the superintendent.

"I think you'll agree with me, sir, when you hear what I've gathered about him one way and another."

Robinson was sure of his audience now. Quite unconsciously, he had applied the chief canon of realism in art. He had conveyed his effect by one striking note. The rest of the picture was quite subsidiary to the bold splurge of color evoked by actually naming the man he suspected of murdering Adelaide Melhuish.

CHAPTER III

THE GATHERING CLOUDS

Thus, it befell that Grant was not worried by officialdom until long after his housekeeper and her daughter had recovered from the shock of learning that they were, in a sense, connected at first hand with a ghastly and sensational crime.

Like Bates and their employer, neither Mrs. Bates nor Minnie had heard or seen anything overnight which suggested that a woman was being foully done to death in the grounds attached to the house. As it happened, Minnie's bedroom, as well as that occupied by her parents, overlooked the lawn and river. Grant's room lay in a gable which commanded, the entrance. He had chosen it purposely because it faced the rising sun. The other members of the household, therefore, though in bed, had quite as good an opportunity as he, working in the dining-room beneath, of having their attention drawn to sounds disturbing the peace of the night in a quiet and secluded spot. Moreover, none of them was asleep. Minnie Bates, in particular, said that the "grandfather's clock" in the hall struck twelve before she "could close an eye."

At last, just as Grant was rising from an almost untasted luncheon, Mrs. Bates, with a voice of scare, announced "the polis," and P.C. Robinson introduced Superintendent Fowler. This time Grant did not resent questions. He expected them, and had made up his mind to give full and detailed answers. Of course, the finding of the body was again described minutely. The superintendent, a man of experience, one whose manner was not fox-like and irritating like his subordinate's, paid close attention to the face at the window.

"There seems to be little room for doubt that Miss Melhuish did enter your grounds about a quarter to eleven last night," he said thoughtfully. "You recognized her at once, you say?"

"I imagined so. Until this horrible thing became known I had persuaded myself that the vision was a piece of sheer hallucination."

"Let us assume that the lady actually came here, and looked in. Evidently, her face was sufficiently familiar that you should know instantly who this unusual visitor was. I understand, though, that you had not the least notion she was staying in Steynholme?"

"Not the least."

"How long ago is it since you last saw her?"

"Nearly three years."

"You were very well acquainted with her, then, or you could not have glanced up from your table, seen someone staring at you through a window, and said to yourself, as one may express it: - 'That is Adelaide Melhuish'."

"We were so well acquainted that I asked the lady to be my wife."

"Ah," said the superintendent.

His placid, unemotional features, however, gave no clew to his opinions. Not so P. C. Robinson, who tried to look like a judge, whereas he really resembled a bull-terrier who has literally, not figuratively, smelt a rat.

Despite his earlier good resolutions, Grant was horribly impatient of this inquisition. He admitted that the superintendent was carrying through an unpleasant duty as inoffensively as possible, but the attitude of the village policeman was irritating in the extreme. Nothing would have tended so effectively to relieve his surcharged feelings as to supply P. C. Robinson then and there with ample material for establishing a charge of assault and battery.

"That is not a remarkable fact, if regarded apart from to-day's tragedy," he said, and there was more than a hint of soul-weariness in his voice. "Miss Melhuish was a very talented and attractive woman. I first met her as the outcome of a suggestion that one of my books should be dramatized, a character in the novel being deemed eminently suitable for her special rôle on the stage. The idea came to nothing. She was appearing in a successful play at the time, and was rehearsing its successor. Meanwhile, I - fell in love with her, I suppose, and she certainly encouraged me in the belief that she might accept me. I did eventually propose marriage. Then she told me she was married already. It was a painful disillusionment - at the time. I only saw her, to speak to, once again."

"Did she reveal her husband's name?"

"Yes - a Mr. Ingerman."

The superintendent looked grave. That was a professional trick of his. He had never before in his life heard of Mr. Ingerman, but encouraged the notion that this gentleman was thoroughly, and not quite favorably, known to him. Sometimes it happened that a witness, interpreting this sapient look by the light of his or her personal and intimate knowledge, would blurt out certain facts, good or bad as the case might be, concerning the person under discussion.

But Grant remained obstinately silent as to the qualities of this doubtful Ingerman, so Mr. Fowler scribbled the name in a note-book, and was particular as to whether it ended in one 'n" or two.

Still, he carried other shots in his locker. In fact, Mr. Fowler, had he taken in youth to nicer legal subtleties than handcuffs and summonses, would have become a shrewd lawyer.

"We'll leave Mr. Ingerman for the moment," he said, implying, of course, that on returning to him there might be revelations. "I gather that you and Miss Melhuish did not agree, shall I put it? as to the precise bearing of the marriage tie on your love affair?"

"I'm afraid I don't quite follow your meaning," and Grant's tone stiffened ominously, but his questioner was by no means abashed.

"I have no great acquaintance with the stage or its ways, but I have always understood that divorce proceedings among theatrical folk were, shall we say? more popular than, in the ordinary walks of life," said Mr. Fowler.

Grant's resentment vanished. The superintendent's calm method, his interpolated apologies, as it were, for applying the probe, were beginning to interest him.

"Your second effort is more successful, superintendent," he said dryly. "Miss Melhuish did urge me to obtain her freedom. It was, she thought, only a matter of money with Mr. Ingerman, and she would be given material for a divorce."

"Ah," murmured Fowler again, as though the discreditable implication fitted in exactly with the life history of a noted scoundrel in a written *dossier* then lying in his office. "You objected, may I suggest, to that somewhat doubtful means of settling a difficulty?"

"Something of the kind."

Assuredly, Grant did not feel disposed to lay bare his secret feelings before this persuasive superintendent and an absurdly conceited village constable. Love, to him, was an ideal, a blend of mortal passion and immortal fire. But the flame kindled on that secret altar had scorched and seared his soul in a wholly unforeseen way. The discovery that Adelaide Melhuish was another man's wife had stunned him. It was not until the fire of sacrifice had died into parched ashes that its earlier banality became clear. He realized then that he had given his love to a phantom. By one of nature's miracles a vain and selfish creature was gifted in the artistic portrayal of the finer emotions. He had worshiped the actress, the mimic, not the woman herself. At any rate, that was how he read the repellent notion that he should bargain with any man for the sale of a wife.

"You might be a trifle more explicit, Mr. Grant," said the superintendent, almost reproachfully.

"In what direction? Surely a three-years-old love affair can have little practical bearing on Miss Melhuish's death?"

"What, then, may I ask, could bear on it more forcibly? The lady admittedly visits you, late at night, and is found dead in a river bordering the grounds of your house next morning, all the conditions pointing directly to murder. Moreover - it is no secret, as the truth must come out at the inquest - she had passed a good deal of her time while in Steynholme, unknown to you, in making inquiries concerning you, your habits, your surroundings, your friends. Surely, Mr. Grant, you must see that the history of your relations with this lady, though, if I may use the phrase, perfectly innocent, may possibly supply that which is at present lacking - a clew, shall I term it, to the motive which inspired the man, or woman, who killed her?"

P.C. Robinson was all an eye and an ear for this verbal fencing-match. It was not that he admired his superior's skill, because such finesse was wholly beyond him, but his suspicious brain was storing up Grant's admissions "to be used in evidence" against him subsequently. His own brief record of the conversation would have been: - "The prisoner, after being duly cautioned, said he kept company with the deceased about three years ago, but quarreled with her on hearing that she was a married woman."

The superintendent seldom indulged in so long a speech, but he was determined to force his adversary's guard, and sought to win his confidence by describing the probable course to be pursued by the coroner's inquest. But Grant, like the dead actress, had two sides to his nature. He was both an idealist and a stubborn fighter, and ideality had been shattered for many a day by that grewsome object hauled in that morning from the depths of the river.

"I am willing to help in any shape or form, but can only repeat that Miss Melhuish and I parted as described. I should add that I have never, to my knowledge, met her husband."

"He may be dead."

"Possibly. You may know more about him than I."

"Even then, we have not traveled far as yet."

Fowler was puzzled, and did not hesitate to show it. He believed, not without reasonable cause, that this young man was concealing some element in the situation which might prove helpful in the quest for the murderer. He resolved to strike off along a new track.

"I am informed," he went on, speaking with a deliberateness meant to be impressive, "that you did entertain another lady as a visitor last night."

Grant allowed his glance to dwell on Robinson for an instant. Hitherto he had ignored the man. Now he surveyed him as if he were a viper.

" It will be a peculiarly offensive thing if the

personality of a helpless and unoffending girl is brought into this inquiry," he cried. "Brought in' is too mild - I ought to say 'dragged in.' As it happens, astronomy is one of my hobbies. Last evening, as the outcome of a chat on the subject, Doris Martin, daughter of the local postmaster, came here to view Sirius through an astronomical telescope. There is the instrument," and he pointed through P.C. Robinson to a telescope on a tripod in a corner of the room. The gesture was eloquent. The burly policeman might have been a sheet of glass. "As you see, it is a solid article, not easily lifted about. It weighs nearly a hundred-weight."

"Why is it so heavy?"

The superintendent had a knack of putting seemingly irrelevant questions. Robinson had been disconcerted by it earlier in the day, but Grant seemed to treat the interruption as a sensible one.

"For observation purposes an astronomical telescope is not of much use unless the movement of the earth is counteracted," he said. "Usually, the dome of an observatory swings on a specially contrived axis, but that is a very expensive structure, so my telescope is governed by a clockwork attachment and moves on its own axis."

Mr. Fowler nodded. He was really a very well informed man for a country police-officer; he understood clearly.

"Miss Martin came here about a quarter to ten," continued Grant, "and left within three-quarters of an hour. She did not enter the house. She was watching

Sirius while I explained the methods whereby the distance of any star from the earth is computed and its chemical analysis determined -"

"Most instructive, I'm sure," put in the superintendent.

He smiled genially, so genially that Grant dismissed the notion that the other might, in vulgar parlance, be pulling his leg.

"Well, that is the be-all and end-all of Miss Martin's presence. It would be cruel, and unfair, if a girl of her age were forced into a distasteful prominence in connection with a crime with which she is no more related than with Sirius itself."

The older man shook his head in regretful dissent.

"That is just where you and I differ," he said. "That very point leads us back to your past friendship with the dead woman."

"Why?"

"Surely you see, Mr. Grant, that Miss Melhuish might be, probably was, watching your star-gazing, especially as your pupil chanced to be, shall I say, a remarkably attractive young lady ... No, no," for Grant's anger was unmistakable - "It does no good to blaze out in protest. An unhappy combination of circumstances must be faced candidly. Here are you and a pretty girl together in a garden at a rather late hour, and a woman whom you once wanted to marry spying on you, in all likelihood. I've met a few coroner's juries in my time, and not one of them but would deem the coincidence strange, to put it mildly."

"What in Heaven's name are you driving at?"

"You must not impute motives, sir. I am seeking them, not supplying them."

"But what am I to say?"

"Perhaps you will now tell me just how Miss Melhuish and you parted."

The fencers were coming to close quarters. Even P. C. Robinson had to admit that his "boss" had cornered the suspect rather cleverly.

Grant realized that there was no room for squeamishness in this affair. If he did not speak out now, his motives might be woefully misunderstood.

"We parted in wrath and tears," he said sadly. "Miss Melhuish could not, or did not, appreciate my scruples. She professed to be in love with me. She even went so far as to threaten suicide. I - hardly believed in her sincerity, but thought it advisable to temporize, and asked for a few days' delay before we came to a final decision. We met again, as I have said, and discussed matters in calmer mood. Ultimately, she professed agreement with my point of view, and we parted, ostensibly to remain good friends, but really to separate for ever."

"Thank you. That's better. What *was* your point of view, Mr. Grant?"

"Surely I have made it clear. I could not regard my wife as purchasable. The proposed compact was, I believe, illegal. But that consideration did not sway me. I had been dreaming, and thought I was roaming in an enchanted garden. I awoke, and found myself in a morass."

The superintendent nodded again. Singularly enough, Grant's somewhat high-flown simile appeared to satisfy his craving for light.

"Do you mind telling me - is there another woman?" he demanded, with one of those rapid transitions of topic in which he excelled.

"No," said Grant.

"You see what I am aiming at. Let us suppose that Miss Melhuish never, in her own mind, abandoned the hope that some day the tangle would straighten itself. Women are constituted that way. If her husband is now dead, and she became free, she might wish to renew the old ties, but, being proud, would want to ascertain first whether or not any other woman had come into your life."

"I follow perfectly," said Grant, with some bitterness. "She would be consumed with jealousy because my companion in the garden last night happened to be a charming girl of nineteen."

"It is possible."

"So she went off and got someone to kill her, and tie her body with a rope, and arrange a dramatic setting whereby it would be patent to the meanest intelligence that I was the criminal?"

Mr. Fowler smiled, and looked fixedly at

P.C. Robinson.

"No, no," he said, quite good-humoredly. "That would be carrying realism to extremes. Still, I am convinced, Mr. Grant, that this mystery is bound up in some way with your romance of three years ago. At present, I admit, I am working in the dark."

He rose. Apparently, the interview was at an end. But, while pocketing his note-book, he said suddenly: -

"The inquest will open at three o'clock tomorrow. You will be present, of course, Mr. Grant?"

"I suppose it is necessary."

"Oh, yes. You found the body, you know. Besides, you may be the only person who can give evidence of identity. In fact, you and the doctor will be the only witnesses called."

"Dr. Foxton?"

"Yes."

"Has he made a post-mortem?"

"He is doing so now. You see, there is clear indication that this unfortunate lady was struck a heavy blow, perhaps killed, before she was put in the river."

"Good Heavens! Somehow, I was so stunned that I never thought of looking for signs of any injury of that sort."

Grant's horror-stricken air was so spontaneous that it

probably justified the severe test of that unexpected disclosure. He was so unnerved by it that the two policemen had gone before he could frame another question.

Once they were in the open road, and well away from The Hollies, Robinson ventured to open his mouth.

"He's a clever one is Mr. Grant," he said meaningly. "You handled him a bit of all right, sir, but he didn't tell you everything he knew, not by long chalks."

The superintendent walked a few yards in silence. Even when he spoke, his gaze was introspective, and seemed to ignore his companion.

"I'm inclined to agree with you, Robinson," he said, speaking very slowly. "We have a big case in our hands, a very big case. We must tread warily. You, in particular, mixing with the village folk, should listen to all but say nothing. Don't depend on your memory. Write down what you hear and see. People's actual words, and the exact time of an occurrence, often have an extraordinarily illuminating effect when weighed subsequently. But don't let Mr. Grant think you suspect him. There is no occasion for that - yet."

Mr. Fowler could be either blunt or cryptic in speech at will. In one mood he was the straightforward, out-spoken official; in another the potential lawyer. P.C. Robinson, though unable to describe his chief's erratic qualities, was unpleasantly aware of them. He was not quite sure, for instance, whether the superintendent was encouraging or warning him, but, being a dogged person, resolved to "take his own line," and stick to it.

Grant passed a distressful day. Work was not to be thought of, and reading was frankly impossible. His mind dwelt constantly on the tragedy which had come so swiftly and completely into his ordered life. He could not wholly discard the nebulous theory suggested by Superintendent Fowler, but the more he surveyed it the less reasonable it seemed. The one outstanding fact in a chaos of doubt was that someone had deliberately done Adelaide Melhuish to death. The murderer had been actuated by a motive. What was that motive? Surely, in a place like Steynholme no man could come and go without being seen, and the murderer must be a stranger to the district, because it was ridiculous to imagine that he was one of the residents.

Yet that was exactly what a dunderheaded policeman believed. P.C. Robinson had revealed himself by many a covert glance and prick-eared movement. Grant squirmed uneasily at the crass conceit, as there was no denying that circumstances tended towards a certain doubt, if no more, in regard to his own association with the crime.

The admission called for a fierce struggle with his pride, but he forced himself to think the problem out in all its bearings, and the folly of adopting the legendary policy of the chased ostrich became manifest. What, then, should he do? He thought, at first, of invoking the aid of a barrister friend, who could watch the inquest in his behalf.

Nevertheless, he shrank from that step, which, to his super-sensitive nature, implied the need of legal protection, and he fiercely resented the mere notion of such a thing. But something must be done. Once the murderer was laid by the heels his own troubles would vanish, and the storm raised by the unhappy fate of Adelaide Melhuish would subside into a sad memory.

He was wrestling with indecision when a newspaper reporter called. Grant received the journalist promptly, and told him all the salient facts, suppressing only the one-time prospect of a marriage between himself and the famous actress.

The reporter went with him to the river, and scrutinized the marks, now rapidly becoming obliterated, of the body having been drawn ashore.

"The rope and iron staple, I understand, were taken from the premises of a man who lets boats for hire on the dam quarter of a mile away," he said casually.

Grant was astounded at his own failure to make any inquiry whatsoever concerning this vital matter. He laughed grimly.

"You can imagine the state of my mind," he said, "when I assure you that, until this moment, it never occurred to me even to ask where these articles came from or what had become of them."

"I can sympathize with you," said the journalist. "A brutal murder seems horribly out of place in this environment. It is a mysterious business altogether. I wonder if Scotland Yard will take it up."

Grant surprised him by clapping him on the back.

"By Jove, my friend, the very thing! Of course, such an investigation requires bigger brains than our local police are endowed with. Scotland Yard *must* take it up. I'll wire there at once. If necessary, I'll pay all expenses."

The newspaper man had his doubts. The "Yard," he said, acted in the provinces only if appealed to by the authorities directly concerned. But Grant was not to be stayed by a trifle like that. He hurried to the post office, hoping that Doris Martin might walk back with him.

The girl and her father were busy behind the counter when he entered. He noticed that Doris was rather pale. She was about to attend to him, but Mr. Martin intervened. It struck Grant that the postmaster was purposely preventing his daughter from speaking to him.

For some inexplicable reason, he felt miserably tongue-tied, and was content to write a message to the Chief Commissioner of Police, London, asking that a skilled detective should be sent forthwith to Steynholme.

Mr. Martin read it gravely, stated the cost, and procured the requisite stamps. In the event, Grant quitted the place without exchanging a word with Doris, while her father, usually a chatty man, said not a syllable beyond what was barely needed.

As he passed down the hill and by the side of the Green he was aware of being covertly watched by many eyes. He saw P.C. Robinson peering from behind a curtained window. Siddle, the chemist, came to the shop door, and looked after him. Hobbs, the butcher, ceased sharpening a knife and gazed out. Tomlin, landlord of the Hare and Hounds Inn, surveyed him from the "snug."

These things were not gracious. Indeed, they were positively maddening. He went home, gave an emphatic order that no one, except Miss Martin, if she called, was to be admitted and savagely buried himself in a treatise on earth-tides.

But that day of events had not finished for him yet. He had, perforce, eaten a good meal, and was thinking of going to the post office in order to clear up an undoubted misapprehension in Mr. Martin's mind, when Minnie Bates came with a card.

"If you please, sir," said the girl, "this gentleman is very pressing. He says he's sure you'll give him an interview when you see his name."

So Grant looked, and read: -

MR. ISIDOR G. INGERMAN

Prince's Chambers, London, W.

CHAPTER IV

A CABAL

Grant stared again at the card. A tiny silver bell seemed to tinkle a sort of warning in a recess of his brain. The name was not engraved in copper-plate, but printed in heavy type. Somehow, it looked ominous. His first impression was to bid Minnie send the man away. He distrusted any first impression. It was the excuse of mediocrity, a sign of weakness. Moreover, why shouldn't he meet Isidor G. Ingerman?

"Show him in," he said, almost gruffly, thus silencing shy intuition, as it were. He threw the card on the table.

Mr. Ingerman entered. He did not offer any conventional greeting, but nodded, or bowed. Grant could not be sure which form of salutation was intended, because the visitor promptly sat down, uninvited.

Minnie hesitated at the door. Her master's callers were usually cheerful Bohemians, who chatted at sight. Then she caught Grant's eye, and went out, banging the door in sheer nervousness.

Still Mr. Ingerman did not speak. If this was a pose on his part, he erred. Grant had passed through a trying day, but he owned the muscles and nerves of an Alpine climber, and had often stared calmly down a wall of rock and ice which he had just conquered, when the least slip would have meant being dashed to pieces two thousand feet below.

There was some advantage, too, in this species of stage wait. It enabled him to take the measure of Adelaide Melhuish's husband, if, indeed, the visitor was really the man he professed to be.

At first sight, Isidor G. Ingerman was not a prepossessing person. Indeed, it would be safe to assume that if, by some trick of fortune, he and not Grant were the tenant of The Hollies, P.C. Robinson would have haled him to the village lock-up that very morning. It was not that he was villainous-looking, but rather that he looked capable of villainy. He was a tall, slender, rather stooping man, with a decidedly well-molded, if hawk-like, face. His aspect might be described as saturnine. Possibly, when he smiled, this morose expression would vanish, and then he might even win a favorable opinion. He had brilliant black eyes, close set, and an abundant crop of black hair, turning gray, which, in itself, lent an air of distinction. His lips were thin, his chin slightly prominent. He was well dressed, and managed a hat, stick, and gloves with ease. Altogether, he reminded Grant of a certain notable actor who is invariably cast for the rôle of a gentlemanly scoundrel, but who, in private life, is a most excellent fellow and good citizen. Oddly enough, Grant recognized in him, too, the type of man who would certainly have appealed to Adelaide Melhuish in her earlier and impressionable years.

Meanwhile, the visitor, finding that the clear-eyed young man seated in an easy chair (from which he had not risen) could seemingly regard him with blank indifference during the next hour, thought fit to say something.

"Is my name familiar to you, Mr. Grant?" he inquired.

The voice was astonishingly soft and pleasant, and the accent agreeably refined. Evidently, there were surprising points about Mr. Ingerman. Long afterwards, Grant learned, by chance, that the man had been an actor before branching off into that mysterious cosmopolitan profession known as "a financier."

"No," said Grant. "I have heard it very few times. Once, about three years ago, and today, when I mentioned it to the police."

The other man's sallow cheeks grew a shade more sallow. Grant supposed that this slight change of color indicated annoyance. Of course, the association of ideas in that curt answer was intolerably rude. But Grant had been tried beyond endurance that day. He was in a mood to be brusque with an archbishop.

"We can disregard your confidences, or explanations, to the police," said Ingerman smoothly. "Three years ago, I suppose, my wife spoke of me?"

"If you mean Miss Adelaide Melhuish - yes."

"I do mean her. To be exact, I mean the lady who was murdered outside this house last night."

Grant realized instantly that Isidor G. Ingerman was a foeman worthy of even a novelist's skill in repartee. Thus far, he, Grant, had been merely uncivil, using a bludgeon for wit, whereas the visitor was making play with a finely-tempered rapier.

"Now that you have established your identity, Mr. Ingerman, perhaps you will tell me why you are here," he said.

"I have come to Steynholme to inquire into my wife's death."

"A most laudable purpose. I was given to understand, however, that at one time you took little interest in her living. I have not seen Mrs. Ingerman for three years - until last night, that is - so there is a chance, of course, that husband and wife may have adjusted their differences. Is that so?"

"Until last night!" repeated Ingerman, almost in a startled tone. "You admit that?"

Grant turned and pointed.

"I saw, or fancied I saw, her face at that window," he said. "She looked in on me about ten minutes to eleven. I was hard at work, but the vision, as it seemed then, was so weird and unexpected, that I went straight out and searched for her. Perhaps 'searched' is not quite the right word. To be exact, I opened the French window, stood there, and listened. Then I persuaded myself that I was imagining a vain thing, and came in."

"What was she doing here?"

"I don't know."

" She arrived in Steynholme on Sunday evening, I

am told."

"I heard that, too."

"You imply that you did not meet her?"

"No need to imply anything, Mr. Ingerman. I did not meet her. Beyond the fanciful notion that I had seen her ghost last night, the first I knew of her presence in the village was when I recognized her dead body this morning."

"Strange as it may sound, I am inclined to believe you."

Grant said nothing. He wanted to get up and pitch Ingerman into the road.

"But who else will take that charitable view?" purred the other, in that suave voice which so ill accorded with his thin lips and slightly hooked nose.

"I really don't care," was the weary answer.

"Not at the moment, perhaps. You have had a trying day, no doubt. My visit at its close cannot be helpful. But -"

"I am feeling rather tired mentally," interrupted Grant, "so you will oblige me by not raising too many points at once. Why should you imagine that conversation with you in particular should add to my supposed distress?"

"Doesn't it?"

"No."

"Why, then, may I ask, do you so obviously resent my questions? Who has so much right to put them as I?"

Grant found that he must bestir himself. Thus far, the honors lay with this rather sinister-looking yet quiet-mannered visitor.

"I am sorry if anything I have said lends color to that belief," he answered. "Candidly, I began by assuming that you forfeited any legal right years ago to interfere in behalf of Miss Melhuish, living or dead. Let us, at least, be candid with each other. Miss Melhuish herself told me that you and she had separated by mutual consent."

"Allow me to emulate your candor. The actual fact is that you weaned my wife's affections from me."

"That is a downright lie," said Grant coolly.

Ingerman's peculiar temperament permitted him to treat this grave insult far more lightly than Grant's harmless, if irritating, reference to the police.

"Let us see just what 'a lie' signifies," he said, almost judicially. "If a lady deserts her husband, and there is good reason to suspect that she is, in popular phrase, 'carrying on' with another man, how can the husband be lying if he charges that man with being the cause of the domestic upheaval?"

"In this instance a hypothetical case is not called for. Three years ago, Mr. Ingerman, you had parted from your wife. Your name was never mentioned.

Apparently, none in my circle had even heard of you. Miss Melhuish had won repute as a celebrated actress. I met her, in a sense, professionally. We became friends. I fancied I was in love with her. I proposed marriage. Then, and not until then, did the ghost of Mr." - Grant bent forward, and consulted the card - "Mr. Isidor G. Ingerman intrude."

"So marriage was out of the question?"

"If you expect an answer - yes."

Ingerman rested the handle of his stick against his lips.

"That isn't how the situation was represented to me at the time," he said thoughtfully.

Grant was still sore with the recollection of the way in which the superintendent of police had forced him to confess the pitiful scheme whereby a woman in love had sought to gain her ends. He refused to sully her memory a second time that day, even to gain the upper hand in this troublesome controversy.

"I neither know nor care what representations may have been made to you," he retorted. "I merely tell you the literal truth."

"Possibly. Possibly. It was not I who used the word 'lie,' remember. But if you are ungracious enough to refuse to withdraw the offensive phrase, let it pass. We are not in France. This deadly business will be fought out in the law courts. I am here to-night of my own initiative. I thought it only fair and reasonable that you and I should meet before we are brought face to face at a coroner's inquest, and, it may be, in an Assize

Court.... No, no, Mr. Grant. Pray do not put the worst construction on my words. *Someone* murdered my wife. If the police show intelligence and reasonable skill, *someone* will be tried for the crime. You and I will certainly be witnesses. That is what I meant to convey. The doubt in my mind was this - whether to be actively hostile or passively friendly to the man who, next to me, was interested in the poor woman now lying dead in a wretched stable of this village."

The almost diabolical cleverness of this long speech, delivered without heat and with singularly adroit stress on various passages, was revealed by its effect on Grant. He was at once infuriated and puzzled. Ingerman was playing him as a fisherman humors a well-hooked salmon. The simile actually occurred to him, and he resolved to precipitate matters by coming straightway to the landing-net.

"Is your friendship purchasable?" he inquired, making the rush without further preamble.

"My wife was, I was led to believe," came the calm retort.

Grant threw scruples to the wind now. Adelaide Mulhuish was being defamed, not by him, but by her husband.

"We are at cross purposes," he said, weighing each word. "Your wife, who knew your character fairly well, I am convinced, thought that you were open to receive a cash consideration for your connivance in a divorce."

"She had told me plainly that she would never live

with me again. I was too fair-minded a man to place obstacles in the way when she wished to regain her freedom."

"So it was true, then. What was the price? One thousand - two? I am not a millionaire."

"Nor am I. As a mere matter of pounds, shillings, and pence, it was a serious matter for me when my wife's earnings ceased to come into the common stock."

"My first, if rather vague, estimate of you was the correct one. You are a good bit of a scoundrel, and, if I guess rightly, a would-be blackmailer."

"You are talking at random, Mr. Grant. The levying of blackmail connotes that the person bled desires that some discreditable, or dangerous, fact should be concealed."

"Such is not my position."

"I - I wonder."

"I can relieve you of any oppressive doubt. I informed the police some few hours ago that you have appeared already in a similar role."

"Oh, you did, did you?" snarled Ingerman, suddenly abandoning his pose, and gazing at Grant with a curiously snakelike glint in his black eyes.

"Yes. It interested them, I fancied."

Grant was sure of his man now, and rather relieved that the battle of wits was turning in his favor.

"So you have begun already to scheme your defense?"

"Hadn't you better go?" was the contemptuous retort.

"You refuse to answer any further questions?"

"I refuse to buy your proffered friendship - whatever that may mean."

"Have I offered to sell it?"

"I gathered as much."

Ingerman rose. He was still master of himself, though his lanky body was taut with rage. He spoke calmly and with remarkable restraint.

"Go through what I have said, and discover, if you can, the slightest hint of any suggested condonation of your offenses, whether avowed or merely suspected. I shall prove beyond dispute that you came between me and my wife. Don't hug the delusion that your three years' limit will save you. It will not. I wish you well of your attempt to prove that I was a consenting party to divorce proceedings. I came here to look you over. I have done so, and have arrived at a very definite opinion. I, also, have been interviewed by the police, and any unfavorable views they may have formed concerning me as the outcome of your ex parte statements are more than counteracted by the ugly facts of a ghastly murder. You were here shortly before eleven o'clock last night. My wife was here, too, and alive. This morning she was found dead, by you. At eleven o'clock last night I was playing bridge with three city men in my flat. When the news of the murder reached me to-day my first thought, after the shock of it had passed, was: - 'That fellow, Grant, may be innocently involved in a terrible crime, and I may figure as the chief witness against him.' I am not speaking idly, as you will learn to your cost. Yet, when I come on an errand of mercy, you have the impudence to charge me with blackmail. You are in for a great awakening. Be sure of that!"

And Isidor G. Ingerman walked out, leaving Grant uncomfortably aware that he had not seen the last of an implacable and bitter enemy.

It was something new and very disturbing for a writer to find himself in the predicament of a man with an absolutely clear conscience yet perilously near the meshes of the criminal law. He had often analyzed such a situation in his books, but fiction diverged so radically from hard fact that the sensation was profoundly disconcerting, to say the least. He did not go to the post office. He was not equal to any more verbal fire-works that evening. So he lit a pipe, and reviewed Ingerman's well-rounded periods very carefully, even taking the precaution to jot down exact, phrases. He analyzed them, and saw that they were capable of two readings. Of course, it could not be otherwise. The plausible rascal must have conned them over until this essential was secured. Grant even went so far as to give them a grudging professional tribute. They held a canker of doubt, too, which it was difficult to dissect. Their veiled threats were perplexing. While their effect, as apart from literal significance, was fresh in his mind, he made a few notes of different interpretations.

He went to bed rather early, but could not sleep until the small hours. Probably his rest, such as it was, would have been even more disturbed had he been able to accompany Ingerman to the Hare and Hounds Inn.

A small but select company had gathered in the bar parlor. The two hours between eight and ten were the most important of the day to the landlord, Mr. Tomlin. It was then that he imparted and received the tit-bits of local gossip garnered earlier, the process involving a good deal of play with shining beer-handles and attractively labeled bottles.

But this was a special occasion. Never before had there been a Steynholme murder before the symposium. Hitherto, such a grewsome topic was supplied, for the most part, by faraway London. To-night the eeriness and dramatic intensity of a notable crime lay at the very doors of the village.

So Tomlin was more portentous than usual; Hobbs, the butcher, more assertive, Elkin, the "sporty" breeder of polo ponies, more inclined to "lay odds" on any conceivable subject, and Siddle, the chemist, a reserved man at the best, even less disposed to voice a definite opinion.

Elkin was about twenty-five years of age, Siddle looked younger than his probable thirty-five years, while the others were on the stout and prosperous line of fifty.

They were discussing the murder, of course, when Ingerman entered, and ordered a whiskey and soda. Instantly there was dead silence. Looks and furtive winks were exchanged. There had been talk of a detective being employed. Perhaps this was he. Mr. Tomlin knew the stranger's name, as he had taken a room, but that was the extent of the available information.

"A fine evenin', sir," said Tomlin, drawing a cork noisily. "Looks as though we were in for a spell o' settled weather."

"Yes," agreed Ingerman, summing up the conclave at a glance. "Somehow, such a lovely night ill accords with the cause of my visit to Steynholme."

"In-deed, sir?"

"Well, you and these other gentlemen may judge for yourselves. It will be no secret tomorrow. I am the husband of the lady who was found in the river outside Mr. Grant's residence this morning."

Sensation, as the descriptive reporters put it. Mr. Tomlin was dumbly but unanimously elected chairman of the meeting, and was vaguely aware of his responsibilities. He drew himself a fresh glass of bitter.

"You don't tell me, sir!" he gasped. "Well, the idee! The pore lady's letters were addressed to Miss Adelaide Melhuish. Perhaps you don't know, sir, that she stayed here!"

"Oh, yes. I was told that by the local police-constable. Have I, by any chance, been given her room?"

"No, sir. Not likely. It's locked, and the police have the key till the inquest is done with."

"As for the name," explained Ingerman, in his suave voice, "that was a mere stage pseudonym, an adopted name. My wife was a famous actress, and there is a sort of tacit agreement that a lady in the theatrical profession shall be known to the public as 'Miss' rather than 'Mrs.'"

"Well, there!" wheezed Tomlin. "Who'd ever ha' thought it?"

The landlord was not quite rising to the occasion. He was, in fact, stunned by these repeated shocks. So Hobbs took charge.

"It's a sad errand you're on, sir," he said. "Death comes to all of us, man an' beast alike, but it's a terrible thing when a lady like Miss - Mrs. -"

"Ingerman is my name, but my wife will certainly be alluded to by the press as Miss Melhuish."

"When a lady like Miss Melhuish is knocked on the 'ead like a -"

Mr. Hobbs hesitated again. He also felt that the situation was rather beyond him.

"But my wife was flung into the river and drowned," said Ingerman sadly.

"No, sir. She was killed fust. It was a brutal business, so I'm told."

"Do you mean that she was struck, her skull battered?" came the demand, in an awed and soul-thrilling whisper.

"Yes, sir. An' the wust thing is, none of us can guess

Louis Tracy

who could ha' done it."

"Lay yer five quid to one, Hobbs, that the police cop the scoundrel afore this day fortnight," cried Elkin noisily.

Then Mr. Siddle put in a mild word.

"Gentlemen," he said, "let me remind you that we four will probably be jurors at the inquest."

That was a sobering thought. Elkin subsided, and Hobbs looked critically at the remains of a gill of beer.

Ingerman took stock of the chemist. He might easily induce the others to believe that Grant was the real criminal, but the quiet man in the black morning-coat and striped cloth trousers was of finer metal. He knew instantly that if he could persuade this one "probable juror" of Grant's guilt, the remainder would follow his lead like a flock of sheep.

But there was no need to hurry. Next day's inquest would be a mere formality. The real struggle would begin a week or a fortnight later.

"You have said a very wise thing, sir," he murmured appreciatively. "Even my feelings must be kept under better control. But this is no ordinary murder. Before it is cleared up there will be astounding revelations. Mark the word - astounding.'

Hobbs, whose heavy cheeks were of a brick-red tint, almost startled the conclave by a sudden outburst which gave him an apoplectic appearance.

"You're too kind'earted, Siddle," he cried. "Wot's the use of talkin' rubbish. We all know where the body was found. We all know that Doris Martin an' Mr. Grant were a'sweet-'eartin' in the garden -"

"Look here, Hobbs, just keep Doris Martin's name out of it!" shouted Elkin, smiting the table with his fist till the glasses danced.

"Gentlemen!" protested Siddle gently.

"It's all dashed fine, but I'm not -" blustered Elkin. He yielded to Ingerman's outstretched hand.

"I seem to have brought discord into a friendly gathering," came the mournful comment. "Such was far from being my intent. Landlord, the round is on me, with cigars. Now, let us talk of anything but this horror. If I forget myself again, pull me up short, and fine me another round."

Siddle half rose, but thought better of it. Evidently, he meant to use his influence to stop foolish chatter.

CHAPTER V

THE SEEDS OP MISCHIEF

Ingerman was a shrewder judge of human nature than the village chemist. As well try to stem the flowing tide as stop tongues from wagging when such a theme offered.

Tomlin created a momentary diversion by clattering in the bar. After this professional interlude, Ingerman ignored his own compact.

"I'm sure you local residents will be interested, at least, in hearing something of my wifes career," he said. "There never was a more lovable and gracious woman, and no couple could be more united than she and I till some three years ago. Then came a break. She was independent of me, of course. She was a celebrity, I a mere nobody, best known, if at all, as 'Miss Melhuish's husband.' Nevertheless, we were devoted to each other until, to her and my lasting misfortune, a certain author wrote a book which, when dramatized, contained a part for which my wife's stage presence and talents seemed to be peculiarly suited."

Siddle stirred uneasily, but the others were still as partridges in stubble. Ingerman did not intend to alarm the shy bird of the covey, however.

"I name no names," he said solemnly. "Nor am I telling you anything that will not be thoroughly exposed before the coroner and elsewhere. From that unhappy period dated our estrangement. My wife fell under a fatal influence which lasted, practically unchecked, until the day, if not the very hour, of her death. Do I blame her? No - a thousand times no! You see me, a plain man, considerably her senior. *I* had not the gift of writing impassioned love passages in which she could display her artistic genius. When I came home from the City, tired after the day's work, *she* was just beginning hers. You know what London fashionable life is - the theater, a supper, a dance, some great lady's 'reception,' and the rest of it. Ah, me! The stage, and literature, and the arts generally are not for poor fellows moiling in a City office. You gentlemen, I take it, are all happily married -"

"I'm not," said Elkin, "but I'll lay you long odds I will be soon."

For some reason, this remark produced a certain uneasiness among his friends. Tomlin stared at the ash of one of the cigars "stood" by this talkative Londoner; Hobbs, whose glass had reached a low level again, examined the dregs almost fiercely; and Siddle seemed to be about to say something, but, with his usual restraint, kept silent. Then Ingerman made a very shrewd guess, and wondered who Doris Martin was, and what Hobbs's cryptic allusion had meant.

"Good luck to you, sir," he said, "but - take no offense - don't marry an actress. There's an old adage, 'Birds of a feather flock together.' I would go farther, and interpolate the word 'should.' If Adelaide Melhuish had never met me, but had married the man who could write her plays, this tragedy in real life would never have been."

"D - n him," muttered Elkin fiercely. "He's done for now, anyhow. He'll turn no more girls' heads for a bit."

"An' five minutes since you yapped at me like a vicious fox-terrier for 'intin' much the same thing," chortled Hobbs.

Siddle stood up.

"You ain't goin', Mr. Siddle?" went on the butcher. "It's 'ardly 'arf past nine."

"I have some accounts to get out. It's near the half year, you know," and Siddle vanished unobtrusively.

Hobbs shook his head, and gazed at Elkin as though the latter was a refractory bullock.

"Siddle's a fair-minded chap," he said. "He can't stand 'earin' any of us 'angin' a man without a fair trial."

Ingerman had marked the chemist for more subtle treatment when an opportunity arose, or could be made. At present, he was not sorry such a restraining influence was removed. The next half hour should prove a golden one if well utilized. He was right. Before the inn was cleared, what between Elkin's savage comments and the other men's thinly-veiled allusions, he knew all that Steynholme could tell with regard to Grant and Doris Martin.

Grant's first thought next morning was of the girl who had been thrust so prominently into his life by the death of another woman. That was, perhaps, the strangest outcome of the tragedy. Doris was easily the prettiest and most intelligent girl in the village, a rare combination in itself, even among young ladies of much higher social position than a postmaster's daughter. But her father was a self-educated man, whose life had been given to books, whose only hobby was the culture and study of bees. He had often refused promotion, solely because his duties at Steynholme were light, and permitted of many free hours. In his only child he found a quick pupil and a sympathetic helper. Of her own accord she took to poetry and music. In effect, had Doris Martin attended the best of boarding-schools and training colleges, she would have received a smattering of French and a fair knowledge of the piano or violin, whereas, after more humble tuition, it might fairly be said of her that few girls of her age had read so many books and assimilated their contents so thoroughly. From her mother she inherited her good looks and a small yearly income, just sufficient to maintain a better wardrobe than her father's salary would permit.

Grant, newly settled in Steynholme, found the postmaster and his daughter intellectually on a par with himself, and this claim could certainly not be made on behalf of the local "society" element. The three became excellent friends. Naturally, the young people spent a good deal of time together. But there had been no love-making - not a hint or whisper of it!

And now, by cruel chance, their names were linked by scandal in its most menacing form, since there was no gainsaying the fact that Doris's star-gazing on that fatal Monday night was indissolubly bound up with the death of Adelaide Melhuish.

Louis Tracy

For the first time, then, the notion peeped up in Grant's mind that the whirligig of existence might see Doris his wife. But the conceit resembled the Gorgon's teeth, which, when sown in the ground, sprang forth as armed men. The very accident which revealed a not unpleasing possibility had established a grave obstacle in the way of its ultimate realization. Already there was a cloud between him and the Martins, father and daughter. To what a tempest might not that cloud develop when the questionings and innuendoes of the inquest established an aura of suspicion and intrigue around a perfectly innocent meeting in the garden of The Hollies!

Grant ate his breakfast in wrath. In wrath, too, he glanced through the morning newspapers, and saw his own name figuring large in the "story" of the "alleged" murder. The reporters had missed nothing. They had even got hold of the "peculiar coincidence" of his (Grant's) glimpse of a face at the window. His play was recalled, and Adelaide Melhuish's success in the title-rôle. Then Mr. Isidor G. Ingerman was introduced. He was described as "a man fairly well known in the City." That was all. The press could say nothing as yet of marital disagreements, nor was any hint concerning Doris Martin allowed to appear. But these journalistic fire-works were only held in reserve. "Dramatic and sensational developments" were promised, and police activity in "an unexpected direction" fore-shadowed.

All of which, of course, was mere journalistic paraphrasing of circumstances already known to the writers, and none the less galling to Grant on that account.

And there was no answer from the Commissioner of

Police at Scotland Yard. True, the overnight telegram might have reached the Department after office hours. Grant, like most members of the general public, held the vague belief that Government officials do very little work. Still, one might reasonably expect better things from the institution which was supposed to safeguard law-abiding citizens.

Calm analysis of Ingerman's nebulous threats had revealed a hostile force not to be despised. Possibly, the man was already in league with that narrow-minded village constable, so every passing hour made more urgent the need of a trained intelligence being brought to bear on the mystery of Adelaide Melhuish's killing. Grant racked his brains to discover who could possibly have a motive for committing the crime. Naturally, his thoughts flew to Ingerman. Surely that sinister-looking person should be forced to give an account of himself instead of, as was probable, being allowed to instill further nonsense into the suspicious mind of P.C. Robinson.

There were two morning deliveries of London letters in Steynholme, one at eight and another at half past ten. Grant waited until the postman had left a publisher's circular (the only letter for The Hollies by the second mail). Then, in a fever of impatience, he jammed on a hat and went out. He would wait no longer. He would telegraph Scotland Yard again, and, incidentally, demand an audience at the post office.

No sooner had he entered the highroad than he saw P.C. Robinson on guard. That important person was standing on the bridge, apparently taking the air. He was nibbling the chin-strap of his helmet; both thumbs were locked in his belt. From that strategic position

Louis Tracy

three roads came under observation.

It was a fine morning, and Grant's sense of humor was not proof against this open espionage. He smiled, and determined to take a rise out of "Sherlock," as Bates had christened the policeman.

The bridge lay a hundred yards to the left. The road was straight until it curved around the house and its shrubberies, so the view was blocked on that side. Grant filled and lighted a pipe with a deliberateness meant to be provoking, glancing several times doubtfully at P.C. Robinson, who, of course, was grandly unaware of his presence. Then he strolled off to the right, and, when hidden, took to his heels for a hundred yards sprint. Turning into a winding bridle-path tucked between hedges of thorn and hazels, he walked to a point where it crossed a patch of furze. At a little distance a hand-bridge spanned the river, and gave access to the eastern end of the village by a steep climb of the wooded cliff. The path, in fact, was a short cut to that part of Steynholme.

He sat on a hump of rock, and waited. It was a boyish trick, but very successful. Within three minutes, at the utmost, P.C. Robinson hurried past, using a stalking, stealthy stride which was distinctly ludicrous.

The eyes of the two men met, but Grant alone was prepared.

"Hello, Robinson!" he cried cheerfully. "What's the rush? Surely our rural peace has not been disturbed again?"

Robinson knew he had been " sold," but rose to

the occasion.

"Excuse me, Mr. Grant," he puffed. "Can't wait now. Have an appointment. I'll see you later."

Honor demanded that he should not relax that swift pace. Unhappily, the path up the cliff was visible throughout from Grant's rock, so, on reaching the summit, Robinson was a-boil in more ways than one. Moreover, peeping through the first screen of trees that offered, he had the mortification of seeing the man who had befooled him go back the way he came.

Purple-faced with heat and anger, the policeman forgot his surroundings, and glowered at Grant with real fury. So he heard no one approaching along the main road until he was hailed a second time with, "Hello, Robinson!"

He turned sharply. This was Mr. Elkin.

"Good morning!" he said. "Have you seen the superintendent?"

"What? Mr. Fowler? No. Is *he* here so early?"

"I must have missed him."

"Well, you'll hardly find him on Bush Walk," which was the name of the path.

"You never can tell," came the dark answer.

At any rate, the policeman elected to abandon his self-imposed vigil, and the two walked together into the village.

"My! You look as though you'd run a mile," commented Elkin.

"This murder has kept me busy," growled the other, frankly mopping his forehead.

"Ay, that's so. And it isn't done with yet, by a long way. Pity you weren't in the Hare and Hounds last night. You'd have heard something. There's a chap staying there, name of Ingerman -"

"I've met him. The dead woman's husband."

"Oh, perhaps you've got his yarn already?"

"It all depends what he said to you."

"Well, he hinted things. Unless I'm greatly mistaken, you'll soon be making an arrest."

"I believe I could put my hand on the murderer this very minute," said Robinson vindictively.

Elkin laughed, somewhat half-heartedly.

"Lay you fifty to one against the time," he said. "I'm the only one near enough for that limit, you know."

The policeman realized that he had allowed annoyance to shake his wits. He looked at Elkin rather sharply, and noticed that the horse-breeder seemed to be nervous and ill.

"I didn't quite mean that I could grab my man this minute," he said, "but, if I can guess him, it amounts to nearly the same thing. What have you been doing to yourself, Mr. Elkin? You look peeky to-day."

"Too much whiskey and tobacco. I'll call at Siddle's for a 'pick-me-up.' Am I wanted for the jury?"

"Yes. I left a notice at your place last evening."

"I didn't get it."

"Been away?"

"No. Fact is, I went home late, and didn't bother about letters this morning. What time is the inquest?"

"Three o'clock, in the club-room of the Hare and Hounds."

"Will that fellow, Grant, be there?"

"Rather. Dr. Foxton warned him yesterday."

"Good! What about Doris Martin? Will she be a witness?"

"Not to-day."

They were entering the village, and could see down the long, wide slope of the hill. Grant had just come into sight at its foot.

Both men scowled at the distant figure, but neither passed any comment. They parted, the policeman walking straight on, Elkin bearing to the left. The chemist's shop stood exactly opposite the post office, so Elkin, arriving first, was aware of his unconscious rival's destination.

Louis Tracy

He had not answered Mr. Siddle's greeting, but gazed moodily through a barricade of specifics piled in the window. Then he swore.

"What's wrong now?" inquired the chemist quietly.

"That Grant. Got a nerve, hasn't he?"

"I can't say, unless you explain."

"He's just gone into the post office."

"Why shouldn't he? He wants stamps, may be; plenty of 'em, I should imagine."

"Oh, you're a fish, Siddle. You aren't crazy about a girl, like I am. The sooner Grant's in jail the better I'll be pleased."

"If you take my advice, which you won't, I know, you will not utter that sort of remark publicly."

"Can't help it. Bet you a fiver I'm engaged to Doris Martin within a week."

Mr. Siddle took thought.

"Why so quickly?" he asked, after a pause.

"I'll catch her on the hop, of course. If she's engaged to me it'll help her a lot when this case comes into court."

"I cannot believe that Doris would accept any man for such a reason."

"I'm not 'any man.' She knows I'm after her. Will you

take my bet, even money?"

"No. I don't bet."

"Well, you needn't put a damper on me. In fact, you can't. Have you that last prescription of Dr. Foxton's handy? My liver wants a tonic."

The chemist thumbed a dog-eared volume, read an entry carefully, and retired to a dispensing counter in the rear of the shop.

"Shall I send it?" came his voice.

"No. I'll wait. Give me a dose now, if you don't mind."

For some reason, Fred Elkin was not himself that day. He was moody, and fretful as a sick colt. But he had diagnosed his ailment and its cause accurately; a discreet doctor was probably aware of his failings, and had considered them in the "mixture."

The post office was not busy when Grant entered. A young man, a stranger, was seated at the telegraphist's desk, tapping a new instrument. The G. P. O., fore-warned, had lent an expert to deal with press messages.

Mr. Martin, sorting some documents, came forward when he saw Grant. His kindly, somewhat pre-occupied face was long as a fiddle.

"Good morning, Mr. Martin," said Grant.

"Good morning. What can I do for you?" was the stiff reply. Grant was in no mind to be rebuffed, however.

"I must have a word with you in private," he said.

"I'm sorry - but my time is quite full."

"I'm sorry, too, but the matter is urgent."

The click of the sounder became less businesslike. There was an element in the tone of each voice that drew the London telegraphist's attention. Martin, usually the mildest-mannered man in Sussex, was obviously ill at ease. But he simply could not hold out against Grant's compelling gaze.

"Come into the back room," he said nervously. "Call me if I'm needed," he added, nodding to his assistant.

Grant did not hesitate an instant when the postmaster reached the "back parlor" through another door. The open window, draped in clematis, gave a delightful glimpse of The Hollies. A window-box of mignonette filled the air with its delicate perfume. Grant hoped that Doris would be there, but the only signs of her recent presence were a hat and an open book on the table.

"Now, Mr. Martin," he said gravely, "you and I should have a serious talk. It is idle to deny that gossip is spreading broadcast certain malicious and absurd rumors which closely concern Doris and myself. To me these things are of slight consequence. To a girl of your daughter's age they are poisonous. If you, her father, know the whole truth, you can regulate your actions so as to defeat the scandalmongers. That is why I am here to-day. That is why I came here yesterday, but your attitude took me aback, and I was idiot enough to go without a word of explanation. I was too shaken then to see my clear course, and follow it regardless of personal feelings. This morning I am master of myself, and I insist that you listen now while I tell you exactly what occurred on Monday night."

"Surely - these matters - are - for the authorities," stammered the older man.

"What? Your daughter's good name?"

Mr. Martin reddened. His agitation was pitiful.

"That is hardly in question, sir," he said brokenly.

"I am speaking of the tongue of slander. Heaven help and direct me! I would suffer death rather than see Doris subjected to the leers and innuendoes of every lout in the village."

Grant's earnestness could hardly fail to impress his friend. But Martin had either made up his mind or been warned not to discuss the murder, and adhered loyally to that line of conduct. He retreated toward the door leading to the post office proper.

"It is too late to interfere now," he said.

"What on earth do you mean?" demanded Grant, yielding to a gust of anger.

"The whole - of the circumstances - are being inquired into by the police," came the hesitating answer.

"Has that prying scoundrel, Robinson, dared to cross-examine Doris?"

"He came here, of course, but Scotland Yard has taken up the inquiry."

"A detective - here?"

"Yes. He is with Doris in the garden at this moment."

Grant knew the topography of the house. Without asking permission, he tore through yet a third door leading to a kitchen and scullery, nearly upsetting a tiny maid who had her ear or eye to the key-hole, and raced into the garden in which the postmaster kept his bees.

Doris, standing with her hands behind her back, was looking at The Hollies , and deep in conversation with an alert and natty little man who was evidently absorbed in what she was saying.

Grant, in a whirl of fury, was only conscious that Doris's companion was slight, almost diminutive, of frame, very erect, and dressed in a well-fitting blue serge suit, neat brown boots and straw hat, when the two heard his footsteps.

Doris was flustered. Her Romney face held a look of scare.

"Oh, here is Mr. Grant!" she said, striving vainly to speak with composure.

The little man pierced Grant with an extraordinarily penetrating glance from very bright and deeply-recessed black eyes.

"Ah, Mr. Grant, is it!" he chirped pleasantly. "Good morning! So *you're* the villain of the piece, are you?"

CHAPTER VI

SCOTLAND YARD TAKES A HAND

It was a singular greeting, to say the least, and the person who uttered it was quite as remarkable as his queer method of expressing himself seemed to indicate.

Grant, though in a fume of hot anger, had the good sense to choke back the first impetuous reprimand trembling on his lips. In fact, wrath quickly subsided into blank incredulity. He saw before him, not the conventional detective who might be described as a superior Robinson - not even the sinewy, sharp-eyed, and well-spoken type of man whom he had once heard giving evidence in a famous jewel-robbery case - but rather one whom he would have expected to meet in the bar of a certain well-known restaurant in Maiden Lane, a corner of old London where literally all the world's a stage, and all the men and women merely players.

During his theatrical experiences he had come across scores of such men, dapper little fellows, wizened of face yet curiously youthful in manner; but they, each and all, were labeled "low comedian." Certainly, a rare intelligence gleamed from this man's eyes, but that is an attribute not often lacking in humorists who command high salaries because of their facility in laughter-making. This man, too, had the wide, thin-lipped, mobile mouth of the actor. His ivory-white, wrinkled forehead and cheeks, the bluish tint on jaws and chin, his voice, his perky air, the very tilt of his straw hat, were eloquent of the footlights. Even his opening words, bizarre and cheerfully impertinent, smacked of "comic relief."

"I figure prominently in this particular 'piece,'" snapped Grant. "May I ask your name, sir?"

"A wise precaution with suspicious characters," rejoined the other, smiling. Grant was suddenly reminded of a Japanese grinning at a joke, but he bent over a card which the stranger had whisked out of a waistcoat pocket. He read:

MR. CHARLES F. FUENEAUX,

Criminal Investigation Department,

NEW SCOTLAND YARD, S.W.

He could not control himself. He gazed at Mr. Charles F. Furneaux with a surprise that was not altogether flattering.

"Did the Commissioner of Police send *you* in response to my telegram?" he said.

"That is what lawyers call a leading question," came the prompt retort. "And I hate lawyers. They darken understanding, and set honest men at loggerheads."

"But it happens to be very much to the point at

this moment."

"Well, Mr. Grant, if you really press for an answer, it is 'Yes' and 'No.' The Commissioner received a certain telegram, but he may have acted on other grounds. Even Commissioners can be creatures of impulse, or expediency, just as the situation demands.

"You are here, at any rate."

"That is what legal jargon terms an admitted fact."

"Then you had better begin by assuming that I am no villain."

"It is assumed. It couldn't well be otherwise after the excellent character you have been given by this young lady."

"She, at least, will speak well of me, I do believe," said Grant, with a strange bitterness, for his heart was sore because of the seeming defection of his friend, the postmaster. "What I actually had in mind was the stupidity of the local policeman, who is convinced that I am both a criminal and a fool."

"The two are often synonymous," said Furneaux dryly. "But I acquitted you on both counts, Mr. Grant, on hearing, and even seeing, how you spent Monday evening."

Grant, who had cooled down considerably, found a hint of badinage in this comment.

"You have evidently been told that Miss Martin and I were star-gazing in the garden of my house," he said.

"It happens to be true."

"Oh, yes. There was a very fine cluster of small stars in Canis Major, south of Sirius, that night."

"You know something about the constellations, then?" was the astonished query.

"Enough for the purposes of Scotland Yard," smirked Furneaux, who had checked P.C. Robinson's one-sided story by referring to Whitaker's Almanack. "It may relieve your mind if I tell you that I have never seen a real live astronomer in the dock. Venus and Mars are often in trouble, but their devoted observers seldom, if ever."

Grant warmed to this strange species of detective, though, if pressed for an instant decision, he would vastly have preferred that one of more orthodox style had been intrusted with an inquiry so vital to his own happiness and good repute. Eager, however, to pour forth his worries into any official ear, he brought back the talk to a definite channel.

"Will you come to my place?" he asked. "I have much to say. Let me assure you now, in Miss Martin's presence, that she is no more concerned in this ghastly business than any other young lady in the village."

"But she is interested. And *you* are. And I am. Why not discuss matters here, for the present, I mean? We have a glorious view of your house and grounds. We can see without being seen. None can overhear. I advise both of you to go thoroughly into this matter here and now."

Furneaux spoke emphatically. Even Doris put in a

timid plea.

"Perhaps that would be the best thing to do," she said. "Mr. Furneaux has been most sympathetic. I am sure he understands things already in a way that is quite wonderful to me."

The very sound of her voice was comforting. Grant might have argued with the detective, but could not resist Doris. Without further demur he went through the whole story, giving precise details of events on the Monday night. Then the recital widened out into a history of his relations with Adelaide Melhuish. He omitted nothing. Doris gasped when she heard Superintendent Fowler's version of the view a coroner's jury might take of her presence in the garden of The Hollies at a late hour. But Grant did not spare her. He reasoned that she ought to be prepared for an ordeal which could not be avoided. He was governed by the astute belief that his very outspokenness in this respect would weaken the inferences which the police might otherwise draw from it.

Furneaux uttered never a word. He was a first-rate listener, though his behavior was most undetective-like, since he hardly looked at Grant or the girl, but seemed to devote his attention almost exclusively to the scenic panorama in front.

However, when Grant came to the somewhat strenuous passage-at-arms of the previous night between Ingerman and himself, the little man broke in at once.

"Isidor G. Ingerman?" he cried. "Is he a tall, lanky, cadaverous, rather crooked person, with black hair turning gray, and an absurdly melodious voice?"

"You have described him without an unnecessary word," said Grant.

Furneaux clicked his tongue in a peculiar fashion.

"Go on!" he said. "It's a regular romance - quite in your line, Mr. Grant, of course, but none the less enthralling because, as you so happily phrased Miss Martin's lesson in astronomy, it happens to be true."

Grant was scrupulously fair to Ingerman. He admitted the "financier's" adroitness of speech, and made clear the fact that if the visit had the levying of blackmail for its object such a possible outcome was only hinted at vaguely. Being a novelist, one whose temperament sought for sunshine rather than gloom in life, he wound up in lighter vein. The ruse which tricked P.C. Robinson into a breathless scamper of nearly a mile on a hot day in June was described with gusto. Doris, who knew the village constable well, laughed outright, while Furneaux cackled shrilly. None who might be watching the little group in that delightful garden, with its scent of old-world flowers and drone of bees, could have guessed that a grewsome tragedy formed their major theme.

The girl was the first to realize that even harmless merriment was in ill accord with the presence of death, for the body of Adelaide Melhuish lay within forty yards of the place where they stood.

"May I leave you now?" she inquired. "Father may be wanting help in the office."

"I shan't detain you more than a few seconds," said Furneaux briskly. "On Monday evening you two young people parted at half past ten. How do you fix the time?"

Doris answered without hesitation:

"The large window of Mr. Grant's study was open, and we both heard a clock in the hall chime the half-hour. I said, 'Goodness me, is that half past ten?' and started for home at once. Mr. Grant came with me as far as the bridge. When I reached my room, in exactly five minutes after leaving The Hollies, I stood at the open window - that window" - and she pointed to a dormer casement above the sitting-room - "and looked out. It was a particularly fine night, mild, but not very clear, as a slight mist often rises from the river after a hot day in summer. I may have been there about ten minutes, no longer, when I saw the study window of The Hollies thrown open, and Mr. Grant's figure was silhouetted by the lamp behind him. He seemed to be listening for something, so I, who must have heard any unusual sound, listened too. There was nothing. I could hear the ripple of the river beneath the bridge, so everything was very still. After a minute, or two, perhaps - no longer - Mr. Grant went in, and closed the window. Then I went to bed."

"Did Mr. Grant draw any blind or curtains?"

"There are muslin curtains attached to each side of the window. One cannot see into the room from a distance."

Furneaux measured an imaginary line drawn from Doris's bedroom to the edge of the cliff, and pro-longed it.

"Nor can you see the river or foot of the lawn from your room," he commented.

"No. In winter I can just make out the edge of the lawn. When the trees are in leaf, all the lower part is hidden."

"You had actually retired to rest about eleven, I suppose?"

"Yes."

"So if Mr. Grant came out again you would not know?" Doris blushed furiously, but her reply was unfaltering.

"I would have known during the next half-hour, at least," she said. "An inclined mirror hangs in my room. I use it sometimes for adjusting a hat. The square of light from Mr. Grant's room is reflected in it, and any sudden increase in the illumination caused by opening the window or pulling the curtains aside would certainly have caught my eye."

"You have an unshakable witness in Miss Martin," said Furneaux, stabbing a finger at Grant. "Now, I'll hurry off. You and I, Mr. Grant, meet at Philippi, otherwise known as the crowner's quest."

Any benevolent intent he may have had in leaving these young people together was, however, frustrated by Doris, whose composure seemed to have fled since her statement about the mirror. She resolutely accompanied the detective, and Grant had to follow. All three passed into the post office, Doris using the private door. Mr. Martin looked up from his desk when they appeared, and requested his daughter to check a bundle of postal orders. The pretext was painfully obvious, but Grant was not so wishful now to clear up matters with Doris's father, as the girl herself might be trusted to pass on an accurate account of the affair from beginning to end.

He was about to reach the street quick on Furneaux's heels when the little man turned suddenly.

"By the way, don't you want a shilling's worth of stamps?" he said.

Grant smiled comprehension, and went back to the counter, where Doris herself served him. She did not try to avoid his glance, but rather met it with a baffling serenity oddly at variance with her momentary loss of self-possession in the garden.

When he entered the street the detective had vanished.

He walked down the hill at a rapid pace, disregarding the eyes peeping at him through open doorways, over narrow window-curtains, and covertly staring when people passed in the roadway. The sensitive side of his temperament shrank from this thinly-veiled hostility. He was by way of being popular in Steynholme, yet not a soul spoke to him. Before he reached the bridge, the other side of him, the man of action, of cool resource in an emergency, rose in rebellion against the league of silly clodhoppers. Back he strode to the post office and dashed off a telegram. It ran:

"Walter Hart, Savage Club, Adelphi, London. Come here and help to lay a ghost."

He signed it in full, name and address. Doris was gone, but her father received it, and read the text in a bewildered way.

"I find myself deserted by my Steynholme friends so I am trying to import one stanch one," said Grant, almost vindictively.

Martin murmured the cost, and Grant stormed out again. This time, passing the Hare and Hounds, he looked at door and windows. He caught a face scowling at him over a brown wire blind bearing the words "Wines and Spirits" on it in letters of dull gold. It was a commonplace type of face, small-featured, ginger-moustached, and crowned by a billy-cock hat set at a rakish angle. Its most marked characteristic was the positive hatred which glowed in the sharp, pale-blue eyes. Grant wondered who this highly censorious young man might be. At any rate, he meant to ascertain whether or not the critic was susceptible of satire at his own expense. He walked up to the window, elevated his eyebrows at the frowning person within, pretended to read the words on the screen, looked again at the man inside, and shook his head gravely in the manner of one who has accurately determined cause and effect.

Fred Elkin was quick-witted enough to appreciate Grant's unspoken comment. He was also unmannerly enough to put out his tongue. Then Grant laughed, and turned on his heel.

Mr. Siddle, quietly observant of recent comings and goings, was standing at the door of the shop, and missed no item of this dumb show. He raised both hands in silent condemnation of Elkin's childishness, whereupon the horse-dealer jerked a thumb toward Grant's retreating figure, and went through a rapid pantomime of the hanging process. His crony disapproved again, and went in. Now, both those men were on the jury panel, so, to all appearance, Grant would be judged by at least one deadly enemy, whose animosity might or might not be fairly balanced by the chemist's impartial mind.

The tenant of The Hollies actually dreaded the loneliness of his dwelling now, though it was that very quality which had drawn him to Steynholme a year earlier. Work or reading was equally out of the question that day. He sought the industrious Bates, who was trenching celery in the kitchen garden.

"Have 'ee made out owt about un, sir?" inquired that hardy individual, pausing to spit on the handle of his spade.

"No," said Grant. "The thing is a greater mystery than ever."

"I'm thinkin' her mun ha' bin killed by a loony," announced Bates.

"Something of the kind, no doubt. But why are the little less dangerous loonies of Steynholme united in the belief that I am the guilty one?"

"Ax me another," growled Bates.

"Who is spreading this rumor? Robinson?"

"'E dussen't, sir. 'E looks fierce, but 'e'll 'old 'is tongue. T'super will see to that."

"Someone is talking. That is quite certain."

"There's a chap in the 'Are an' 'Ounds - kem 'ere last night."

"Ingerman?"

"Ay, sir, that's the name. 'E's makin' a song of it, I hear."

"Anybody else?"

"Fred Elkin is gassin' about. Do 'ee know un? Breeds 'osses at Mount Farm, a mile that-a-way," and Bates pointed to the west.

Grant hazarded a guess, and described the face of condemnation seen at the inn. Bates nodded.

"That's un," he said. Then he drove the spade into the rich loam. "They do say," he added, apparently as an after-thought, "as Fred Elkin is mighty sweet on Doris, but her'll 'ave nowt to do wi' un."

Grant whistled softly. This explanation threw light on a dark place.

"The plot thickens," he said. "Mr. Elkin becomes more interesting than he looks. Are there other disappointed swains in the offing?"

"What's that, sir?"

"Has Miss Martin any other suitors?"

" Lots of 'em 'ud be after her like wasps round a

plum-tree if she'd give 'em 'alf a chance. But *you* put a stopper on 'em."

Bates was blunt of speech, though a philosopher withal.

"Elkin is my only serious rival, then?" laughed Grant, passing off as a joke a thrust which was shrewder than the gardener knew.

"'E 'as plenty of brass, but I reckon nowt on 'im," was the contemptuous answer.

"Well, he is not a likely person to kill a woman he had never before seen. Miss Martin will marry whom she chooses, no doubt. The present problem is to find out who murdered Miss Melhuish. Now, had *I* been the victim you would be thinking hard, Bates."

"I tell 'ee, sir, it wur a loony."

Nor was Bates to be moved from that opinion. He held to it, through thick and thin, for many days.

Grant wandered into the front garden. His eyes rose involuntarily to the distant post office, and he noticed at once that the dormer window was closed. Yet Doris shared his own love of fresh air, and that window had always been open till that very hour. Somehow, this simple thing seemed to shut him out of her life. He walked to the river, and gazed at the spot where the body was drawn ashore. In the absence of rain the water ran clear as gin, and the marks made by the feet of Adelaide Melhuish's murderer were still perceptible. If only those misshapen blotches could reveal their secret! If only some Heaven-sent ray of intuition would enable him to put the police on the track of the criminal! Theoretically, a novelist and essayist should be a first-rate detective, yet, brought face to face with an actual felony, here was one who perforce remained blind and dumb.

Yet he was not blameworthy for failing to solve a mystery which was rapidly establishing a record for bewildering elements. Wherein he did err most lamentably was in his reading of a woman's heart.

No answering telegram came from his friend in London. The day wore slowly till it was time to attend the inquest. He found a crowd gathered in front of the Hare and Hounds. Superintendent Fowler was there, and quite a number of policemen, whose presence was explained when a buzz of excitement heralded Grant's arrival. He decided not to stand this sort of persecution a moment longer.

Before the superintendent could interfere, he leaped on to a set of stone mounting-steps which stood opposite the door. Instantly, seeing that he was about to speak, the angry murmuring of the mob was hushed. He looked into a hundred stolid faces, and stretched out his right hand.

"I cannot help feeling," he said, in slow, incisive accents which carried far, "that a set of peculiar circumstances has led you Steynholme folk to suspect me of being responsible, in some way, for the death of the lady whose body was found in the river near my house. Now, I want to tell you that I am not only an innocent but a much-maligned man. The law of the land will establish both facts in due season. But I want to warn some of you, too, I shall not trouble to issue writs for libel. If any blackguard among you dares to insult me openly, I shall smash his face."

He knew when to stop. Superintendent Fowler's nudge was not called for, as the orator simply met the scrutiny of all those eyes without another word.

Curiously enough, the sense of justice is inherent in every haphazard gathering of the public. Grant's soldierly bearing, his calm defiance of hostile opinion, the outspoken threat which he so plainly meant, won instant favor. Someone shouted, "Hear, hear!" and the crowd applauded. From that moment he had little to complain of in the attitude of the community as a whole. There were subtle and dangerous enemies to be fought and conquered, but Steynholme looked on, keen to learn of any new sensation, of course, but placidly content that the final verdict should be left in the hands of the authorities.

CHAPTER VII

"ALARUMS AND EXCURSIONS"

The inquest was surprisingly tame after the stirring events which had led up to it. Indeed, save for two incidents, the proceedings were almost dull.

The coroner, a Knoleworth solicitor named Belcher, prided himself on conducting this *cause célèbre* with as little ostentation as he would have displayed over an ordinary inquiry. Messrs. Siddle, Elkin, Tomlin and Hobbs, with eight other local tradesmen and farmers, formed the jurors, and the chemist was promptly elected foreman; no witnesses were ordered out of court; the formalities of "swearing in" the jury and "viewing" the body were carried through rapidly. Almost before Grant had time to assimilate these details Superintendent Fowler, who marshalled the evidence, called his name. The coroner's officer tendered him a well-thumbed Bible, while the coroner himself administered the oath.

Grant eyed the somewhat soiled volume, and opened it before putting it to his lips. The action probably did not please the jury. Elkin nudged Tomlin, and sniggered at the rest of his colleagues, as much as to say: "What did I tell you? The cheek of him!"

Louis Tracy

Elkin, by the way, looked ill. When his interest flagged for an instant his haggard aspect became more noticeable.

Ingerman was there, of course. Furneaux sat beside Mr. Fowler. A stranger, whom Grant did not recognize, proved to be the County Chief Constable. There was a strong muster of police, and the representatives of the press completely monopolized the scanty accommodation for the public. To Grant's relief, Doris Martin was not in attendance.

He told the simple facts of the finding of Adelaide Melhuish's corpse. A harmless question by the coroner evoked the first "scene" which set the reporters' pencils busy.

"Did you recognize the body!" inquired Mr. Belcher.

"I did."

"Then you can give the jury her name?"

Before Grant could answer, Ingerman sprang up, his sallow face livid with passion.

"I protest, sir, against this man being permitted to identify my wife," he said.

He was either deeply moved, or proved himself an excellent actor. His flute-like voice vibrated with an intense emotion. Thus might Mark Antony have spoken when vowing that Brutus was an honorable man.

"Who are you?" demanded the coroner sharply.

"Isidor George Ingerman, husband of the deceased lady," came the clear-toned reply.

"Well, sit down, sir, and do not interrupt the court again," said the coroner.

"I demand, sir, that you note my protest."

"Sit down! Were you any other person I would have you removed. As it is, I am prepared to regard your feelings to the extent of explaining that the witness is not identifying the body but relating a fact within his own knowledge."

Ingerman bowed, and resumed his seat.

For some reason, Grant stared blankly at Furneaux. The latter did not meet his glance, but put a finger on those thin lips. It might, or might not, be a warning to repress any retort he had in mind. At any rate, obeying a nod from the coroner, he merely said:

"She was a well-known actress, Miss Adelaide Melhuish."

Mr. Belcher's pen hesitated a little. Then it scratched on. Undoubtedly, he was himself exercising the restraint he meant to impose on others.

"You are quite sure?" he said, after a pause.

"Quite."

"Thank you, Mr. Grant. Wait here until you sign your deposition. Of course, you are aware that this inquiry will stand adjourned, and the whole matter will be gone into fully at a later date."

"So I have been informed, sir."

Ingerman was the next witness. *He*, like a good democrat, kissed the cover of the Bible. The coroner began by giving him some advice.

"This is a purely formal inquiry, to permit of a death certificate being issued. You will oblige me, therefore, by answering my questions without introducing any extraneous subject."

Ingerman adhered to these instructions. Having already shot a carefully-prepared bolt, he meant avoiding any further conflict with the authorities. His evidence was brief and to the point. The deceased was his wife. They were married at a London registrar's office on a given date, six years ago. His wife acted under her maiden name. There was no family.

The court was well lighted by four long windows in the eastern wall, which each witness faced, so Grant was free to study his avowed enemy at leisure. He thought he made out a crafty underlook in Ingerman which he had failed to detect the previous night. That slow, smooth voice seemed to weigh each syllable. Such a man would never blurt out an unconsidered admission. He was a foe to be reckoned with. The subtle malignancy of that well-timed outburst was proof positive in that respect.

The jury, apparently, attached much weight to his words. On some faces there was an expectancy which merged into marked disappointment when his evidence came to an end. The foreman alone displayed the judicial attitude warranted by the oath he had taken. Somehow, Grant had faith in Mr. Siddle. The man looked intellectual. When spoken to in his shop his manner was invariably reserved. But that was his general repute in Steynholme - a quiet, uninterfering person, who had come to the village a young man, yet had never really entered into its life. For instance, he neither held nor would accept any public office. At first, people wondered how he contrived to eke out a living, but this puzzle was solved by his admitted possession of a small annuity.

Dr. Foxton, general practitioner, who held undisputed sway in the district, told how he had conducted an autopsy on the body of the deceased. He found a deep, incised wound on the back of the skull, a wound which would have caused death in any event. The instrument used must have been a heavy and blunt one. Miss Melhuish was dead or dying when thrown into the river. The body was well nourished, and the vital organs sound. Undoubtedly she had been murdered.

Bates followed, and evoked a snigger by the outspokenness of blunt Sussex.

"I hauled 'um in," he said, "an' knew it wur a dead 'un by the feel of the rope."

The coroner was not curious. He merely wished to put on record the time and manner in which Mr. Grant summoned assistance.

Then P. C. Robinson entered the box, and contrived to bring about the second "incident."

He told how, "from information received," he went to

The Hollies, and found Mr. Grant standing near the river with a dead body at his feet.

"One side of Mr. Grant's face was covered with blood," he went on.

If the policeman was minded to create a sensation, he certainly succeeded. A slight hum ran through the court, and then all present seemed to restrain their breathing lest a word of the evidence should be lost. The mention of "blood" in a murder case was a more adroit dodge than Robinson himself guessed, perhaps. Few of his hearers troubled to reflect that a smudge of fresh gore on Grant's cheek could hardly have any bearing on the death of a woman whose body had admittedly lain all night in the river. It sufficed that Robinson had introduced a touch of the right color into the inquiry. Even the coroner was worried.

"Well!" he said testily.

"I took down his statement, sir," said the witness, well knowing that he had wiped off Grant's morning score in the matter of Bush Walk.

"Never mind his statement. That must await the adjourned hearing. What did you do with the body?"

"Took it to the stable of the Hare and Hounds, sir."

"Where it was viewed recently by the jury?"

"Yes, sir."

"It is the body identified by Mr. Ingerman as that of his wife?"

"Yes, sir."

"That will do.... Superintendent Fowler, will this day week at ten o'clock suit you?"

"Yes, sir," said the superintendent.

"Then the inquest stands adjourned until that day and hour. Gentlemen of the jury, you must be here punctually."

"Can't we ask any questions?" cried Elkin, in an injured tone.

"No. You cannot," snapped the coroner emphatically.

After a few formalities, which included the reading and signing of the depositions, the courthouse emptied. The whole thing was over in half an hour. Grant, determined to have a word with the representative of Scotland Yard, went openly to Furneaux, and asked him to come to The Hollies and join him in a cup of tea.

"No," was the curt answer. "I'm busy. I'll see you later."

It was difficult to reconcile the detective's present stand-off manner with his earlier camaradie, to say nothing of the seemingly friendly hint conveyed by the signal to pass no comment on Ingerman's interruption.

Rather sick at heart, Grant went out into the sunshine. He was snap-shotted a dozen times by press photographers. One man, backing impudently in front of him in order to secure a sharp focus, tripped over the raised edge of a cartway into a yard, and sat down violently.

The onlookers laughed, but Grant helped the photographer to rise.

"If you want a really good picture of the Steynholme murderer, come to my place, and I'll give you one," he said.

The pressman was grateful, because Grant's action had tended to mitigate his discomfiture.

"No one but a fool thinks of you as a murderer, Mr. Grant," he said. "What I really want is a portrait of 'the celebrated' author in whose grounds the body was found."

"Come along, then, and I'll pose for you."

The photographer was surprised, but joyfully accepted the gifts the gods gave. He could not guess that his host was pining for human companionship. He could not fathom Grant's disappointment, on reaching The Hollies, at finding no telegram from a trusted friend, Walter Hart. And he was equally unconscious of the immense service he rendered by compelling his host to talk and act naturally. He enlightened Grant, too, in the matter of inquests.

"Next week there will be a gathering of lawyers," he said. "The police will be represented, probably by the Treasury, if the case is thought sufficiently important. That chap, Ingerman, too, will employ a solicitor, I expect, judging from his attitude to-day. In fact, any one whose interests are affected ought to secure legal assistance. One never knows how these inquiries twist and turn."

"Thank you," said Grant, smiling at the journalist's tact. "I'll order tea to be got ready while you're taking your pictures. By the way, what sort of detective is Mr. Charles F. Furneaux?"

"A pocket marvel," was the enthusiastic answer. "Haven't you heard of him before? Well, you wouldn't, unless you followed famous cases professionally. He seldom appears in the courts - generally manages to wriggle out of giving direct evidence. But I've never known him to fail. He either hangs his man or drives him to suicide. If I committed a crime, and was told that Furneaux was after me, I'd own up and save trouble, because I wouldn't have the ghost of a chance of winning clear."

"He strikes one as too flippant for a detective."

"Yes. Lots of people have thought that, and they're either disappearing in quicklime beneath some corridor of a prison, or doing time at Portland. I wonder if Winter also is coming down on this job."

"Who is 'Winter'?"

"The Chief Inspector at the 'Yard.' A big, cheerful-looking fellow - from his appearance might be a gentleman-farmer and J. P., with a taste for horses and greyhounds. He and Furneaux are called the Big 'Un and the Little 'Un, and each is most unlike the average detective. But Heaven help any wrong-doer they set out to trail! They'll get him, as sure as God made little apples."

"Then the sooner Mr. Winter visits Steynholme the better I shall be pleased. This tragedy is becoming a perfect nightmare. You heard that fat-headed police-man speak of my face being covered with blood. He did it purposely. I made a fool of him this morning, so he paid me out, the literal truth being that a branch of that Dorothy Perkins rose there caught my cheek as I entered this room on Tuesday morning - before I discovered the body - and broke the skin. I suppose the cut is visible still? I saw it to-day while shaving."

"Yes," said the other, chortling over the "copy" his colleagues were missing. "The mark is there right enough. Queer how inanimate objects like a rose-tree can make mischief. I remember a case in which a chestnut in a man's pocket sent him to penal servitude. There was absolutely no evidence against him, except a possible motive, until that chestnut was found and proved to be one of a particular species, grown only in a certain locality."

"How fortunate that the Dorothy Perkins is popular!" laughed Grant. "Will your paper publish photographs of the principals in this affair?"

"I expect so. I've a fine collection - the jury, all in a row - and you, making that speech to the mob."

"Oh! Will that appear?"

"By Jove, yes, sir. It was wired off before the inquest opened."

Grant reddened slightly. His own impetuous action had blurted out to the whole world that which Steynholme was only thinking. No wonder Furneaux had warned him to go slow. Perhaps the little man was annoyed because of his challenge to the village crowd? Well, be it so. He meant, and would live up to, every word of it!

The afternoon dragged after the pressman's departure. What Grant really hungered for was a heart-to-heart talk between Doris Martin and himself. But, short of a foolish attempt to carry the post office by storm, he saw no means of realizing his desire. He must, perforce, await the less troubled hours of the morrow or next day. Doris would surely give her father an exact account of the conversation between Grant, Furneaux, and herself that morning, and that greatly perplexed man could hardly fail to see how unjust was the tittle-tattle of the village.

So, avoiding Mrs. Bates, whose fell intent it was to ask him what he wanted for dinner, he struck off along the road to Knoleworth, walked eight miles in two hours, and reached The Hollies about seven o'clock, rather inclined for a meal and much more contented with life.

Minnie announced that a gentleman "who brought a bag" had been awaiting him since half-past five, and was now asleep on the lawn! A glance at the aforesaid bag, still reposing in the entrance hall, sent Grant quickly into the garden. A long, broad-shouldered person was stretched on a wicker chair, and evidently enjoying a nap. A huge meerschaum pipe and tobacco pouch lay on the grass. The newcomer's face was covered by a broad-brimmed, decidedly weather-beaten slouch hat, which, legend had it, was purchased originally in South America in the early nineties, and had won fame as the only one of its kind ever worn in the Strand.

Louis Tracy

"Hullo! Wally! Glad to see you!" shouted Grant joyously.

The sleeper stirred.

"No, not another drop!" he muttered. "You fellows must have heads of triple brass and stomachs of leather!"

"Get up, you rascal, or I'll spill you out of the chair!" said Grant.

A lazy hand removed the hat, and a pair of peculiarly big and bright eyes gazed up into his.

"Oh, it's you, is it?" drawled a quiet voice. "Why the blazes did you send for me? And, having sent, why wake me out of the best sleep I've had for a week?"

"But why didn't you let me know you were coming? I would have met the train."

"I did. Here's the telegram. That pink-cheeked maid of yours nearly had a fit when I opened it to show her that I was expected."

"You wired from Victoria, I suppose?"

"Would you have preferred Charing Cross, or the Temple? Isn't Victoria respectable?"

Grant laughed as they shook hands. Hart was the most casual adventurer in existence. His specialty was revolutions. Wherever the flag of rebellion was raised against a government, thither went Walter Hart post-haste by train, steamer, or on horseback. He had been sentenced to death five times, and decorated by successful Jack Cades twice as often.

"I'm a sort of outlaw. That's why I sought your help," explained Grant.

"I know all about you, Jack," said Hart slowly, picking up the pipe and filling it from the pouch. The meerschaum was carved to represent the head of a grinning negro, and was now ebon black from use.

"I felt like a pint of Sussex ale after a hot journey in the train, so hied me to the village inn, where several obliging gentlemen told me your real name. Two of them, Ingerman and Elkin, apparently make a hobby of enlightening strangers as to your right place in society."

"I must interview Elkin."

"Not worth while, my boy. Ingerman is the crafty one. I thought I might be doing you more harm than good, or I would have given him a thick ear this afternoon ... Oh, by the way, what time is it?"

"Seven o'clock."

"A little fellow named Furneaux is coming here to dinner at seven-thirty. Said he would drop in by the back door, and mutter 'Hush! I'm Hawkshaw, the detective.' He resembles a cock-sparrow, so I asked him why he didn't fly in through an attic window. He took my point at once, and remarked that he wanted none of my lip, or he would ask me officially what became of Don Ramon de Santander's big pink pearl. It's a queer yarn. There was a bust-up in Guatemala -"

"Look here, Wally," broke in Grant anxiously. "Are you serious? Did Furneaux really say he was coming here?"

"He did, and more - he expressed a partiality for a chicken roasted on a spit. You have a spit in your kitchen, he says, and a pair of chickens in your larder."

"How did you contrive to meet him?"

"You're a poor guesser, Jack. *He* met *me*. 'That you, Mr. Hart?' he said. 'Mr. Grant's house is the first on the right across the bridge. Tell him' - and the rest of it."

"Have you warned Mrs. Bates?"

"Mrs. Bates being?"

"My housekeeper."

"No, sir. If she's anything like your housemaid, I'm glad I didn't, or I should have been chucked into the road. I had the deuce of a job to reach the lawn. Had I ordered dinner I might now have been in the village lockup."

Grant hurried away, and placated Mrs. Bates after a stormy interlude. Precisely at 7.30 p. m. Minnie came and said that "Mr. Hawkshaw" had arrived.

"Bring him out here," said Grant. "Fetch some sherry and glasses, and give us five minutes' notice before dinner is served."

"Please, sir," tittered Minnie, "the gentleman prefers to stay indoors. He said his complexion won't stand the glare."

"Very well," smiled Grant, rising. "Put the sherry and bitters on the sideboard."

"Say," murmured Hart, "is this chap really a detective?"

"Yes. He stands high at Scotland Yard."

"Never more than five feet four, I'll swear. But I wouldn't have missed this for a pension. I have a revolver in my hip pocket, of course. One would feel lonely without it, even in England. But I hope you can stage a few knives and daggers, and a red light. I can cut masks out of a strip of black velvet. That girl will have a piece stowed away somewhere."

The two entered the dining-room study, where the table was now laid for dinner. Furneaux was seated on the edge of a chair in the darkest corner. His eyes gleamed at them strangely.

"Can you trust Bates?" he said to Grant.

It was a wholly unexpected question, and Grant answered sharply:

"Of course, I can."

"Tell him to make sure that no one trespasses on your lawn between now and ten o'clock. Close that window, draw the blind and curtains, and block that small window, the one through which you saw the ghost."

"Ye gods!" cackled Hart ecstatically.

"Why all these precautions?" demanded Grant, rather amused now.

"I'm supposed to be on the very verge of arresting you, and it would weaken the faith of my allies if I were seen drinking your wines and eating your chicken."

"By the way, how did you know I had chickens in store, and a spit on which to roast them?"

"I looked you over at five-thirty this morning, having traveled from London by the mail train. I must lecture you on your inefficient window-catches, Mr. Grant. Several self-respecting burglars of my acquaintance would give your house the go-by as being too easy. And, one other matter. I suggest that any man who mentions the Steynholme murder again before the coffee arrives shall be fined a sovereign for each offense, such fine, or fines, to form a fund for the relief of his hearers. *Cré nom d'un pipe!* Three intelligent men can surely discuss more interesting topics while they eat!"

CHAPTER VIII

AN INTERRUPTED SYMPOSIUM

"Have a cigarette," said Grant to Furneaux, when the blinds were drawn, a lamp lighted, and the sherry dispensed.

"Thank you."

The self-invited guest took one. He sniffed it, broke the paper wrapping, and crumbled some of the tobacco between finger and thumb.

"Ah, those Greeks!" he said sadly. "They simply can't go straight. This brand of Turk used to be made of a tobacco grown on a slope above Salonica. A strip of sun-baked soil built up a reputation which is now being bartered for filthy lucre by the use of Egyptian 'fillings.'"

"You're a connoisseur, Mr. Hawknose - try these," said Hart, proffering a case, from which the detective drew a cigarette, throwing the other one aside.

"Why 'Hawknose'?" he inquired.

"A blend. First syllable of Hawkshaw and second of Furneaux - the latter Anglicized, of course."

"And vulgarized."

"You prefer Furshaw, perhaps?"

"Either effort is feeble for a man who can write about South America, and be lucid. Do you smoke this stuff, may I ask?" While talking, he had smelt and destroyed the second cigarette.

"If it's a fair question, what the devil do *you* smoke?" cried Hart.

"Nothing. I'm a non-smoker. My profession demands a clear intellect, not a brain atrophied by nicotine."

"Piffle! Carlyle and Bismarck were smokers."

"Who reads Carlyle now-a-days? And what modern German pays heed to Bismarck's dogmas? Look at that pipe of yours. It was once a pure ivory white. Now it is black - soiled by tobacco juice. Your lungs are slowly emulating it, and your wits will cloud in time. Read Tolstoi, Mr. Hart. He will teach you how nicotine deadens the conscience."

"At last I know why I smoke like a Thames tug," laughed Hart, "but I'm blest if I can understand why *you* make such a study of the vile weed."

"Most criminals are addicted to the habit. I classify them by their brand of tobacco. For instance, a clever forger would never descend to thick twist, while a swell mobsman would turn with horror from a woodbine."

Minnie entered, and nodded, whereupon Grant led the

others upstairs to wash. From the bathroom he looked out over a darkening landscape. Doris's dormer window was open. She was leaning on the sill, but he could not tell whether or not her eyes were turned his way. Her attitude was pensive, disconsolate, curiously forlorn for a girl normally high-spirited. He was on the point of signaling to her when he remembered Furneaux's presence. There was something impish, almost diabolically clever, in that little man's characteristics which induced wariness.

The dinner was a marvel, considering the short notice given to the cook. Luckily, Mrs. Bates, a loyal soul, had resolved to tempt her employer's appetite that evening. Village gossip had it that the police were about to arrest him, and she was determined he should enjoy at least one good meal before being haled to prison. Hence, the materials were present. The rest was a matter of quantities, and Sussex seldom stints itself in that respect.

The chatter round the table was light and amusing. The three were well matched conversationally. Furneaux evidently held the opinion once expressed by a notable Walrus - that the time had come

> To talk of many things:
> Of shots - and ships - and sealing-wax -
> Of cabbages - and kings.

He was in excellent form, and the others played up to him. Hart's slow drawl was ever trenchant and witty, and Grant forgot his woes in congenial company. As for the mercurial detective himself, it might be said of him as of the school-master of Auburn:

And still they gazed, and still the wonder grew, That one small head could carry all he knew.

It was he who dropped them with a bounce from the realm of fancy to the unpleasing region of ugly fact. No sooner had Minnie cleared the table, and brought in the coffee, than he whisked around on Grant as though hitherto he had been only awaiting an opportunity of scarifying him.

"Now," he said, propping an elbow on the table, and supporting his chin on a clenched fist, "the embargo is off the Steynholme affair. *You* didn't kill Adelaide Melhuish, Mr. Grant. Who did?"

"I wish I could tell you," was the emphatic answer.

"Do you suspect anybody? You needn't fear the libel law in confiding your secret thought to me, and I assume that Mr. Hart is trustworthy - where his friends are concerned?"

"Why that unkind differentiating clause, my pocket Vidocq?" put in Hart.

"Because two Kings and a baker's dozen of Presidents have, at various times, sent most unflattering reports to this country about you."

"I must have annoyed 'em most damnably."

"You had. I congratulate you, but Heaven only knows where I may convoy you some day on an extradition warrant....Proceed, Mr. Grant."

"I assure you, on my honor, that the only reasonable

suggestion I can make is that put forward by my gardener to-day," said Grant. "He thinks that the murder must have been committed by a lunatic. I can offer no other hypothesis."

"Your gardener may be right. But what lunatic, barring yourself and the horse-coper, Elkin, is in love with Doris Martin?"

Like Elkin the previous night, Grant struck the table till things rattled.

"Keep her name out of it," he cried fiercely. "You are a man of the world, not a suspicious idiot of the Robinson type. You heard to-day the full and true explanation of her presence here on Monday night. It was a sheer accident. Why harp on Doris Martin rather than any member of the Bates family?"

"Who, may I ask, is Doris Martin?" put in Hart.

"The Steynholme postmaster's daughter," said Furneaux. "A remarkably pretty and intelligent girl. If her father was a peer she would be the belle of a London season. As it is, her good looks seem to have put a maggot in more than one nut in this village."

Hart waved the negro's head in the air.

"The lunatic theory for mine," he declared. "If one woman's lovely face could bring a thousand ships to Ilion, why should not another's drive men to madness in Steynholme?"

"Well phrased, sir," cackled Furneaux delightedly. "I'll wangle that in on a respected colleague of mine, who is a whale at deducing a proposition from given premises, but cannot induce a general fact from particular instances to save his life ... Now, stifle your romantic frenzy, Mr. Grant, and listen to me. If you were minded to instruct me in the art of writing good English, I would sit at your feet an attentive disciple. When I, Furneaux, of the 'Yard,' lay down a first principle in the investigation of crime, I expect deference on your part. I tell you unhesitatingly that if Doris Martin didn't exist, Adelaide Melhuish would be alive now. That, as a thesis, is nearly as certain a thing as that the sun will rise to-morrow. I go farther, and hazard the guess, not the fixed belief, though my guesses are usually borne out by events, that if Doris Martin had not been in this garden at half past ten on Monday night, Adelaide Melhuish would not have been killed some twenty minutes later. It is useless for you to fume and rage in vain effort to disprove either of these presumptive facts. You are simply beating the air. This mystery centers in and around the post-master's daughter. Come, now, you are a reasonable person. Admit the cold, hard truth, and then give play to your fancy."

"Sir," said Hart, brandishing his pipe again, "I suggest that you and I, here and now, form a mutual admiration society."

"It is a cruel and bitter thing that an innocent girl should be dragged into association with a foul crime," said Grant stubbornly. "I am not disputing the force of your acumen, Mr. Furneaux. My only desire is to shield the good name of a very charming young lady."

"What's done can't be undone," countered the detective, well knowing that Grant confessed himself beaten.

"But what is all the bother about? You heard from Miss Martin's own lips absolutely the whole truth, and nothing but the truth. Put her in the witness-box, and what more can she tell you?"

"I am not worrying about her appearance in the witness-box," said Furneaux dryly. "Long before that stage is reached I shall be hunting a star burglar, or, perhaps, looking into the Foreign Office *dossier* of our worthy friend here, as to-day's papers hint at trouble in Venezuela. No, sir. The county police will get all the credit. P.C. Robinson will be swanking about then, telling the yokels what *he* did. I, with Olympic nod, say, 'There's your man!' and the handcuffs' brigade do the rest. So far as I can foresee, Miss Martin's name may be spared any undue prominence in this inquiry. I go even farther, and promise that anything I can do in that way shall be done."

"That is very kind and considerate of you," said Grant gratefully.

"Don't halloo till you're out of the wood." said Furneaux, sitting back suddenly and nursing his left knee with clasped hands. "I can't control other people's actions, you know. What I insist on to-night is that you shall envisage this affair in its proper light. We have a long way to travel before counsel rises with his smug 'May it please you, me lud, and gentlemen of the jury.' But, having persuaded you to agree that, willy nilly, Miss Doris is the hub of our little universe for the hour, I now swear you and this fire-eater in as assistants. There must be no more speeches, no punching of heads, very little love-making, and that by order -"

"Has the postmaster's daughter a delectable sister, O Liliputian cop?" demanded Hart.

"No. Two of 'em would have caused a riot long since. Mr. Grant will do all, and more than all, necessary in that direction."

Grant leaned forward. He spoke very earnestly.

"I want you to believe me when I tell you," he said, "that I never gave serious thought to the notion of marrying Miss Martin until such a possibility was suggested last night by that swab, Ingerman."

"Ah, Ingerman! You kept a record of what he said, I gather?"

"Yes, here it is."

Grant rose, and went to a writing-desk with nests of drawers which stood against the wall on the left of the door. He never used it for its primary purpose. When the table was laid for meals, Minnie or her mother had orders to remove all papers and books to the top of the desk. The house contained no other living-room of size. The hall was spacious; a smoking den next the dining-room had degenerated into a receptacle of guns, fishing-rods, golf-clubs, Alpenstocks, skis and other such sporting accessories. The remainder of the ground-floor accommodation was given up to the Bateses.

Unlocking a drawer, Grant produced a notebook, which he handed to Furneaux. The detective laid it on the table. He was sitting with his back to the large window. Hart faced him. Grant's chair was between the two.

"By the way, as you're on your feet, Mr. Grant," said Furneaux, "you might just show me exactly where you were standing when you saw the face at the window."

"For the love of Mike, what's this?" gurgled Hart. "'The face at the window'; 'the postmaster's daughter.' How many more catchy cross-heads will you bring into the story?"

"Poor Adelaide Melhuish undoubtedly came here on Monday night and looked in at me while I was at work," said Grant sadly. "You know the history of my calf love three years ago, Wally."

"Shall I ever forget it? You bored me stiff about it. Then, when the crash came, you walked me off my legs in the Upper Engadine. Ugh! That night on the Forno glacier. It gives me a chill to think of it now. Furneaux, pass the port. Your name is wrongly spelt. It should be fourneau, not Furneaux. A little oven. Hot stuff. Got me?"

"My *dear* Hart, you flatter me," retorted the detective instantly.

"How long am I to pose here?" snapped Grant.

"Sorry," said Furneaux. "These interruptions are banal. Is that where you were?"

"Yes. I had my hand outstretched for a book. It's dark in this corner. When I want to find a book I light a candle, which is always placed on the ledge of the window for the purpose. The blind was not drawn that night. It seldom is. I had the book in my hand, and had found the required passage when I chanced to look at the window and saw *her* face."

"Do you mind reconstructing the scene. This lamp was on the table, I suppose?"

"Yes."

"Well, pull up the blind, light your candle, and find the book. Act the whole incident, in fact."

Grant obeyed. He held the candlestick until he had picked out the particular volume; then he placed it in the recess of the window, and searched through the pages of the book.

Furneaux bent forward so as to watch the rehearsal and catch the effect of the light externally. The hour was not so late as when Adelaide Melhuish, or her ghost, gazed in through one of those narrow panes, but the night was dark enough to lend the necessary *vraisemblance*. Hart, deeply interested, looked on with rapt, eager eyes. For a full minute the tableau remained thus. Then, with a rapidity born of many a close 'scape in wild lands, Hart drew a revolver from a hip pocket, and fired at the window.

He alone was in a position to see through all parts of it. Grant was still thumbing a small brown volume in the manner of one who knew that a certain passage would be found therein but was ignorant of its exact place in the text. Furneaux, intent on his every movement, had only a side-long view of the window, which, it will be remembered, formed a tiny rectangle in a thick wall.

The revolver was a heavy-caliber weapon, and the explosion blew out the lamp. The flame of the candle flickered, owing either to the passage of the bullet or the disturbance of the air. But it burnt steadily again within the fifth part of a second, and they all saw a starred hole in the center pane of glass of the second tier from the bottom.

"What fool's game are you playing?" shrilled Furneaux, nevertheless active as a wildcat in his spring to the French window, there to snatch at the blind and turn the knob which controlled a lever bolt.

"Laying another ghost - one with whiskers," said Hart coolly. "I got him, too, I think."

"You must be mad, mad!" shrieked the detective, tearing open the window, and vanishing.

"For Heaven's sake, Wally, no more shooting!" cried Grant, running after Furneaux.

Minnie and her mother appeared at the dining-room door. Finding the place in semi-obscurity, and reeking with gunpowder, they screamed loudly.

"You Steynholme folk are all on the jump," said Hart. "Cheer up, fair dames! Thunder relieves the atmosphere, you know, and one live cartridge is often more effective than an ocean of talk."

"Bub-bub-but who's shot, sir?" gasped Minnie.

"A ghost, a most scoundrelly apparition, with fearsome eyes, offensive whiskers, and a hat which is a base copy of mine."

"Owd Ben!" sighed Mrs. Bates, collapsing straightway in a faint.

Luckily, Minnie caught her mother and broke her fall, because the housekeeper was large and solid, and might have been seriously injured otherwise. Hart was distressed by this development, but, being eminently a ready person in an emergency, he rose to the occasion by extracting the empty case from the revolver, and holding it to the poor woman's nostrils, while supporting her with an arm and a knee.

"This is far more effective than burnt brown paper, Minnie," he said. "Now, don't get excited, but mix some brandy and water, and we'll have your mother telling us who Owd Ben is, or was, before Hawk-eye comes back to disturb us. Judging by the noises I hear, he's busy outside."

"That's father!" shrieked Minnie hysterically.

"Good Lord! Has your father -"

For an instant, Hart was nearly alarmed, but Grant's voice came authoritatively:

"It's all right, Bates. Let go, I tell you!"

"Phew!" said Hart. "I was on the point of confusing your respected dad with Owd Ben ... That's it, ma! Sniff hard! As a cook you're worth your weight in gold, which is some cook."

Meanwhile, Furneaux, seeing that no dead body was stretched on the strip of grass beneath the window, dashed into the shrubbery to the right, and was clutched in a mighty embrace by an older but much more powerful man in Bates, who had hurried from the front of the house on hearing the pistol-shot. Most fortunately, the gardener, deeming his vigil a needless one, had not armed himself with a stick, or the consequences might have been grave. As it was, no one except Hart had been vouchsafed sight or sound of the latest specter, which, however, had left a very convincing souvenir of its visit in the shape of a soft felt hat with two bullet holes through the crown.

Furneaux, quivering with silent wrath, soon abandoned the search when this *pièce de conviction* was found at the root of the Dorothy Perkins rose-tree. Seeing the lamp relighted, he peremptorily bade Grant and Bates come in with him. He closed the window, adjusted the blind again, and poured generous measures of port wine into two glasses. Handing one to Bates, he took the other himself.

"Friend," he said, "some men have fame thrust upon them, but you have achieved it. To-night you pierced the heel of Achilles. Here's to you!"

"I dunno wot 'ee's saying mister, but 'good health'," said Bates, swigging the wine with gusto.

"Now, for your master's sake, not a word to a soul about this hubbub."

"Right you are, sir! But that there pryin' Robinson wur on t' bridge five minutes since. And, by gum, here he is!"

A determined knock and ring came at the front door. Minnie, helped by Hart, had just escorted Mrs. Bates to the kitchen.

"Let *me* go!" said Furneaux, darting out into the hall. He opened the door, and thrust his face into the police-constable's, startling the latter considerably. Before Robinson could utter a syllable, the detective hissed a question.

"Did anyone cross the bridge after that shot was fired?"

"Nun - No, sir," stuttered the other.

"You saw no one running along the road?"

"Saw nothing, sir."

"Very well. Glad to find you're on the job. Don't let on you met me here. Good-night!"

Mighty is Scotland Yard with the provincial police. Robinson was back on his self-imposed beat before he well realized that he knew neither why nor by whom nor by what sort of weapon the commotion had been created. But he was quite sure the noise came from the garden front of Mr. Grant's house.

"That little hop-o'-me-thumb thinks he's smart, dam smart," he communed angrily, "but I've taken a line of me own, an' I'll stick to it, though the Yard sends down twenty men!"

He heard footsteps coming down a paved footpath which ran like a white riband through the cobble-beaded width of the high-street, and withdrew swiftly to the shelter of a disused tannery adjoining the village end of the bridge. A cloaked female figure sped past. Though the night was rather dark for June, he had no difficulty in recognizing Doris Martin's graceful movements. No other girl in Steynholme walked like her. She was slim enough to dispense with tight corsets, and tall enough to wear low-heeled shoes, nor did she need to pinch her toes in order to gain the semblance of small feet.

After her went Robinson, keyed to exultation by this outcome of his watchfulness. She was going to The Hollies, of course. The road led to Knoleworth, and no young woman of her age in the village would dream of taking a lonely walk in the country at ten o'clock at night.

For a man of his height and somewhat ponderous build, the policeman followed with real stealth. Thus, when she turned in at the gate, he was there by the time she had reached the front door. He heard her pull the bell. Curiously enough, to his thinking, Furneaux again appeared.

"Is Mr. Grant at home?" he heard Doris say.

"Yes. Will you come in?" replied the detective.

"Is he - is all well here?"

"Quite, I assure you. But *do* come in. I'll escort you home. I'm going to the inn in five minutes."

Doris, after hesitating a little, entered.

Robinson crept on tiptoe over a stretch of gravel, and took to the shrubbery. It was high time, he thought, that the local constabulary learnt what was going on in that abode of mystery.

CHAPTER IX

HE WHOM THE CAP FITS -

Several minutes had elapsed between the two unexpected visits. During those minutes a somewhat acrimonious discussion broke out in the dining-room. Bates went to reassure his wife, and Hart sauntered back from the kitchen. He was received by Furneaux and Grant more in sorrow than in anger, a pose on their part which he blandly disregarded. He helped himself to the remains of the decanter of port.

"The next point of vital interest in the narrative is to establish, by such evidence as is available, who Owd Ben is, or was," he said. "I presume, since he had attained local celebrity as a ghost, he has passed over, as the spiritists say."

"Sit down!" cried Furneaux savagely.

Hart sat down, and began filling that portentous pipe.

"You fellows merely ran into each other outside, I take it," he said, apparently by way of a chatty remark. "The crack of the pistol-shot and the supposed resurrection of Owd Ben threw Mrs. Bates temporarily off her balance, so I helped in reviving her. Between such a cook and such a ghost, who would hesitate?"

When Furneaux was really irritated, he swore in French.

"Nom d'un bon petit homme gris!" he almost squealed, "why did you whip out that infernal revolver? You spoiled everything, everything! Have you no sense in that picturesque head of yours? Your skull is big enough to hold brains, not soap-bubbles."

"Did your French father marry a Jap?" inquired Hart, with sudden interest.

"And now you're insulting my mother," yelped the detective.

"Not I. You know nothing about the finest race of little women in the world, or you would not even imagine such rubbish."

"But why, why, didn't you tell me that you saw someone outside?"

"You wouldn't have believed me. The goblin was disappearing. I had to shoot quick."

"Why shoot at all?"

"Sir, there are certain manifestations I object to on principle. What self-respecting ghost ever wore whiskers?"

"This was no ghost. You shot the man's hat off."

"Then what the blazes are you growling at? Had I, in blood-curdling whisper, told you that once again there was a face at the window, you would have scoffed at me. The ill-looking scamp caught my eye after his first glance at Grant. He was mizzling when I fired. You would have sat there and argued about hypnosis, with our worthy author's skilled support. And there would have been no hat! I do an admirable bit of trick shooting, yet I am only reviled for my dexterity. Really, Charles François!"

"Ah! You remember, at last," and the detective smiled sourly.

"*Parfaitement*! as they say in Paris, where you and I met once, though 'twas in a crowd. But *I* didn't steal the blessed pearl. I believe it was that blatant patriot, Domengo Suarez."

"You've got *some* brains, then. Why not use them? Don't you see what a fix we three would have found ourselves in had you shot the man?"

"But, consider, Carlo mio! A spook with whiskers! What court would find me guilty? Let me produce the authentic record of Owd Ben, and I have no doubt but that the Lord Chief Justice himself would have potted his representative. He'd be bound to confess it."

Furneaux was cooling down.

"You've shaken my confidence," he said. "Unless I have your promise that you will never do such a thing again while in my company, I shall ban you from this inquiry with bell, book, and candle."

"Very well. It's a bargain. Now let us ponder Exhibit A."

He stretched a long arm over the table, and took the hat.

"Put it on!" commanded the detective.

Hart did so, and scowled frightfully. Furneaux bent forward and squinted.

"Notice the line of those bullet-holes," he said to Grant.

"Any man wearing that hat must have had his scalp ploughed up," said Grant instantly.

"Well, we know that nothing of the kind happened. Why?"

"It was perched on top of a wig," drawled Hart.

Furneaux was slightly disappointed - there was no denying it. Being a vain little person, he liked to show off in a minor matter such as this.

"Yes," he admitted, "and what's the corollary?"

"That the wearer is probably a clean-shaven person with thin hair, a daring scoundrel who is well posted in the leading characteristics of Owd Ben. Charles le Petit, time is now ripe for details of that hairy goblin."

"Where did you dig him up from, anyhow?" said the detective testily.

"Mrs. Bates recognized him from my vivid description."

"Her husband can tell us the story," put in Grant. "I'll fetch him."

He had not moved ere the front door bell rang a second time.

"Here is Owd Ben himself, I expect," said Hart.

"If it's that Robinson - " growled Furneaux vexedly, hastening to forestall Minnie.

But it was Doris Martin, and very pretty she looked as she entered the room, her high color being the joint outcome of a rapid walk and a very natural embarrassment at finding the frankly admiring eyes of a stranger fixed on her.

"I don't quite know why I'm here," she said, with a nervous laugh, addressing Grant directly. "You will think I am always gazing in the direction of The Hollies, but my room commands this house so fully that I cannot help seeing or hearing anything unusual. A few minutes ago I heard what I thought was a muffled gunshot. I looked out, and saw your window thrown open, though the light was dim, and only a candle was showing in the smaller window. I was alarmed, so came to inquire what had happened. You'll pardon me, I'm sure."

"Say you don't, Jack, I implore you, and let me apologize for you," pleaded Hart.

"Doris, this is my good friend, Wally Hart," smiled Grant. "Won't you sit down? We have an exciting story for you."

"Father will be horribly anxious if he knows I have gone out."

Nevertheless, there was sufficient spice of Mother Eve in Doris that she should take the proffered chair.

"Sorry to interrupt," broke in Furneaux. "Did you meet P.C. Robinson!"

"No."

"You came by way of the bridge?"

"There is no other way, unless one makes a detour by Bush Walk."

The detective whirled round on Grant.

"What room is over this one?"

"Minnie's."

"She's in the kitchen, with her mother. See that she doesn't come upstairs while I'm absent. You three keep on talking."

"Thanks," said Hart.

Doris, more self-possessed now, read the meaning of the quip promptly.

"Mr. Grant has often spoken of you," she said. "You talk, and we'll listen."

"Not so, divinity," came the retort. "I may be a parrot, but I don't want my neck wrung when you've gone."

"Don't encourage him, Doris," said Grant, "or you'll be here till midnight."

"If that's the best you can do, you had better leave the recital to me," laughed Hart.

Meanwhile, Furneaux had stolen noiselessly to the bedroom overhead. The casement window was open - he had noted that fact while in the garden. He peeped out, and was just in time to see Robinson emulating a Sioux Indian on the war-path. The policeman removed his helmet, and was about to peer cautiously through the small window. The detective's blood ran cold. What if Hart discovered yet another ghost?

"Robinson - go home!" he said, in sepulchral tones.

The constable positively jumped. He gaped on all sides in real terror. He, too, had heard hair-raising tales of Owd Ben.

"Go home!" hissed Furneaux, leaning out.

Then the other looked up.

"Oh, it's you, sir!" he gasped, sighing with relief.

"Man, you've had the closest shave of your life! There's a fellow below there who shoots at sight."

"But I'm on duty, sir."

"You'll be in Kingdom Come if you gaze in at that window. Be off!"

"I -"

"Robinson, you and I will quarrel if you don't do as I bid you. And that would be a pity, because I want to inform Mr. Fowler that he has a particularly smart man in Steynholme."

"Very well, sir, if *you're* satisfied, I *must* be."

And away went the eavesdropper, crushed, still tingling with that fear of the supernatural latent in every heart, but far from convinced.

Furneaux tripped downstairs. The routing of Robinson had put him into a real good humor. He found the three in the dining-room gazing spell-bound at the felt hat.

"Now, young lady, you're coming with me," he said, grinning amiably. "The Sussex constabulary is quelled for the hour."

"But, Mr. Furneaux, I recognize that hat!" said Doris, and it was notable that even Hart remained silent.

The detective looked at her strangely, but put no question.

"I am almost sure it belongs to our local Amateur Dramatic Society," went on the girl. "It was worn by Mr. Elkin last November. He played a burlesque of Svengali. I was Trilby, and caught a horrid cold from walking about without shoes or stockings."

"Don't tell me any more," was Furneaux's surprising comment. "I'll do the rest. But let me remark, Miss Martin, that I experienced great difficulty, not so long ago, in persuading friend Grant that you were the only important witness this case has provided thus far.

Playing in a burlesque, were you? We've been similarly engaged to-night. The farce must stop now. It makes way for grim tragedy. Not one word of to-night's events to anyone, please.... Are you ready?"

Doris stood up. Hart thrust the negro's head at the detective.

"Fouché," he said, "do you honestly mean slinging your hook without making any inquiry as to Owd Ben?"

"Oh, the ghost!" said Doris eagerly. "The Bateses would think of him, of course. An old farmer named Ben Robson used to live in this house about the time of Napoleon. He was suspected by the authorities to be an agent of the smugglers, and the story goes that his own daughter quarreled with him and betrayed him. He narrowly escaped hanging, owing to his age, I believe, and was sentenced to a long term of imprisonment. At last he was released, being then a very old man, and he came straight here and strangled his daughter. It is quite a terrible story. He was found dead by her side. Then people remembered that she had spoken of someone scaring her by looking in through that small window some nights previously. Naturally, a ghost was soon manufactured. I really wonder why the man who rebuilt and renamed the place in the middle of last century didn't have the window removed altogether."

"Glad I began the work of demolition tonight," said Hart, and, for once, his tone was serious.

"Why did you never tell me that scrap of history, Doris?" inquired Grant.

"You liked the place so much that father and I agreed not to mar your enthusiasm by recalling an unpleasant legend," she said frankly. "Not that what I've related isn't true. The record appears in a Sussex Miscellany of those years .... Oh, my goodness, can it be eleven o'clock!"

The hall clock had no doubt on the point. Furneaux pocketed the written notes regarding Ingerman, and grabbed the hat off the table. Grant, for some reason, was aware that the detective repressed an obvious reference to the last occasion on which the girl had heard that same clock announce the hour.

Furneaux would allow no other escort. He and Doris made off immediately.

When they were gone, Hart stared fixedly at an empty decanter.

"My dim recollection of your port, Jack, is that it was a wine of many virtues and few vices," he mused aloud.

Grant took the hint, and went to a cellar. Returning, he found his crony poring over the book which, singularly enough, figured prominently on each occasion when the specter-producing window was markedly in evidence. Hart glanced up at his host, and nodded cheerfully at a dust-laden bottle.

"What is there in 'The Talisman' which needed so much research?" he asked.

"Some lines by Sir David Lindsay, quoted by Scott," was the answer.

"Are these they?" And Hart read:

> One thing is certain in our Northern land;
> Allow that birth, or valor, wealth, or wit,
> Give each precedence to their possessor,
> Envy, that follows on such eminence,
> As comes the lyme-hound on the roebuck's trace,
> Shall pull them down each one.

"Yes," said Grant.

"Love isn't mentioned. The fair Doris will be true. You're in luck, my boy. But somebody is out for your blood, and here is clear warning. Gee whizz! If I remain in Steynholme a week I shall become an occultist. What is a lyme-hound?"

"'Lyme,' or 'leam,' is the old-time word for 'leash.'"

"Good!" said Hart. "That will appeal to Furneaux. Have him in to dinner every day, Jack. He's a tonic!"

Furneaux, for some reason known only to himself, did not accompany Doris to the post office. Once they were across the bridge, and the broad village street, more green than roadway, was seen to be empty, he tapped her on the shoulder and said pleasantly:

"Run away home now, little girl. Sleep well, and don't worry. The tangle will right itself in time."

"Poor Mr. Grant is suffering," she ventured to murmur.

"And a good thing, too. It will steady him. Hurry, please. I'll wait here till you are behind a locked door."

"No one in Steynholme will hurt me," she said.

"You never can tell. I'm not taking any chances to-night, however."

So Doris sped swiftly up the hill. Arrived at her house, she waved a hand to the detective, who flourished his straw hat in response. A fine June night in England is never really dark, so the two could not only see each other but, when Doris disappeared, Furneaux, turning sharply on his heel, was able to make out the sudden straightening of a pucker in the blind of a ground-floor room in P.C. Robinson's abode.

The detective walked straight there, and tapped lightly on the window. Robinson, after an affected delay, came to the door.

"Who's there?" he demanded.

"As if you didn't know," laughed Furneaux.

Robinson turned a key, and looked out.

"Oh, it's you, sir?" he cried.

"You'll get tired of saying that before I quit Steyn-holme," said the detective. "May I come in? No, don't show a light here. Let's chat in the back kitchen."

"I was just going to have a bite of supper, sir," began Robinson apologetically. "It's laid in the kitchen. On'y bread and cheese an' a glass of beer. Will you join me?"

"With pleasure, if I hadn't stuffed myself at Grant's

place. Nice fellow, Grant. Pity you and he don't seem to get on together. Of course, we policemen cannot allow friendship to interfere with duty, but, between you and me, Robinson - strictly in confidence - Grant had no more to do with the actual murder of Miss Melhuish than either of us two."

Robinson had turned up a lamp, and hospitably installed Furneaux in his own easy-chair.

"The 'actual murder,' you said, sir?" he repeated.

"Yes. It was his presence at The Hollies which brought an infatuated woman there, and thus directly led to her death. That is all. Grant is telling the truth. I assure you, Robinson, I never allow myself to break bread with a man whom I may have to convict. So, I'll change my mind, and take a snack of your bread and cheese."

The village constable, by no means a fool, grinned at the implied tribute. What he did not appreciate so readily was the fact that his somewhat massive form was being twiddled round the detective's little finger.

"Right you are, sir," he cried cheerily. "But, if Mr. Grant didn't kill Miss Melhuish, who did!"

"In all probability, the man who wore that hat," chirped Furneaux, taking a nondescript bundle from a coat pocket, and throwing it on the table.

Robinson started. This June night was full of weird surprises. He set down a jug of beer with a bang - his intent being to fill two glasses already in position, from which circumstance even the least observant visitor might deduce a Mrs. Robinson, *en negligé*, hastily flown upstairs.

He examined the hat as though it were a new form of bomb.

"By gum!" he muttered. "Are these bullet-holes?"

"They are."

"An' is this what someone fired at?"

"Yes."

"But how in thunder -"

He checked himself in time. He did not want to admit that he had been watching the only recognized road to Grant's house all the evening.

"Quite so!" chortled Furneaux, with admirable misunderstanding. "You're quick on the trigger, Robinson - almost as quick as that friend of Grant's who arrived by the 5.30 from London. You perceive at once that no ordinary head could have worn that hat without having its hair combed by the same bullet. It was stuck on to a thick wig. Now, tell me the man, or woman, in Steynholme, who wears a wig and a hat like that, and you and I will guess who killed Miss Melhuish."

Robinson suspected that, as he himself would have put it, his leg was being pulled rather violently. Furneaux read his face like a printed page. Chewing, much against his will, a mouthful of bread and cheese, he mumbled in solemn, broken tones:

"Think - Robinson. Don't - answer - offhand. Has - anybody - ever worn - such things - in a play?"

Then the policeman was convinced, galvanized by memory, as it were.

"By gum!" he cried again. "Fred Elkin - in a charity performance last winter."

Furneaux choked with excitement.

"A horsey-looking chap, on to-day's jury," he gurgled.

"That's him!"

"The scoundrel!"

"No wonder he looked ill."

"No wonder, indeed. How oft the sight of means to do ill deeds makes ill deeds done!"

"But, sir -"

Robinson was flabbergasted. He could only murmur "Fred Elkin!" in a dazed way.

"Have a drink," said Furneaux sympathetically. "I'll wet my whistle, too. Only half a glass, please. Now, we mustn't jump to conclusions. This Elkin looks a villain, but may not be one. That is to say, his villainy may be confined to dealings in nags. But you see, Robinson, what a queer turn this affair is taking. We must get rid of preconceived notions. Superintendent Fowler and you and I will go into this matter thoroughly to-morrow. Meanwhile, breathe not a

Louis Tracy

syllable to a living soul. If I were you, I'd let Mr. Grant understand that we regard him as rather outside the scope of our inquiry. This beer is very good for a country village. You know a good thing when you see it, I expect. Pity I don't smoke, or I'd join you in a pipe. I must get a move on, now, or that fat landlord will be locking me out. Good night! Yes. I'll take the hat. *Good* night!"

While walking up the hill Furneaux fanned himself with the straw hat.

"One small bit of my brain is evidently a hereditary bequest from a good-natured ass!" he communed. "Here am I, Furneaux, plagued beyond endurance by a first-class murder case, and I must go and busy myself with the love affair of a postmaster's daughter and a feather-headed novelist!"

When Tomlin admitted him to the Hare and Hounds, he buttonholed the landlord, who, at that hour, was usually somewhat obfuscated.

"Sir," said the detective gravely, "I am told that you Steynholme folk indulge occasionally in such frivolities as amateur theatricals?"

"Once in a way, sir. Once in a way. Afore I lock up the bar, will you -"

"Not to-night. I've mixed port and beer already, and I'm only a little fellow. Now you, Mr. Tomlin, can mix anything, I fancy?"

"I've tried a few combinations in me time, sir."

"But, about these theatrical performances - is there any scenery, costumes, 'props' as actors call them?"

" Yes, sir. They're stored in the loft over the club-room - the room where the inquest wur held."

"What, *here*?"

Furneaux's shrill cry scared Mr. Tomlin.

"Y-yes, sir," he stuttered.

"Is that my candle?" said the detective tragically. "I'm tired, dead beat. To-night, Mr. Tomlin, you are privileged to see the temporary wreck of a noble mind. God wot, 'tis a harrowing spectacle."

Furneaux skipped nimbly upstairs. Tomlin proceeded to lock up.

"It's good for trade," he mumbled, "but I'll be glad when these 'ere Lunnon gents clears out. They worry me, they do. Fair gemme a turn, 'e did. A tec', indeed! He's nothin' but a play-hactor hisself!"

CHAPTER X

THE CASE AGAINST GRANT

Next morning, after a long conference with Superintendent Fowler, from which, to his great chagrin, P. C. Robinson was excluded, Furneaux went to the post office, dispatched an apparently meaningless telegram to a code address, and exchanged a few orthodox remarks with Doris and her father about the continued fine weather. While he was yet at the counter, Ingerman crossed the road and entered the chemist's shop.

"Let me see," said the detective musingly, "by committing a slight trespass on your left-hand neighbor's garden, can I reach the yard of the inn?"

"What the eye doesn't see the heart doesn't grieve over," smiled Doris. "Mrs. Jefferson went to Knoleworth early to-day, and took her maid. By shopping at the stores there, they save their fares, and have a day out each week."

"May I go that way, then?" he said. "Suppose you send that goggle-eyed skivvy of yours on an errand."

This was done, and Furneaux made the desired transit.

Now, Tomlin, to whom the comings and goings of all and sundry formed the staple of the day's gossip, had seen the detective go out, but could "take his sollum davy" that the queer little man had not returned. He, too, had watched Ingerman going to Siddle's. Ten minutes later Elkin came down the hill, and headed for the same rendezvous. Five minutes more, and Hobbs, the butcher, joined the others. Tomlin was seething with curiosity, but there were some casual customers in the "snug," so he could not abandon his post.

Soon, however, Ingerman led Elkin and Hobbs to the inn. Evidently, the "financier" had been making some small purchases. He was in high spirits. Ordering appetizers before the mid-day meal, he announced that he was returning to London that afternoon, but would be in Steynholme again for the adjourned inquest.

"No matter how my business suffers, I mean to see this affair through," he vowed. "You gentlemen can pretty well guess my private convictions. You were good enough to give me your friendship, so I spoke as openly as one dares when no charge has actually been laid against any particular person."

"Ay," said Elkin, with whom sunshine seemed to disagree, because he looked miserably ill. "We know what you mean, Mr. Ingerman. If the police were half sharp they'd have nabbed their man before this ... Did you put any water in this gin, Tomlin?"

"Water?" wheezed Tomlin indignantly. *"Water?"*

"Well, no offense. I can't taste anything. I believe I could swallow dope and not feel it on my tongue."

"You do look bad, an' no mistake, Fred," agreed Hobbs. "Are you vettin' yerself? Don't. Every man to his trade, sez I. Give Dr. Foxton a call."

"I'm taking his medicine regular. Perhaps I need a change."

"'Ave a week-end in Lunnon," said Hobbs, with a broad wink.

"Change of medicine, I mean. I'm not leaving Steynholme till things make a move. My next trip to London will be my honeymoon."

"You look like a honeymooner, I don't think," guffawed Hobbs.

"You wouldn't laugh if I told *you* what you really look like," cried Elkin angrily. "Bet you a level fiver I'm married this year. Now, put up or shut up!"

Furneaux peeped in, through a door, always open, which led to the stairs.

"Can I have my account, Mr. Tomlin?" he said. "I'm going to town by the next train."

"You don't mean to say, Mr. Furneaux, that you are abandoning the case so soon?" broke in Ingerman.

"Did I say that?" inquired the detective meekly.

"No. One can't help drawing inferences occasionally."

"Great mistake. Look at our worthy landlord. He's been drawing inferences as well as corks, and he's beat to the world."

Tomlin was, indeed, gazing at his smaller guest open-mouthed.

"S'elp me!" he gurgled. "I could ha' sworn -"

"Bad habit," and Furneaux crooked a waggish fore-finger at him. "Even the wisest among us may err. Last night, for instance, I blundered. I really fancied I had a clew to the Steynholme murderer. And where do you think it ended? In the loft of your club-room, Mr. Tomlin. In a box of old clothes at that. Silly, isn't it?"

"Wot! Them amatoor play-hactin' things?"

"Exactly."

Elkin grunted, though intending to laugh.

"Not so sharp for a London 'tec, I must say," he cried. "Why, those props have been there since before Christmas."

"Yes. I know now," was the downcast reply. "Twelve hours ago I thought differently. Didn't I, Mr. Tomlin?"

Tomlin tried hard to look knowing.

"Oh, is that wot you wur drivin' at?" he said. "Dang me, mister, I could soon ha' put you right 'ad you tole me."

"Well, well. Can't be helped. I may do better in London. What do *you* say, Mr. Ingerman? The City is the real mint of money and crime. Who knows but that a stroll through Cornhill may have some bearing on the Steynholme mystery?"

"May be you'd get a bit nearer if you took a stroll along the Knoleworth Road, and not so very far, either," guffawed Elkin.

"Who knows?" repeated Furneaux sadly. "Good-day, gentlemen. Some of this merry party will meet again, of course, if not here, at the Assizes. Don't forget my bill. Mr. Tomlin. By the way, one egg at breakfast had seen vicissitudes. It shouldn't be rated too highly."

"I'm traveling by your train," cried Ingerman.

"So I understood," said Furneaux over his shoulder.

There was silence for a moment after he had gone. Ingerman looked thoughtful, even puzzled. He was casting back in his mind to discover just how and when the detective "understood" that his departure was imminent, since he himself had only arrived at a decision after leaving the chemist's.

"That chap is no good," announced Elkin. "I'll back old Robinson against him any day."

"Sh-s-sh! He may 'ear you," muttered the landlord.

"Don't care if he does. Cornhill! What the blazes has Cornhill to do with the murder at The Hollies?"

Ingerman appreciated the value of that concluding phrase. Elkin had used it once before in Siddle's shop, and was quietly reproved by the chemist for his outspokenness.

Ingerman, however, did not inform the company that his office lay in an alley off Cornhill. He elected to rub in Elkin's words.

"Mr. Siddle seemed to object to The Hollies being mentioned as the scene of the crime," he said. "I wonder why?"

"Because he's an old molly-coddle," snapped the horse-dealer. "Thinks everyone is like himself, a regular slow-coach."

Tomlin closed the door into the passage, closed it for the first time in living memory, whereat Furneaux, on the landing above, grinned sardonically, and ran downstairs.

"Wot's this about them amatoor clo'es?" he inquired portentously. "Oo 'as the key of that box?"

"*I* have," said Elkin. "I locked it after the last performance, and, unless you've been up to any monkey tricks, Tomlin, the duds are there yet."

"You're bitin' me 'ead off all the mornin', Fred," protested the aggrieved landlord. "Fust, the gin was wrong, an' now I'm supposed to 'ave rummidged yur box. Wot for?"

Furneaux popped in.

"My bill ready?" he squeaked.

"No, sir. The train -"

"Leaves at two, but I'm driving to Knoleworth with

Superintendent Fowler."

The door closed behind him. Tomlin shook his head.

"Box! Jack-in-the-box, I reckon," he said darkly, turning to a dog-eared ledger.

Neither at Knoleworth nor Victoria did Ingerman catch sight of the detective, though he was anxious either to make the journey in the company of the representative of Scotland Yard or arrange an early appointment with him. True, he was not inclined to place the strange-mannered little man on the same high plane as that suggested by certain London journalists to whom he had spoken. But he wanted to win the confidence of "the Yard" in connection with this case, and the belief that he was being avoided was nettling. He found consolation, of a sort, in the illustrated papers. One especially contained two pages of local pictures. "Mr. Grant addressing the crowd," with full text, was very effective, while there were admirable studies of The Hollies and the "scene of the tragedy." His own portrait was not flattering. The sun had etched his Mephistophelian features rather sharply, whereas Grant looked a very fine fellow.

Ingerman would have been more than surprised were he privileged to overhear a conversation which began and ended before he reached his flat in North Kensington.

Furneaux, who had jumped into the fore part of the train at Knoleworth, and was out in a jiffy at Victoria, handed his bag to a station detective, and turned into Vauxhall Bridge Road, one of the quietest of London's main thoroughfares. There he met a big man, dressed in tweeds, whose manifest concern at the moment seemed to center in a rather bad wrapping of a very good cigar.

"Ah! How goes it, Charles?" cried the big man heartily, affecting to be aware of Furneaux's presence when the latter had walked nearly a hundred yards down a comparatively deserted street.

"What's wrong with the toofa?" inquired Furneaux testily.

"My own carelessness. Stupid things, bands on cigars.... Well, what's the rush?"

"There's a train to Steynholme at five o'clock. I want you to take hold. I must have help. Like your cigar, this case has come unstuck."

Mr. James Leander Winter, Chief Inspector under the Criminal Investigation Department, whistled softly.

"Tut, tut!" he said. "One can never trust the newspapers. Reading this morning's particulars, it looked dead easy."

"Tell me how it struck you. Sometimes the uninformed brain is vouchsafed a gleam of unconscious genius."

Winter appeared to be devoting his mind to circumventing the vagaries of a fragile tobacco-leaf. He was a man of powerful build, over forty, heavy but active, deep-chested, round-headed, with bulging blue eyes which radiated kindliness and strength of character. The press photographer described him accurately to Grant. The average Londoner would have taken him for a county gentleman on a visit to the Agricultural Show at Islington, with a morning at Tattersall's as a variant. Yet, Sam Weller's extensive and peculiar knowledge of London compared with his as a freshman's with a don's of a university. It would be hard to assess, in coin of the realm, the value of the political and social secrets stowed away in that big head.

"First, I must put a question or two," he said, smiling at a baby which cooed at him from the shaded depths of a passing perambulator. "Is there another woman?"

"Yes, the postmaster's daughter, Doris Martin."

"Shy, pretty little bird, of course?"

"Everything that is good and beautiful."

"Is Grant a Lothario?"

"Excellent chap. Quarter of an hour before the murder he was giving Doris a lesson in astronomy in the garden of The Hollies."

"Never heard it called *that* before."

"This time the statement happens to be strictly accurate."

"Honest Injun?"

"I'm sure of it. If anything, the death of Adelaide Melhuish cleared the scales off their eyes. Those two have never kissed or squeezed - yet. They'll be starting quite soon now."

"How old is Doris?"

"Nineteen."

"But a really good-looking girl of nineteen must have had admirers before Grant went to the village."

"She had, and has. Having educated herself out of the rut, however, she left many runners at the post. One is persistent - a youngish horse-coper named Elkin. Adelaide Melhuish probably saw her with Grant. Neither Doris nor Grant knew that Adelaide Melhuish, as such, was in Steynholme. That is to say, the girl had seen Miss Melhuish in the post office, and recognized her as a famous actress, but that is all. And now I shan't tell you any more, or you'll know all that I know, which is too much."

The cigar was behaving itself at last, having burnt down to the fracture, so Winter's thoughts could be given exclusively to the less important matter of the Steynholme affair.

"To begin with," he said instantly. "Ingerman can establish a cast-iron alibi."

"So I imagined. But he's a bad lot. I throw in that item gratuitously."

The oddly-assorted pair walked in silence until Vauxhall Bridge was in sight. Winter pulled out a watch.

"What time did you say my train left Victoria?" he inquired.

"Plenty of time yet to make your guess and listen to further details," scoffed Furneaux.

"Frankly, I give it up. But, if I must share in the hunt, I tell you now that, metaphorically speaking, I shall cling to the postmaster's daughter till torn away by sheer force of evidence."

Furneaux dug his colleague in the ribs.

"That's the effect of constant association with me, James," he cackled gleefully. "Ten years ago you would have pounced on Elkin. You've hit it! I'm a prood mon the day. The pupil is equaling the master."

"You little rat, I had hanged my first murderer before you knew the meaning of *habeas corpus*! Let's turn now, and get to business."

Few Treasury barristers, leading for the Crown, could have marshaled the facts with such lucidity and fairness as Furneaux during that saunter to Victoria Station.

"Nothing extenuate, nor set down aught in malice," said Othello to Lodovico, and these Scotland Yard men, charged with so great a responsibility, never forgot the great-hearted Moor's advice.

When Winter took his seat in the train at five o'clock he could have drawn a plan of Steynholme, which he had never seen, and marked thereon the exact position of each house mentioned in this record. Moreover, he was acquainted with the chief characters by sight, as it were. And, finally, he and Furneaux had arranged a plan of campaign.

Furneaux refreshed a jaded intellect by an evening at the opera. Next morning, at eleven o'clock, he was inquiring for Mr. Ingerman at an office in a certain alley off Cornhill.

A smart youth interposed a printed formula between the visitor and a door marked "Private." Furneaux wrote his name, and put "Steynholme" in the space reserved for "business." He was admitted at once. Mr. Ingerman, apparently, was immersed in a pile of letters, but he swept them all aside, and greeted the caller affably.

"Glad to see you, Mr. Furneaux," he said. "I missed you on the train yesterday. Did you -"

"Nice quiet place you've got here, Mr. Ingerman," interrupted the detective.

"Yes. But, as I was about to -"

"Artistically furnished, too," went on Furneaux dreamily. "Oak, self-toned carpets and rugs, restful decorations. Those etchings, also, show taste in the selection. 'The Embankment - by Night.' Fitting sequel to 'The City - by Day.' I'm a child in such matters, but, 'pon my honor, if tempted to pour out my hard-earned savings into the lap of a City magnate, I would disgorge here more readily than in some saloon-bar of finance, where the new mahogany glistens, and the typewriters click like machine-guns."

Ingerman was nettled. He glanced at his correspondence.

" You have a somewhat far-fetched notion of my

position," he said, with a staccato quality in his velvet voice. "I am not a magnate, and I toil here to make, not to lose, money for my clients."

"A noble ideal. Forgive me if my rhapsody took the wrong line."

"And I'm sure you will forgive me if I now put the question which leads to the probable cause of your visit. Did you travel by the two o'clock train yesterday?"

"Yes. I avoided you purposely."

"May I ask, why?"

"My mind was weary. I wanted my wits about me when I tackled you."

Ingerman smiled, and leaned back, resting both elbows on the arms of the chair, and bringing the tips of his fingers together.

"Proceed," he said.

"You prefer that I should drag out a statement piecemeal rather than receive it *en bloc*?"

"Put it that way, if you like."

"I shall even enjoy it. To clear the ground, are you the Isidor G. Ingerman who exploited the A1 Mine in Abyssinia?"

Ingerman's finger-tips whitened under a sudden pressure, but his voice remained calm.

"An unfortunate episode," he said.

"And the Aegean Transport Company, Limited?"

"Into which I was inveigled by Greeks. But why this history of ruined enterprises?"

"It's a sort of schooling. I have noticed that the smartest counsel invariably begin with a few fireworks in order to induce the proper frame of mind in a witness."

"Does that mean that you want me to blurt out bitter and prejudiced accusations against Mr. Grant?"

"I want to hear what you have to say about the death of your wife. You forced the cross-examining role on me. I'm doing my best."

Ingerman kept silent during many seconds. When he spoke, his cultured voice was suave as ever.

"Perhaps it was my fault, Mr. Furneaux," he said. "You gave me a strong hint. I should have taken it, and we might have started an interesting chat on pleasanter lines. So, with apologies for my insistence about the train, I make a fresh start. I believe firmly that Grant was directly concerned in the murder. And I shall justify my belief. Within the past fortnight a *rapprochement* between my wife and myself became possible. It was spoken of, even reduced to the written word. I have her letters. Mine should be found among her belongings. May I take it that they *have* been found?"

"Yes," said Furneaux.

"Ah. So far, so good. My poor wife reached the parting of the ways. She saw that her life was becoming an empty husk. I think the theater was palling on her. But I see now that she still cherished the dream of winning the man she loved - not me, her husband, but that handsome dilettante, Grant. I take it, therefore, that she went to Steynholme to determine whether or not the glamour of the past was really dead. Unfortunately, she witnessed certain idyllic passages between her one-time lover and a charming village girl. Imagine the effect of this discovery on one of the artistic temperament. 'Hell hath no fury like a woman scorned,' and my unhappy wife would lash herself into an emotional frenzy. She would tear a passion to rags. Her very training on the stage would come to her aid in scathing words - perhaps threats. If Grant remained cold to her appeal the village beauty should be made to suffer. Then *he* would flame into storm. And so the upas-tree of tragedy spread its poisonous shade until reason fled, and some demon whispered, 'Kill!' I find no flaw in my theory. It explains the inexplicable. Now, how does it strike you, Mr. Furneaux?"

"As piffle."

"Is that so? I have the advantage, of course, in knowing my wife's peculiarities. And I have made some study of Grant. He admits already that he is under suspicion. Why, if he is innocent? Mind you, I pay little heed to the crude disposal of the body. Horace, I think, has a truism that art lies in concealing art. My wife's presence in Steynholme was no secret. She would have been missed from the inn. Search would be made. The murder must be revealed sooner or later, and the murderer himself was aware that by no twisting or turning could his name escape association with that of his victim. Why not face the music at once? He would argue. The very simplicity of the means adopted to fasten a kind of responsibility on him might prove his best safeguard. Even now I doubt whether any jury will find him guilty on the evidence as it stands, but my duty to my unhappy wife demands that I shall strengthen the arm of justice by every legitimate means in my power."

"Is that your case, Mr. Ingerman?"

"At present, yes."

"It assumes that the police adopt your view."

"Not necessarily. The police must do their work without fear or favor. But Grant can be committed for trial on a coroner's warrant."

"Grant is certainly in an awkward place."

"Only a little while ago you dismissed my theory of the crime as airy persiflage."

"That was before you quoted Horace. I have a great respect for Horace. His ode to the New Year is a gem."

"Would you care to see my wife's recent letters?"

"If you please."

"They are at my flat, I'll send you copies. The originals are always at your disposal for comparison, of course. Now may I, without offense, ask a question?"

"Yes."

"Is it wise that the emissary of Scotland Yard should leave Steynholme?"

"But didn't I tell you that I might obtain light in the neighborhood of Cornhill?"

"True. I could have given you the facts in Steynholme."

"I'm a greater believer in what the theater people call 'atmosphere.' Some of your facts, Mr. Ingerman, remind me of an expert's report in a mining prospectus. When tested by cyanide of potassium the gold in the ore often changes into iron pyrites. But don't hug the delusion that I shall neglect Steynholme. The murderer is there, not in London, and, unless my intellect is failing, he will be tried for his life at the next Lewes Assizes. Meanwhile, may I give you a bit of advice?"

"By all means."

"Employ a sound lawyer, one who will avoid needless mud-slinging. Good day! Send those letters to the Yard by to-night's post if practicable."

"It shall be done."

When the door closed on Furneaux, Ingerman smiled.

"I've given that little Frenchman furiously to think," he murmured.

But the "little Frenchman" was smiling, too. He had elaborated the scheme already discussed with Winter. It was much to his liking, though unorthodox, rather crack-brained, more than risky, and altogether opposed to the instructions of the Police Manual. Each of these drawbacks was a commendation to Furneaux. In fact, the Steynholme mystery had taken quite a favorable turn during that talk with Ingerman.

Louis Tracy

CHAPTER XI

P. C. ROBINSON TAKES ANOTHER LINE

About the time Furneaux was whisked past The Hollies in Superintendent Fowler's dogcart, Grant and Hart were finishing luncheon, and planning a long walk to the sea. Grant would dearly have liked to secure Doris's company, but good taste forbade that he should even invite her to share the ramble. Thus, the death of a woman with whom he had not exchanged a word during three years had already set up a barrier between Doris and himself. Though impalpable, it was effective. It could neither be climbed nor avoided. Quiet little Steynholme had suddenly become a rigid censor of morals and etiquette. Until this evil thing was annihilated by slow process of law, Doris and he might meet only by chance and never remain long together.

When the two were ready to start, Hart elected to dispense with his South American sombrero.

"I am sensitive to ridicule," he professed. "The village urchins will christen me 'Owd Ben,' and the old gentleman's character was such that I would feel hurt. So, for to-day, I'll join the no hat brigade."

"I wonder if we'll meet Furneaux," said Grant, selecting a walking-stick. "It's odd that we should have seen nothing of him this morning."

"It would be still more odd if we had, remembering the precautions he took not to be observed coming here last night."

"Well, that's so. I forgot to ask the reason. There was one, I suppose."

"Of the best. That little man is a live wire of intelligence. He's wasted on Scotland Yard. He ought to be a dramatist or an ambassador."

"Quaint alternatives, those."

"Not at all. Each profession demands brains, and is at its best in coining cute phrases. I've met scores of both tribes, and they're like as peas in a pod."

A bell rang.

"That's the front door," said Grant. "It's Furneaux himself, I hope."

But the visitor was P.C. Robinson, who actually smiled and saluted.

"Glad I've caught you before you went out, sir," he said. "Mr. Furneaux asked me to tell you he had to hurry back to London. I was also to mention that he had got the whiskers."

"What whiskers? Whose whiskers?"

"That's all he said, sir - he'd got the whiskers."

"Why, Owd Ben's whiskers, of course. How dense you are, Jack!" put in Hart.

Now, this was the first Robinson had heard of whiskers in connection with the crime. He remembered Elkin's make-up as Svengali, of course, and could have kicked himself for not associating earlier a set of sable whiskers with the black wig and the bullet-torn hat.

But, Owd Ben! What figure did that redoubtable ghost cut in the mystery?

"There are certain *lacunae* in your otherwise vigorous and thrilling story, constable," went on Hart.

"Very likely, sir," agreed Robinson, much to the surprise of his hearers. He had not the slightest notion what a *lacuna*, or its plural, signified. He was only adopting Furneaux's advice, and trying to be civil.

"Ah, you see that, do you?" said Hart. "Well, fill 'em in. When, where, and how did the midget sleuth obtain the specter's hairy adornments?"

The policeman, whose wits were thoroughly on the alert, realized that he had scored a point, though he knew not how.

"He did not tell me, sir," he answered. "It's a rum business, that's what it is, no matter what way you look at it."

Grant, agreeably aware of the village constable's change of front, accepted the olive branch readily.

"We're just going for a walk," he said. "If you have ten

minutes to spare, Mrs. Bates will find you some luncheon, I have no doubt."

"Well, sir, meals are a trifle irregular during a busy time like this," admitted Robinson, feeling that his luck was in, because tongues would surely be loosened in the kitchen to an official guest introduced by the master of the establishment. He was right. No member of the Bates family dreamed of reticence, now that the household was restored to favor with "the force." Before Robinson departed, he was full of information and good food.

What more natural, then, an hour later, than that he should contrive to meet Elkin as the horse-dealer was taking home a lively two-year-old pony he had been "lungeing" on a strip of common opposite his house?

Each was eager to question the other, but Elkin opened fire.

"Anything fresh?" he cried. "You have a fair course now, Robinson. That little London 'tec has bunked home."

"Has he?" In the language of the ring, Robinson thought fit to spar for an opening.

"Oh, none of your kiddin'," said Elkin, stroking the nervous colt's neck. "You know he has. You don't miss much that's going on. Bet you half a thick 'un you'd have put someone in clink before this if the murder at The Hollies had been left in your hands."

"That's as may be, Mr. Elkin. But this affair seems to have gripped you for fair. You look thoroughly run down. Sleepin' badly?"

"Rotten! Hardly got a wink last night."

"You shouldn't be out so late. Why, on'y a week ago you were in bed regular at 10.15."

"That inquest broke up the day yesterday, so I was delayed at Knoleworth."

"What time did you reach home?"

"Dashed if I know. After twelve before I was in bed. By the way, what's this about things missing from a box owned by the Amateur Dramatic Society? That silly josser of a detective - What's his name?"

"Furneaux," said Robinson, who was clever enough not to appear too secretive, and was thanking his stars that Elkin had introduced the very topic he wanted to discuss.

"Ay, Furneaux. I remember now. He worried old Tomlin last night about that box, which is kept in the loft over the club-room. So Tomlin and I, and Hobbs, just to satisfy ourselves, went up there as soon as Furneaux left to-day. And, what do you think? The box was unlocked, though I locked it myself, and have the key; and a hat and wig and whiskers I wore when we played a skit on 'Trilby' were missing. If that isn't a clew, what is?"

"A clew!" repeated the bewildered Robinson.

"Yes. I'm telling you, though I kept dark before the other fellows. Didn't you say Grant's cheek was bleeding on Tuesday morning?"

"I did."

"Well, the whiskers were held on by wires that slip over the ears. One wire was sharp as a needle. I know, because it stuck into a finger more than once. Why shouldn't it scratch a man's cheek, and the cut open again next morning?"

"By jing, you've got your knife into Mr. Grant, an' no mistake," commented Robinson.

"You yourself gave him a nasty jab at the inquest," sneered Elkin.

"I was just tellin' the facts."

"So am I. I think you ought to know about that hat and the other things. I would recognize them anywhere. Furneaux had something up his sleeve, too, or he wouldn't have pumped Tomlin... Woa, boy! So long, Robinson! I must put this youngster into his stall."

"I'll wait, Mr. Elkin," said Robinson solemnly. "I want to have a word with you."

The policeman was glad of the respite. He needed time to collect his thoughts. The story of the dinner-party and its excitement disposed completely of Elkin's malicious theory with regard to Grant, but, since the horse-dealer was minded to be communicative, it would be well to encourage him.

"Come in, and have a drink," said Elkin, when the colt had been stabled.

Louis Tracy

"No, thanks - not when I'm on duty."

Elkin raised his eyebrows sarcastically. He could not possibly guess that Robinson was adopting Furneaux's pose of never accepting hospitality from a man whom he might have to arrest.

"Well, blaze away. I'm ready."

The younger man leaned against a gate. He looked ill and physically worn.

"Your business has kept you out late of a night recently, you say, Mr. Elkin," began the other, speaking as casually as he could contrive. "Now, it might help a lot if you can call to mind anyone you met on the roads at ten or eleven o'clock. For instance, last night -"

Elkin laughed in a queer, croaking way.

"Last night my mare brought me home. I was decidedly sprung, Robinson. Glad you didn't spot me, or there might have been trouble. What between the inquest, an' no food, an' more than a few drinks at Knoleworth, I'd have passed Owd Ben himself without seeing him, though I believe I did squint in at The Hollies as I went by."

"What time would that be?"

"Oh, soon after eleven."

"Sure."

"I can't be certain to ten minutes or so. The pubs hadn't

closed when I left Knoleworth. What the devil does it matter, anyhow?"

It mattered a great deal. Robinson could testify that Elkin did not cross Steynholme bridge "soon after eleven."

"Nothing much," was the answer. "You see, I'm anxious to find out who might be stirring at that hour, an' you know everybody for miles around. I'd like to fix your journey by the clock, if I could."

"Dash it all, man, I was full to the eyes. There! You have it straight."

"Were you out on Monday night?"

"The night of the murder?"

"Yes."

"I left the Hare and Hounds at ten, and came straight home."

"Who was there with you?"

"The usual crowd - Hobbs, and Siddle, and Bob Smith, and a commercial traveler. Siddle went at half past nine, but he generally does."

"You met no one on the road?"

"No."

The monosyllable seemed to lack Elkin's usual confidence. It sounded as if he had been making up his mind what to say, yet faltered at the last moment.

Robinson ruminated darkly. As a matter of fact, long after eleven o'clock on that fateful night, he himself had seen Elkin walking homeward. He was well aware that the licensing hours were not strictly observed by the Hare and Hounds when "commercial gentlemen" were in residence. Closing time was ten o'clock, but the "commercials," being cheery souls, became nominal hosts on such occasions, and their guests were in no hurry to depart. Robinson saw that he had probably jumped to a conclusion, an acrobatic feat of reasoning which Furneaux had specifically warned him against. At any rate, he resolved now to leave well enough alone.

"Well, we don't seem to get any forrarder," he said. "You ought to take more care of your health, Mr. Elkin. You're a changed man these days."

"I'll be all right when this murder is off our chests, Robinson. You won't have a tiddley? Right-o! So long!"

Robinson walked slowly toward Steynholme. At a turn in the road he halted near the footpath which led down the wooded cliff and across the river to Bush Walk. He surveyed the locality with a reflective frown. Then, there being no one about, he made some notes of the chat with Elkin. The man's candor and his misstatements were equally puzzling. None knew better than the policeman that the vital discrepancy of fully an hour and a half on the Monday night would be difficult to clear up. Tomlin, of course, would have no recollection of events after ten o'clock, but the commercial traveler, who could be traced, might be induced to tell the truth if assured that the police needed the information solely for purposes in connection with their inquiry into the murder. That man must be found. His testimony should have an immense significance.

That evening, shortly before seven o'clock, a stalwart, prosperous-looking gentleman in tweeds "descended" from the London express at Knoleworth. The local train for Steynholme stood in a bay on the opposite platform, and this passenger in particular was making for it when he nearly collided with another man, younger, thinner, bespectacled, who hailed him with delight.

"You, too? Good egg!" was the cry.

The gentleman thus addressed did not seem to relish this geniality.

"Where the deuce are you off to?" he demanded.

"To Steynholme - same as you, of course."

"Look here, Peters, a word in your ear. If you know me during the next few days, you'll never know me again. I suppose you'll be staying at the local inn - there's only one of any repute in the place?"

"That's so. I've got you. May I take it that you will reciprocate when the time comes?"

"Have I ever failed you?"

"No. We meet as strangers."

Peters bustled off. He had the reputation of being the

Louis Tracy

smartest "writer up" in London of mystery cases. The Steynholme affair had interested both him and a shrewd news-editor.

The pair arrived at the Hare and Hounds within a few minutes of each other. The big man registered as "Mr. W. Franklin, Argentina." Peters ordered a chop, and went off at once to interview the local policeman. Mr. Franklin took more pains over the prospective meal.

"Have you a nice chicken?" he inquired.

Yes, Mr. Tomlin had a veritable spring chicken in the larder at that moment.

"And do you think your cook could provide a *tourne-dos*?"

"A what-a, sir?" wheezed Tomlin.

The visitor explained. He liked variety, he said. Half the chicken might be deviled for breakfast. The two dishes, with plain boiled potatoes and French beans, would suit him admirably. He was sorry he dared not try Tomlin's excellent claret, but a dominating doctor had put him on the water-cart. In effect, Mr. Franklin impressed the landlord as a man of taste and ample means.

Peters had gobbled his chop before Franklin entered the dining-room, but they met later in the snug, where Elkin was being chaffed by Hobbs anent his carryin's on in Knoleworth the previous night.

Siddle came in, but the chatter was not so free as when the habitués had the place to themselves.

Now, Peters had marked the gathering as one that suited his purpose exactly, so he gave the conversation the right twist.

"I suppose you local gentlemen have been greatly disturbed by this sensational murder?" he said.

Hobbs took refuge in a glass of beer. Siddle gazed contemplatively at his neat boots. Tomlin meant to say something; Elkin, eying the stranger, and summing him up as a detective, answered brusquely:

"The murder is bad enough, but the fat-headed police are worse. Three days gone, and nothing done!"

"What murder are you discussing, may I ask?" put in Franklin.

Peters turned on him with astonishment in every line of a peculiarly mobile face.

"Do you mean to say, sir, that you haven't heard of the Steynholme murder?" he gasped.

"I seldom, if ever, read such things in the newspapers, and, as I landed in England only a week ago from France, my ignorance, though abyssmal, is pardonable. Moreover, I can say truly that I am far more interested in pedigree horses than in vulgar criminals."

Peters explained fluently. This was no ordinary crime. A beautiful and popular actress had been done to death in a brutal way, and the country was already deeply stirred by the story.

Elkin waited impatiently till the journalist drew breath.

Then he broke in.

"Pedigree horses you mentioned, sir," he said, his rancor against Grant being momentarily conquered by the pertinent allusion to his own business. "What sort? Racing, coaching, roadsters, or hacks?"

"All sorts. The Argentine, where I have connections, offers an ever-open door to good horseflesh."

"Are you having a look round?"

"Yes. There are several decent studs within driving distance of Steynholme. Isn't that so, landlord?"

"Lots, sir," said Tomlin. "An' the very man you're talkin' to has some stuff not to be sneezed at."

"Is that so?" Mr. Franklin gazed at Elkin in a very friendly manner. "May I ask your name, sir?"

Elkin produced a card. Every hoof in his stables appreciated in value forthwith, but he was far too knowing that he should appear to rush matters.

"Call any day you like, sir," he said. "Glad to see you. But give me notice. I generally have an appetizer here of a morning about eleven."

"An' you want it, too, Fred," said Hobbs. "Dash me, you're as thin as a herrin'. Stop whiskey an' drink beer, like me."

"And you might also follow that gentleman's example," interposed Siddle quietly, nodding towards Mr. Franklin.

"What's that?" snapped Elkin.

"Don't worry about murders."

"That's a nice thing to say. Why should *I* worry about the d - d mix-up?"

The chemist made no reply, but Hobbs stepped into the breach valiantly.

"Keep yer 'air on, Fred," he vociferated. "Siddle means no 'arm. But wot else are yer a-doing of, mornin', noon, an' night?"

Elkin laughed, with his queer croak.

"If you stay here a day or two, you'll soon get to know what they're driving at, sir," he said to Franklin. "The fact is that this chap, Grant, who found the body, and in whose garden the murder was committed, has been making eyes at the girl I'm as good as engaged to. That would make anybody wild - now, wouldn't it?"

"Possibly," smiled Franklin. "Of course there is always the lady's point of view. The sex is proverbially fickle, you know. 'Woman, thy vows are traced in sand,' Lord Byron has it."

"Ay, an' some men's, too," guffawed Hobbs. "Wot about Peggy Smith, Fred?"

Elkin blew a mouthful of cigarette smoke at the butcher.

"What about that tough old bull you bought at Knoleworth on Monday?" he retorted.

Hobbs's face grew purple. Mr. Franklin beckoned to Tomlin.

"Ask these gentlemen what they'll have," he said gently. The landlord made a clatter of glasses, and the threatened storm passed.

"You've aroused my curiosity," remarked Franklin to Peters, but taking the company at large into the conversation. "This does certainly strike one as a remarkable case. Is there no suspicion yet as to the actual murderer?"

"None whatever," said Peters.

"That's what you may call the police opinion," broke in Elkin. "We Steynholme folk have a pretty clear notion, I can assure you."

"The matter is still *sub judice*, and may remain so a long time," said Siddle. "It is simply stupid to attach a kind of responsibility to the man who happens to occupy the house associated with the crime. I have no patience with that sort of reasoning."

Hobbs, who did not want to quarrel with Elkin, suddenly championed him.

"That's all very well," he rumbled. "But the hevidence you an' me 'eard, Siddle, an' the hevidence we know we're goin' to 'ear, is a lot stronger than that."

"I'm sure you'll pardon me, friends," said Siddle, rising with an apologetic smile, "but I happen to be foreman of the coroner's jury, and I feel that this matter is not for me, at any rate, to discuss publicly."

Out he went, not even heeding Tomlin's appeal to drink the ginger-ale he had just ordered.

"Just like 'im," sighed Hobbs. "Good-'earted fellow! Would find hexcuses for a black rat."

Elkin talked more freely now that the chemist's disapproving eye was off him. Ultimately, Mr. Franklin elected to smoke a cigar in the open air, and strolled forth. He sauntered down the hill, stood on the bridge, and admired the soft blue tones of the landscape in the half light of a summer evening. Shortly before closing time, Robinson appeared, it being part of his routine duty to see that no noisy revelers disturbed the peace of the village. He noticed the stranger at once, and elected to walk past him.

Thus, he received yet another shock when Mr. Franklin addressed him by name.

"Good evening, Robinson," said the pleasant, clear-toned voice. "I've been expecting you to turn up. Kindly go back home, and leave the door open. I want to slip in quietly. I am Chief Inspector Winter, of Scotland Yard."

"You don't say so, sir!" stammered Robinson.

"But I do say it, and will prove it to you, of course. I'll be with you in a minute or two. There's someone coming. You and I must not be seen together."

Robinson made off, and Winter lounged along the Knoleworth road. He met Bates, going to the post with letters.

Naturally, Bates looked him over. Returning from the post office, he kept a sharp eye for the unknown loiterer, but saw him not. He even walked quickly to the bend of the road, but the other man had vanished.

Grant and Hart were talking of anything but the murder when Bates thrust his head in. He was grasping his goatee beard, sure sign of some weight on his mind.

"Beg pardon," he said, "but I thought you'd like to know. The place is just swarmin' with 'em."

"Bees?" inquired Hart.

Bates stared fixedly at the speaker for a second or two.

"No, sir, 'tecs," he said. "There's a big 'un now - just the opposite to the little 'un, Hawkshaw. I 'ope I 'aven't to tackle this customer, though. He'd gimme a doin', by the looks of 'im."

Bates had disappeared before Grant remembered that the press photographer had mentioned the Big 'Un and the Little 'Un of the Yard.

"Now, I wonder," he said.

His wonder could hardly have equaled Winter's had he heard the gardener's words. The guess was a distinct score for blunt Sussex, though it was founded solely on the assumption that all comers now, unless Bates was personally acquainted with them, were limbs of the law.

CHAPTER XII

WHEREIN WINTER GETS TO WORK

Winter had identified Bates at the first glance. The letters in the man's hand, too, showed his errand, so, while the gardener was climbing the hill, the detective slipped into Robinson's cottage.

He found the policeman awaiting him in the dark, because a voice said:

"Beg pardon, sir, but the other gentleman from the 'Yard' asked me to take him into the kitchen. A light in the front room might attract attention, he thought."

"Just what Mr. Furneaux would suggest, and I agree with him," said Winter, quite alive to the canny discretion behind those words, "the other gentleman."

Robinson led the way. Supper was laid on the table. Poor Mrs. Robinson had again beaten a hasty retreat.

"Now, Robinson," said the Chief Inspector affably, "before we come to business I'll prove my bona fides. Here is my official card, and I'll run quickly through events until 1.30 p.m. to-day. I met Mr. Furneaux at Victoria, and he posted me fully up to that hour."

Louis Tracy

So the policeman listened to a clear summary of the Steynholme case as it was known to the authorities.

"I did not warn either Mr. Fowler or you of my visit because a telegram could hardly be explicit enough," concluded Winter. "At the inn I am Mr. Franklin, an Argentine importer of blood stock in the horse line. At this moment the only other man beside yourself in Steynholme who is aware of my official position is Mr. Peters, and he is pledged to secrecy. To-morrow or any other day until further notice, you and I meet as strangers in public. By the way, Mr. Furneaux asked me to tell you that he found the wig and the false beard in the river early this morning. The wearer had apparently flung them off while crossing the foot-bridge leading from Bush Walk, having forgotten that they would not sink readily. Perhaps he didn't care. At any rate, Mr. Hart's bullet seems to have laid Owd Ben's ghost. Now, what of this fellow, Elkin? He worries me."

"Can I offer you a glass of beer, sir?"

"With pleasure. May I smoke while you eat? You see, I differ from Mr. Furneaux in both size and habits."

Robinson poured out the beer. He was preternaturally grave. The somewhat incriminating statements he had wormed out of the horse-dealer that afternoon lay heavy upon him. But he told his story succinctly enough. Winter nodded to emphasize each point, and congratulated him at the end.

"You arranged that very well," he said. "I gather, though, that Elkin spoke rather openly."

"Just as I've put it, sir. He tripped a bit over the time on Monday night. But it's only fair to say that he might have had Tomlin's license in mind."

"That issue will be settled to-morrow. I'll find out the commercial traveler's name, and send a telegram from Knoleworth before noon.... Who is Peggy Smith?"

Robinson set down an empty glass with a stare of surprise.

"Bob Smith's daughter, sir," he answered.

"No doubt. But, proceed."

"Well, sir, she's just a village girl. Her father is a blacksmith. His forge is along to the right, not far. She'll be twenty, or thereabouts."

"Frivolous?"

"Not more than the rest of 'em, sir."

"Have you seen her flirting with Elkin?"

Robinson took thought.

"Now that I come to think of it, she might be given a bit that way. Her father shoes Elkin's nags, so there's a lot of comin' an' goin' between the two places. But folks would always look on it as natural enough. Yes, I've seen 'em together more than once."

"In that case, he can hardly grumble if the postmaster's daughter has an eye for another young man."

"Miss Martin!" snorted Robinson. "She wouldn't look the side of the road he was on. Fred Elkin isn't her sort."

"But he said to-night in the Hare and Hounds that he and Miss Martin were practically engaged."

"Stuff an' nonsense! Sorry, sir, but I admire Doris Martin. I like to see a girl like her liftin' herself out of the common gang. She's the smartest young lady in the village, an' not an atom of a snob. No, no. She isn't for Fred Elkin. Before this murder cropped up everybody would have it that Mr. Grant would marry her."

"How does the murder intervene?"

Robinson shifted uneasily in his chair. He knew only too well that he himself had driven a wedge between the two.

"Steynholme's a funny spot, sir," he contrived to explain. "Since it came out that Doris an' Mr. Grant were in the garden at The Hollies at half past ten on Monday night, without Mr. Martin knowin' where his daughter was, there's been talk. Both the postmaster an' the girl herself are up to it. You can see it in their faces. They don't like it, an' who can blame 'em!"

"Who, indeed? But this Elkin - surely he had some ground for a definite boast, made openly, among people acquainted with all the parties?"

"There's more than Elkin would marry Doris if she lifted a finger, sir."

"Can you name them?"

"Well, Tomlin wants a wife."

Winter laughed joyously.

"Next?" he cried.

"They say that Mr. Siddle is a widower."

"The chemist? Foreman of the jury?"

"Yes, sir."

"From appearances, he is a likelier candidate than either Elkin or Tomlin. Anybody else?"

"I shouldn't be far wrong if I gave you the name of most among the young unmarried men in the parish."

"Dear me! I must have a peep at this charmer. But I want those names, Robinson."

Winter produced a note-book, so he was evidently taking the matter seriously. The policeman, however, was flustered. His thoughts ran on Elkin, whereas this masterful person from London insisted on discussing Doris Martin.

"My difficulty is, sir, that she has never kep' company with any of 'em," he said.

"Never mind. Give me the name of every man who, no matter what his position or prospects, might be irritated, if no more, if he knew that Miss Martin and Mr. Grant were presumably spooning in a garden at a rather late hour."

It was a totally new line of inquiry for Robinson, but he bent his wits to it, and evolved a list which, if published, would certainly be regarded with incredulous envy by every other girl in the village than the postmaster's daughter; as for Doris herself, she would be mightily surprised when she saw it, but whether annoyed or secretly gratified none but a pretty girl of nineteen can tell.

Winter departed soon afterwards. Before going to the inn he had a look at the forge. A young woman, standing at the open door of the adjoining cottage, favored him with a frank stare. There was no light in the dwelling. When he returned, after walking a little way down the road, the door was closed.

Next morning, Bates heard of Peters as the detective and of Mr. Franklin as a 'millionaire" from South America. Moreover, he scrutinized both in the flesh, and saw Robinson salute Peters but pass the financial potentate with indifference.

Alas, that a reputation, once built, should be destroyed!

"I was mistook, sir," he reported to Grant later. "There's another 'tec about, but 'e ain't the chap I met last night. They say this other bloke is rollin' in money, an' buyin' hosses right an' left."

"Then he'll soon be rolling in the mud, and have no money," put in Hart.

"Who is he?" inquired Grant carelessly.

"A Mr. Franklin, from South America, sir."

Grant and Hart exchanged glances. Curiously enough, Hart remained silent till Bates had gone.

"I must look this joker up, Jack," he said then. "To me the mere mention of South America is like Mother Gary's chickens to a sailor, a harbinger of storm."

But Hart consumed Tomlin's best brew to no purpose - in so far as seeing Mr. Franklin was concerned, since the latter was in Knoleworth, buying a famous racing stud. Being in the village, however, this fisher in troubled waters was not inclined to return without a bag of some sort.

He walked straight into the post office. Doris and her father were there, the telegraphist being out.

"Good day, everybody," he cried cheerfully. "Grant wants to know, Mr. Martin, if you and Miss Doris will come and dine with him, us, this evening at 7.30?"

The postmaster gazed helplessly at this free-and-easy stranger. Doris laughed, and blushed a little.

"This is Mr. Hart, a friend of Mr. Grant's, dad," she explained. "I'm afraid we cannot accept the invitation. We are so busy."

"The worst of excuses," said Hart.

"But there is a London correspondent here who hands in a long telegram at that hour."

"What's his name?"

"Mr. Peters."

"Great Scott! Jimmie Peters here? I'll soon put a stopper on him. He'll come, too - jumping. See if he doesn't. Is it a bargain? Short telegram at six. Dinner for five at 7.30. Come, now, Mr. Martin. It's up to you. I can see 'Yes' in Doris's eye. Over the port - most delectable, I assure you - I'll give full details of the peculiar case of a man in Worcestershire whose crop of gooseberries increased fourfold after starting an apiary. And what does it matter if you do lose a queen or two in June? The drones will attend to that trifle.... It's a fixture, eh? Where's Peters? In the Pull and Push? I'll rout him out."

The whirlwind subsided, but quickly materialized again.

"Peters nearly fell on his knees and wept with joy," announced Hart. "He believes he was given a bull steak for luncheon. He pledges himself to have only five hundred words on the wire at five o'clock."

Meanwhile, father and daughter had decided that there was no valid reason why they should not dine with Mr. Grant. Martin already regretted his aloofness on the day of the inquest, though, truth to tell, Hart's expert knowledge of bee-culture was the determining factor. On her part, Doris was delighted. Her world had gone awry that week, and this small festivity might right it.

Not one word of the improvised dinner-party did Hart confide to Grant. He informed the only indispensable person, Mrs. Bates, and left it at that. Grant, a restless being these days, took him for another long walk. It chanced that their road home led down the high-street. The hour was a quarter past seven, and Peters hailed them.

Hart introduced the journalist, saying casually:

"Jimmie is coming to dinner, Jack."

"Delighted," said Grant, of course.

Peters looked slightly surprised, but passed no comment. Then Doris and her father appeared. They joined the others, shook hands, and, to Grant's secret perplexity, the whole party moved off down the hill in company. When the Martins turned with the rest to cross the bridge, Grant began to suspect his friend.

"Wally," he managed to whisper, "what game have you been playing?"

"Aren't you satisfied?" murmured Hart. "Sdeath, as they used to say in the Surrey Theater, you're as bad as Furshaw!"

There were others far more perturbed by that odd conjunction of diners than the puzzled host, who merely expected Mrs. Bates to belabor him with a rolling pin. Mr. Siddle, for instance, had just closed his shop when the five met. That is to say, the dark blue blind was drawn, but the door was ajar. He came to the threshold, and watched the party until the bridge was neared, when one of them, looking back, might have seen him, so he stepped discreetly inside. Being a non-interfering, self-contained man, he seemed to be rather irresolute. But that condition passed quickly. Leaning over the counter, he secured a hat and a pair of field-glasses, and went out. He, too, knew of Mrs. Jefferson's weakness for shopping in Knoleworth, and that good lady had gone there again. Her train was due in ten minutes. A wicket gate led to a narrow passage communicating with the back door of her residence. He entered boldly, reached the garden, and hurried to the angle on the edge of the cliff next to the Martins' strip of ground.

Yes, a spacious dinner-table was laid at The Hollies. Doris, Mr. Martin, and Peters soon strolled out on to the lawn. The pedestrians had obviously gone upstairs to wash after their tramp.

Mr. Siddle rather forgot himself. He stared so long and earnestly through the field-glasses that he ran full tilt into Mrs. Jefferson and maid before regaining the high-street. But the chemist was a ready man. He lifted his hat with an inquiring smile.

"Didn't you say you wanted some anti-arthritic salts early in the week?" he asked.

"Yes," said Mrs. Jefferson, "but I got some to-day in Knoleworth, thank you."

"Well, I was just making up an indent, and might as well include your specific if you really needed it."

Which was kind and thoughtful of Mr. Siddle, but not quite true, though it fully explained his presence at Mrs. Jefferson's gate.

Mr. Franklin, escorting a fragrant Havana up the hill (he had traveled by the same train) saw the meeting, and, being aware of Mrs. Jefferson's frugal habits, since Furneaux had omitted no item of his movements in Steynholme, remembered it later during the nightly gathering in the inn.

Elkin greeted Mr. Franklin respectfully when the great man joined the circle.

"Did you see anything worth while at Knoleworth, sir?" he said.

"No. I was unlucky. All the principals were at a race meeting."

"By gum! That's right. It's Gatwick today. Dash! I might have saved you a journey."

"Oh, it doesn't matter. In my business there is no call for hurry."

Elkin looked around.

"Where's our friend, the 'tec?" he said.

"I think you're wrong about 'im, meanin' Mr. Peters," said Tomlin. "'E's 'ere for a noospaper, not for the Yard."

"That's his blarney," smirked Elkin. "A detective doesn't go about telling everybody what he is."

"Whatever his profession may be," put in Siddle's quiet voice, "I happen to know that he is dining with Mr. Grant. So are Mr. Martin and Doris. By mere chance I called at Mrs. Jefferson's. I went to the back door, and, finding it closed, looked into the garden. From there I couldn't help seeing the assembly on the lawn of The Hollies."

"Dining at Grant's?" shouted Elkin in a fury. "Well, I'm -"

"'Ush, Fred!" expostulated Tomlin with a shocked glance at Mr. Franklin. "Wot's wrong wi' a bit of grub, ony ways? A very nice-spoken young gent kem 'ere twiced, an' axed for Mr. Peters the second time. He's a friend o' Mr. Grant's, I reckon."

"What's wrong?" stormed the horse-dealer. "Why, everything's wrong! The bounder ought to be in jail instead of giving dinner-parties. Imagine Doris eating in that house!"

"Ay! Sweetbreads an' saddle o' lamb," interjected Hobbs with the air of one imparting a secret.

Elkin was pallid with wrath. He glared at Hobbs.

"What I had in my mind was the impudence of the blighter," he said shrilly. "That poor woman's body leaves here to-morrow for some cemetery in London, and Grant invites folk to a small dinner to-night!"

A sort of awe fell on the company. None of the others had as yet put the two events in juxtaposition, and they had an ugly sound. Even Mr. Siddle stifled a protest. Elkin had scored a hit, a palpable hit, and no one could gainsay him. He felt that, for once, the general opinion was with him, and drove the point home.

"Hobson - the local joiner and undertaker" - he explained for Mr. Franklin's benefit - "came this morning to borrow a couple of horses for the job. It's to be done in style - 'no expense spared' was Mr. Ingerman's order - and the poor thing is in her coffin now while Grant -"

He stopped. Mr. Siddle coughed.

"You've said enough, Elkin," murmured the chemist. "This excitement is harmful. You really ought to be in bed for the next forty-eight hours, dieting yourself carefully, and taking Dr. Foxton's mixture regularly. He has changed it, I noticed."

"Bed! Me! Not likely. I'm going to kick up a row. What are the police doing? A set of blooming old women, that's what they are. But I'll stir 'em up, if I have to write to the Home Secretary."

"Gentlemen," said Mr. Franklin, smiling genially, "I cannot help taking a certain interest in this affair. May I, then, as a complete stranger to all concerned, tell you how this minor episode strikes me. Mr. Grant, I understand, denies having seen or spoken to Miss Melhuish during the past three years. None of the others now in his house had met her at all. Really, if a man may not give a dinnerparty in these conditions, dining-out would become a lost art."

Elkin was obviously seeking for some retort which, though forcible, would not offend a possible patron. But Siddle answered far more deftly than might be looked for from the horse-dealer.

"Your contention, sir, is just what the man of the world would hold," he said, "but, in this village, where we live on neighborly terms, such an incident would be impossible in almost any other house than The Hollies."

Mr. Franklin nodded. He was convinced. Tomlin, Hobbs, and a local draper bore out the chemist's reasonable theory. Next morning Steynholme was again united in condemning Grant, while the postmaster and his daughter were not wholly exempted from criticism.

The dinner itself was an altogether harmless and cheery meal. By common consent not one word was said about the murder. Hart was amusing on the question of bees - almost flippant, Mr. Martin deemed him. Peters had a wide store of strange experiences to draw on, while Grant, if rather silent in deference to two such brilliant talkers, found much satisfaction in regarding Doris as a hostess.

The next day being Saturday, or market day, the village was busy. At eleven o'clock there was a somewhat unnecessary display of nodding plumes and long-tailed black horses at the removal of the coffin to the railway station. For some reason, the funeral arrangements had not been bruited about until Elkin made that envenomed attack on Grant in the Hare and Hounds the previous night. Ingerman had sent a gorgeous wreath, the only one forthcoming locally. This fact, of course, invited comment, though no whisperer in the crowd troubled to add that the interment was only announced in that day's newspapers.

Peters, meeting Mr. Franklin on the stairs of the inn, put a note into his hand. It read:

"Why don't you have a chat with Grant? The public mind is being inflamed against him. It's hardly fair."

Mr. Franklin, meeting Peters in the passage, winked at him, and the journalist tortured his brains to turn out some readable stuff which should grip the million on Sunday yet not to be damaging to the man whose hospitality he enjoyed over night.

In a word, the passing of Adelaide Melhuish was exploited thoroughly as an indictment of her one-time lover, and the only two in Steynholme not aware of the fact were Grant, himself, and Wally Hart.

By a singular coincidence, not ridiculously beyond the ken of a verger, when Doris went to church on Sunday morning, she found herself beside Mr. Franklin.

At the close of the service the same big man whom she had noticed as a neighbor in the pew overtook her at the post office door. He lifted his hat. A passer-by heard him say distinctly:

"Pardon me for troubling you, but can you tell me at what time the mail closes for London?"

"At four-thirty," said Doris.

No other person overheard Mr. Franklin's next words:

"I am now going to drop a letter in the box. It's for you. Get it at once. It is of the utmost importance."

Doris was startled, as well she might be. But - she went straight for the letter. It was marked: "Private and Urgent," and ran:

DEAR MISS MARTIN. I am here *vice* Mr. Furneaux, who is engaged on other phases of the same inquiry. My business is absolutely unknown. I figure at the inn as "Mr. W. Franklin, Argentina." Indeed, Mr. Furneaux left the village because he realized the difficulties facing him in that respect. Now, I trust you, and I hope you will justify my faith. You know Superintendent Fowler. I want you to meet me and him this afternoon

Louis Tracy

at two o'clock at the crossroads beyond the mill. A closed car will be in waiting, and we can have half an hour's talk without anyone in Steynholme being the wiser. Remember that this village, like the night, has a thousand eyes. Naturally, I would not trouble you in this way if the cause was not vital to the ends of justice. Whether or not you decide to keep this appointment, I have every confidence that you will respect my wish that *no one*, other than yourself, shall be informed of my identity. But I believe you will be wise, and come.

I am,

Yours faithfully,

J.L. WINTER,
Chief Inspector, C.I.D., Scotland Yard, S.W.

A card was inclosed, as a sort of credential. But, somehow, it was not needed. Doris had seen "Mr. Franklin" more than once, and she had heard him singing the hymns in church. He looked worthy of credence. His written words had the same honest ring. She resolved to go.

Her father, sad to relate, had found three dead queens in the hives. He was busy, but spared a moment to tell her that Mr. Siddle was coming to tea at four o'clock. Doris was rather in a whirl, and seemed to be unnecessarily astonished.

"Mr. Siddle! Why?" she gasped.

" Why not!" said her father. "It's not the first time. You can entertain him. I'll look after the letters."

"I must get some cakes. We have none."

"Well, that's simple. I wonder if that fellow Hart really understands apiaculture? You might invite him, too."

With that letter in her pocket Doris had suddenly grown wary. Hart and Siddle would not mix, and her woman's intuition warned her that Siddle had chosen the tea-hour purposely in order to have an uninterrupted conversation with her. She disliked Mr. Siddle, in a negative way, but the very nearness of the detective was stimulating. Let Mr. Siddle come, then, and come alone!

"No, dad," she laughed. "Mr. Hart's knowledge will be available to-morrow. In his presence, poor Mr. Siddle would be dumb."

CHAPTER XIII

CONCERNING THEODOEE SIDDLE

Winter, being a cheerful cynic, had not erred when he appealed to that love of mystery which, especially if it is spiced with a hint of harmless intrigue, is innate in every feminine heart. Indeed, he was so assured of the success of his somewhat dramatic move that as he walked to a rendezvous arranged with Superintendent Fowler on the Knoleworth road he reviewed carefully certain arguments meant to secure Doris's assistance.

Passing The Hollies, he smiled at the notion that Furneaux would undoubtedly have brought Grant to the conclave. It was just the sort of difficult situation in which his colleague would have reveled. But the Chief Inspector was more solid, more circumspect, even, singularly enough, more sensitive to the probable comments of a crusty judge if counsel for the defense contrived to elicit the facts.

"Anything fresh?" inquired the superintendent, when a smart car drew up, and Winter entered.

Mr. Fowler was in plain clothes, and the blinds were half drawn. No one could possibly recognize either of the occupants unless the car was halted, and the inquisitor literally thrust his head inside. The motor was a private one, borrowed for the occasion.

"Yes, a little," said Winter, as the chauffeur put the engine in gear. "Your man, Robinson, has been drawing Elkin, or Elkin drew him - I am not quite sure which, but think it matterless either way."

He sketched Robinson's activities briefly, but in sufficient outline.

"A new figure has come on the screen - Siddle, the chemist," he added thoughtfully.

"Siddle!" Mr. Fowler was surprised. "Why, he is supposed to be a model of the law-abiding citizen."

"I don't say he has lost his character in that respect," said Winter. "Still, he puzzles me. Elkin is a loud-mouthed fool. The verbal bricks he hurls at Grant are generally half baked, and crumble into dust. Hitherto, Siddle has tried to repress him, with a transparent honesty that rather worried me. On Friday night, however, Siddle attacked Grant with poisoned arrows. He did more damage in two minutes than Elkin could achieve in as many months."

"How?"

"He showed very clearly that Grant was guilty of gross bad taste in inviting Mr. Martin and his daughter to dinner that evening. I'm inclined to agree with him, if the story has been told fairly. But that is beside the main issue. Siddle aroused the sleeping dogs of the village, and the pack is in full cry again. Grant seems to have been popular here; he had almost recovered from the blow of Miss Melhuish's death by the straightforward speech he made before the inquest. But Siddle threw him back into the mud by a few skillful words. What is Siddle's record? Is he a local man?"

"I think not. Robinson can tell us."

"Robinson says he 'believes' Siddle is a widower. That doesn't argue long and close knowledge."

"We must look into it. Robinson has been stationed here four years. Siddle is not old, but he has been in business in Steynholme more years than that. But - you'll pardon me, I'm sure, Mr. Winter - may I take it that you are really interested in the chemist's history?"

The superintendent was perplexed, or he would not have adopted his professional method of semi-apologetic questions with a man from the C.I.D.

"I hardly know what I'm interested in," laughed Winter. "Grant didn't kill the lady. I shall be slow to credit Elkin with being the scoundrel he looks. Siddle, and Tomlin, if you please, are regarded as starters in the Doris Martin Matrimonial Stakes, and I don't think Tomlin could ever murder anything but the King's English. It is Siddle's *volte face* that bothers me."

"Um!" murmured Mr. Fowler. He was not an uneducated man, but *volte face*, correctly pronounced, was unfamiliar in his ears.

"The change was so marked," went on the detective. "I gather that Siddle is a stickler for charity and fair dealing. He didn't abandon the role, of course. It was the sheer ingenuity of his method that caught my attention. So I simply catalogue him for research."

"Has Miss Martin promised to meet us?" inquired the other, feeling that he was on the track of *volte face*.

"No. But there she is!" cried Winter. "She has just heard the car. Tell your chauffeur to slow up. The road is empty otherwise. By the way, you help her in. She might be a bit shy of me, and I don't want a second's delay."

Winter's judgment was not at fault. Doris *was* feeling a trifle uncertain, seeing that she was about to encounter a complete stranger. Moreover, she had come a good half mile from the shop whence the cakes for tea were to be procured at the back door, and as a favor. Her eyes were fixed on the slowing car with a timid anxiety that betrayed no small degree of doubt as to the outcome of this Sunday afternoon escapade. She was pale and nervous. At that moment Doris wished herself safe at home again.

"One word," broke in the superintendent hurriedly. "Why are you so sure that Grant is innocent, Mr. Winter?"

"I'm sure of nothing with regard to this case. But I have great faith in Furneaux's flair for the true scent. It has never failed yet."

Mr. Fowler wished his companion would not use such uncommon words. However, he got out, and took off his hat with a courteous sweep. Doris had to look twice at him. Hitherto, she had always seen him in uniform. Winter smiled at the unmistakable expression of relief in her face. She was almost self-possessed as she took the seat by his side.

"Good day, Mr. Winter," she said.

"Mr. Franklin, please. Better become used to my pseudonym.... Plenty of room for your feet, Mr. Fowler? That's it. Now we're comfy. The chauffeur will bring us back here in half an hour, Miss Martin. Will that suit your convenience?"

"Oh, yes. I am free till nearly four o'clock. We have a guest to tea then."

"I have a well-developed bump of curiosity these days. Who is it, may I ask?"

"Mr. Siddle, the local chemist."

"Indeed. An old friend, I suppose?"

"We have known him seven years, ever since he came to Steynholme."

"Ah. He is not a native of the place?"

"No. He bought Mr. Benson's business. He's a Londoner, I believe."

"Is there - a Mrs. Siddle?"

"No. I - er - that is to say, gossip has it that he was married, but his wife died."

"He doesn't speak of her? Is that it? One would have thought that in a house where he is well known -"

"We don't really know him well. No one does, I think."

"You've invited him to tea, at any rate," laughed Winter.

"No," said Doris. "He invited himself. At least, so I gathered from dad."

"Ah, well. He feels lonely, no doubt, and wishes to chat about recent strange events in Steynholme. And that brings me to the reason why I sought this chat under such peculiar conditions. You realize my handicap, Miss Martin? If I were seen talking to you, or even entering your house as apart from the post office, people would begin to wonder. You follow that, don't you?"

Yes, Doris did follow it. What she did not follow was the veiled admiration in Superintendent Fowler's glance at the detective. Those few inconsequential questions had shed a flood of light on Siddle's past and present, yet the informant was blissfully unaware of their real purport. And the way was opened so deftly. The purchase of a chemist's business would almost certainly be negotiated through a local lawyer. Let him be found, and Siddle's pre-Steynholme days could be "looked into," as the police phrase has it. The superintendent had the rare merit of being candid with himself. He had no previous experience of Scotland Yard men or methods, and was inclined to be skeptical about Furneaux. But Winter's prompt use of a chance opening, and the restraint which cut off the investigation before the girl could suspect any ulterior motive, displayed a technique which the Sussex Constabulary had few opportunities of acquiring.

"Now, Miss Martin," began Winter, "if ever you have the misfortune to fall ill - touch wood, please - and call in a doctor, you'll tell him the facts, eh?"

"Why consult him at all, if I don't?" she smiled.

"Exactly. To-day I'm somewhat in the position of a Harley-street specialist, summoned to assist an eminent local practitioner in Dr. Fowler. That's a sort of gentle preliminary, leading up to the disagreeable duty of putting some questions of a personal nature. What you may answer will not go beyond ourselves. I promise you that. You will not be quoted, or requested to prove your statements. Such a thing would be absurd. If I were really a doctor, and you needed my advice, you might easily describe your symptoms all wrong. It would be my business to listen, and deduce the truth, and I would never dream of rating you for having misled me. You see my point?"

"Yes, but Mr. Win - Mr. Franklin, I know nothing whatever about the murder."

"I'm sure you don't. It was a wicked trick of Fate that took you to Mr. Grant's garden last Monday night."

"It was really an astronomical almanac," retorted Doris, who now felt a growing confidence in this nice-spoken official. "Sirius is a star remarkable for its beautiful changing lights, and on Monday evening was at its best. I think I ought to explain," and she blushed delightfully, "that the village gossip about Mr. Grant and me is entirely mistaken. We are not - well, I had better use plain English - we are not lovers. My father and I are just on close, friendly terms with Mr. Grant. I - my position hardly warrants even that relationship with an author of some distinction. But please set aside any notion of us as likely to become engaged. For one thing, it is preposterous. For another, I shall not leave my father."

Poor Doris! She little guessed how accurately this skilled student of human nature read the hidden thought behind that vehement protest. Even the note of vague rebellion against social disabilities was pathetic yet illuminating. Of course, he took her quite seriously.

"Let us keep to the hard road of fact," he said. "What you really mean is that Mr. Grant has never made love to you. But I must be candid, young lady. There is no earthly reason why he shouldn't, though I could name offhand half a dozen why he should.... Well, well, I must not pay compliments. My friend, Mr. Furneaux, can manage that with much greater facility, being half a Frenchman. And now I'm going to say an unpleasant thing. I ask your forgiveness in advance. Both Mr. Furneaux and I agree in the opinion that your imaginary love affair is indissolubly bound up with the mystery of Miss Melhuish's death. In a word, I have brought you here today to discuss your prospective marriage, and nothing else. That astonishes you, eh? Well, it's the truth, as I shall proceed to make clear. There's a Mr. Fred Elkin, for instance -"

Doris uttered a little laugh of dismay. Winter's emphatic words had astounded her, but the horse-dealer's name acted as comic relief.

"I can't bear the man," she protested.

"I have no doubt. But you ought to know that he is loudly proclaiming his determination to marry you before the year is out."

The girl's face reddened again, and her eyes sparkled.

"I wouldn't marry him if he were a peer of the realm," she said indignantly.

"Quite so. But he is an avowed suitor. Now don't be vexed. Has he never declared his intentions to *you*?"

"He would never dare. I sing and act a little, at village concerts and dramatic performances, and he has annoyed me at times by an officious pretense that he was deputed by my father to see me home. I came here quite a little girl, so people learnt to use my Christian name. I don't object to it at all. But I simply hate hearing it on Mr. Elkin's lips."

"Exit Fred!" said Winter solemnly. "Next!"

Doris, after a period of calm, was now profoundly uncomfortable. This kind of prying was the last thing she had expected. She had come prepared to defend Grant, but, beyond one exceedingly personal reference, the detective had studiously shut him out of the conversation.

"What am I to say?" she cried. "Do you want a list of all the young men who make sheep's eyes at me?"

"No. I can get that from the Census Bureau. Come, now, Miss Martin. *You* know. Has any man in the village led you to suspect, shall we put it? that sometime or other, he might ask you to become his wife?"

Lo, and behold! Doris's pretty eyes filled with tears. Superintendent Fowler was so pleased at hearing

Scotland Yard introducing a parenthetical query into its sentences that he, sitting opposite, was taken aback when Winter said in a fatherly way:

"I've been rather clumsy, I'm afraid. But it cannot be helped. I must go blundering on. I'm groping in the dark, you know, but it's a thousand pities I shall have to tread on *your* toes."

"It isn't that," sobbed Doris. "I hate to put my thoughts into words. That's all. There *is* a man whom I'm - afraid of."

"Siddle?"

She turned on Winter a face of sudden awe.

"How can you possibly guess?" she said wonderingly, and sheer bewilderment dried her tears.

"My business is nine-tenths guesswork. At any rate, we are on firm ground now. If you could please yourself, I suppose, Mr. Siddle would not come to tea to-day!"

"He certainly would not," declared the girl emphatically.

"You believe he is coming for a purpose?"

"Yes."

"Elkin - I must drag him in again for an instant - pretends that the commotion aroused in the village by this murder would incline you favorably to a proposal of marriage. Mr. Siddle may have discovered some virtue in the theory."

"Did Mr. Elkin really hint that I needed *him* as a shield?"

Doris was genuinely angry now. She little imagined that Winter was playing on her emotions with a master hand.

"Don't waste any wrath on Elkin," he soothed her. "The fellow isn't worth it. But his crude idea might be developed more subtly by an abler man."

"I think it odd that Mr. Siddle should choose to-day, of all days, for a visit," she admitted.

Winter relapsed into silence for a while. The car was running through a charming countryside, and a glimpse of the sea was obtainable from the crest of each hill. Mr. Fowler was too circumspect to break in on the thread of his coadjutor's thoughts. The inquiry had taken a curious turn, and was momentarily beyond his grasp.

"It's singular, but it's true," said the detective musingly when next he spoke, "that I am now going to ask you to act differently than was in my mind when I sought this interview. I should vastly like to be present when Siddle bares his heart to you this afternoon.

"I can invite you to tea."

Alas! that won't serve our ends. But, if you feel you have a purpose, you will be nerved to deal with him. Bring him out into that secluded garden of yours - "

"The first thing he will suggest," and Doris's voice waxed unconsciously bitter. "He knows that dad will be busy with the mails for an hour after tea."

"Good!"

"I think it bad, most disagreeable."

"You won't find the position so awkward if you are playing a part. And that is what I want - a bit of clever acting. Lean on those railings, and make Siddle believe that your heart is on Mr. Grant's lawn. You know the kind of thing I mean. Dreamy eyes, listless manner, inattention, with smiling apologies. You will annoy Siddle, and a cautious man in a temper becomes less cautious. Force him to avow his real thoughts. You will learn something, trust me."

"About what?"

There were no tears in Doris's eyes. They were wide open in wonderment.

"About his attitude to this tragedy. Do this, and you will be giving Mr. Grant the greatest possible help. He needs it. Next Wednesday, at the adjourned inquest, he will be put on the rack. Ingerman will fee counsel to be vindictive, merciless. Such men are to be hired. Their reputation is built up on the slaughter of reputations. I want to understand Siddle before Wednesday. By the way, what's his other name?"

"Theodore."

"Theodore Siddle. Unusual. Well, your half hour is nearly up. Will you do what I ask?"

"I'll try. May I put one question?"

"Yes."

"You said you had something altogether different in view before we met. What was it?"

"I'll tell you - let me see - I'll tell you on Thursday."

"Why not now?"

"Because it is the hardest thing in the world for a woman to be single-minded, in the limited sense of concentration, I mean. Focus your wits on Siddle to-day. I don't suggest any plan. I leave that to your own intelligence. Vex him, and let him talk."

"Vex him!"

"Yes. What man won't get mad if he notices that his best girl is thinking about a rival."

This time Doris did not blush. She was troubled and serious, very serious.

"I'll do what I can," she promised. "When shall I see you again?"

"Soon. There's no hurry. All this is preparatory for Wednesday."

"Am I to tell my father nothing?"

"Please yourself. Not at present. I recommend you."

The car had stopped. It sped on when Doris alighted. She would be home with her cakes at three o'clock, and Mr. Martin would never have noticed her absence.

"A fine bit of work, if I may say so," exclaimed Fowler appreciatively. "But I am jiggered if I can imagine what you're driving at."

Winter was cutting the end off a big cigar. He finished the operation to his liking before answering earnestly:

"We stand or fall by the result of that girl's efforts. Furneaux thinks so, and I agree with him absolutely. After five days, where are we, Mr. Fowler? In the dark, plus a brigand's hat and hair. But there's a queer belief in some parts of England that a phosphorescent gleam shows at night over a deep pool in which a dead body lies. That's just how I feel about Siddle. The man's an enigma. What sort of place is Steynholme for a chemist of his capacities? Dr. Foxton has the highest regard for him professionally, and I'm told he doctors people for miles around. Yet he lives the life of a recluse. An old woman comes by day to prepare his meals, and tidy the house and shop. His sole relaxation is an hour of an evening in the village inn, his visits there being uninterrupted since the murder. He was there on the night of the murder, too. For the rest, he is alone, shut off from the world. Without knowing it, he's going to fall into deep waters to-day, and he'll emit sparks, or I'm a Chinaman.... I'll leave you here. Good-by! See you on Tuesday, after lunch."

The superintendent drove on alone. He pondered the Steynholme affair in all its bearings, but mostly did he weigh up Winter and Furneaux. At last, he sighed.

"London ways, and London books, and London detectives!" he muttered. "We're not up to date in Sussex. Now, if I could please myself, I'd be hot-foot after Elkin. I see what Winter has in his mind, but

Louis Tracy

surely Elkin fills the bill, and Siddle doesn't.... What was that word - volt what!"

Doris was lucky. She met Mr. Siddle as she emerged from the back passage to the cake-shop. Resolving instantly that if an unpleasant thing had to be done it should at least be done well, she smiled brightly.

"See what you have driven me to - breaking the Sabbath," she cried, holding up the bag of cakes.

"Tea and bread-and-butter with you would be a feast for the gods," said Siddle.

"Now you're adapting Omar Khayyam."

"Who's he?"

"A Persian poet of long ago."

"I never read poetry. But, if your tastes lie that way, I'll accomplish some more adaptation."

"Oh, no, please. Cakes for you, Mr. Siddle; poets for giddy young things like me."

There was a sting in the words. Doris preened herself on having carried out the detective's instructions to the letter thus far.

Arrived in the house she found her father still in the garden, examining some larvae under a microscope. He looked severe rather than studious. He might have been an omnipotent being who had detected a male-factor in a criminal act. Was Steynholme and its secret felon being regarded in that way by the providence which, for some inscrutable purpose, permitted, yet would infallibly punish, a dreadful murder? She was a girl of devout mind, and the notion was appalling in its direct application to current events.

In the meantime the chemist, evidently taking a Sunday afternoon constitutional, came on Winter, who was leaning on a wall of the bridge and looking down stream - Grant's house being on the left.

He would have passed, in his wonted unobtrusive way, but the detective hailed him with a cheery "Good day, Mr. Siddle. Are you a fisherman?"

"No, Mr. Franklin, I'm not," he answered.

"Well, now, I'm surprised. You are just the sort of man whom I should expect to find attached to a rod and line - even watching a float."

"I tried once when I was younger, but I could neither impale a worm nor extract a hook. My gorge rose against either practice. I am a vegetarian, for the same reason. If it were not for this disturbing tragedy you would have heard Hobbs, the butcher, rallying me about my rabbit-meat, as he calls my food."

"Well, well!" laughed Winter. "Your ideas and mine clash in some respects. I look on a well-grilled steak as a gift from Heaven, and after it, or before it - I don't care which - let me have three hours whipping a good trout stream. With the right cast of flies I could show a fine bag from this very stretch of water."

"Why not ask Mr. Grant's permission? It would be interesting to learn whether he will allow others to try their luck."

Mr. Siddle strolled on. Winter bent over, keen to discern the gray-backed fish which must be lurking in those clear depths and rippling shallows.

CHAPTER XIV

ON BOTH SIDES OF THE RIVER

The sun, transmuted into Greenwich time, exercised an extraordinary influence on the seemingly humdrum life of Steynholme that day. A few minutes after three o'clock - just too late to observe either Winter or Siddle - P.C. Robinson strolled forth from his cottage. He glanced up the almost deserted high-street, in which every rounded cobble and white flagstone radiated heat. A high-class automobile had dashed past twice in forty minutes, but the pace was on the borderland of doubt, so the guardian of the public weal had contented himself with recording its number on the return journey.

But his thoughts were far a-field from joyriders, stray cattle, hawkers without licenses, and other similar small fry which come into the constabulary net. It would be a feather in his cap if he could only strike the trail of the veritable Steynholme murderer. The entrancing notion possessed him morning, noon, and night. Mrs. Robinson declared that it even dominated his dreams. Robinson was sharp. He knew quite well that the brains of the London detectives held some elusive quality which he personally lacked. They seemed to peer into the heart of a thing so wisely and thoroughly. He did not share Superintendent Fowler's somewhat derogatory estimate of Furneaux, with whom he was much better acquainted than was his superior officer, while Chief Inspector Winter's repute stood so high that it might not be questioned. Still, to the best of his belief, the case had beaten both these doughty representatives of Scotland Yard; there was yet a chance for the humble police-constable; so Robinson squared his shoulders, seamed his brows, and marched majestically down the Knoleworth road.

He had an eye for The Hollies, of course, though neither he nor anybody else could discern more than the bare edge of the lawn from bridge or road, owing to the dense screen of evergreen trees and shrubs planted by the tenant who remodeled the property.

But the spot where the body of Adelaide Melhuish was drawn ashore was visible, and the sight of it started a dim thesis in the policeman's mind which took definite shape during less than an hour's stroll. Thus, at four o'clock exactly, he was pulling the bell at The Hollies. Almost simultaneously, Mr. Siddle knocked modestly on the private door of the post office, to reach which one had to pass down a narrow yard.

"Mr. Grant at home?" inquired Robinson, when Minnie appeared.

Yes, the master was on the lawn with Mr. Hart. The policeman found the two there, seated in chairs with awnings. They had been discussing, of all things in the world, the futurist craze in painting. Hart held by it, but Grant carried bigger guns in real knowledge of the artist's limitations as well as his privileges.

Hart was the first to notice the newcomer's presence,

and greeted him joyously.

"Come along, Robinson, and manacle this reprobate," he shouted. "He's nothing but a narrow-minded pre-Rafaelite. A period in prison will dust the cobwebs out of his attic."

"Hello, Robinson!" said, Grant. "Anything stirring?"

"Not much, sir. I just popped in to ask if you remembered exactly how the body was roped?"

"Indeed, I do not. Some incidents of that horrible half hour have gone into a sad jumble. I recollect you calling attention to the matter, but what your point was I really cannot say now. Perhaps it may come back if you explain."

"Well, we don't seem to be making a great deal of progress, sir, and I was wondering whether you two gentlemen might help. I don't want it mentioned. I'm taking a line of me own."

Grant repressed a smile. He recalled well enough the first "line" the policeman took, and the mischief it had caused. Being an even-minded person, however, he admitted that his own behavior had not been above suspicion on the day the crime was discovered. In allotting blame, as between Robinson and himself, the proportion was six of one and half a dozen of the other.

"Propound, justiciary," said Hart. "You've started well, anyhow. The connection between a line and a rope should be obvious even to a judge.... As a pipe-opener, have a drink!"

Robinson had removed his helmet, and was flourishing a red handkerchief, not without cause, the day being really very hot.

"Not for a few minutes, thank you, sir," said the policeman. "May I ask Bates for a sack and a cord?"

He went to the kitchen. Hart was "tickled to death," he vowed.

"We are about to witness the reconstruction of the crime, a procedure which the French delight in, and the intellect of France is a hundred years ahead of our effete civilization," he chortled.

Grant was not so pleased. The memory of a distressing vision was beginning to blur, and this ponderous policeman must come and revive it. Yet, even he grew interested when Robinson illustrated a nebulous idea by knotting a clothesline around a sack stuffed with straw, having brought Bates to bear him out in the matter of accuracy.

"There you are, gentlemen!" he said, puffing after the slight exertion. "That's the way of it. How does it strike you?"

"It's what a sailor calls two half hitches," commented Hart instantly. "A very serviceable knot, which will resist to the full strength of the rope."

"We have no sailors in Steynholme, sir," said the policeman.

"Oh, it's used regularly by tradesmen," put in Grant. "A draper, or grocer - any man accustomed to tying parcels securely, in fact - will fashion that knot nine times out of ten."

"How about a - a farmer, sir?" That was as near as Robinson dared to go to "horse-dealer."

"I think a farmer would be more likely to adopt a timber hitch, which is made in several ways. Here are samples." And Grant busied himself with rope and sack.

Robinson watched closely.

"Yes," he nodded. "I've seen those knots in a farm-yard.... Well, it's something - not much - but a trifle better than nothing.... All right, Bates. You can take 'em away."

"Have you shown that knot to Mr. Furneaux?" inquired Grant.

"No, sir. I've kept that up me sleeve, as the sayin' is."

"But why?"

Robinson shuffled uneasily on his feet.

"These Scotland Yard men will hardly listen to a uniformed constable, sir," he said. "I'll tell 'em all about it at the inquest on Wednesday."

"In effect, John P. Robinson he sez they didn't know everythin' down in Judee," quoted Hart.

"You've got my name pat," grinned the policeman, whose Christian names were "John Price."

"My name is Walter, not Patrick," retorted Hart. Robinson continued to smile, though he failed to grasp the joke until late that evening.

"Did you make up that verse straight off, sir," he asked.

"No. It's a borrowed plume, plucked from an American quill pen."

Hart gave "plume" a French sound, and Robinson was puzzled to know why Grant bade his friend stop profaning a peaceful Sunday afternoon.

"You'll have a glass of beer now?" went on the host.

"I don't mind if I do, sir, though it's tea-time, and I make it a rule on Sundays to have tea with the missis. A policeman's hours are broken up, and his wife hardly ever knows when to have a meal ready."

Minnie was summoned. It took her a couple of minutes to draw the beer from a cool cellar. So it chanced that when Doris led Mr. Siddle to the edge of the cliff about twenty-five minutes past four, the first thing they saw was the local police-constable on the lawn of The Hollies putting down a gill of "best Sussex" at a draught.

"Well!" cried the chemist icily, "I wonder what Superintendent Fowler would say to that if he knew it?"

"What is there particularly wrong about Robinson drinking a glass of beer?" demanded Doris, more alive to the insinuation in Siddle's words than was quite permissible under the role imposed on her by Winter.

She waved her hand to the party on the lawn. Grant, whose eyes ever roved in that direction, had seen her white muslin dress the moment she appeared.

"Who the deuce is that with Miss Martin?" he said, returning her signal.

"Siddle, the chemist," announced Robinson, not too well pleased himself at being "spotted" so openly. "Well, gentlemen, I'll be off," and he vanished by the side path through the laurels.

"Siddle!" repeated Grant vexedly. "So it is. And she dislikes the man, for some reason."

"Let's go and rescue the fair maid," prompted Hart.

"No, no. If Doris wanted me she would let me know."

"How? At the top of her voice?"

"You're far too curious, Wally."

"Semaphore, of course," drawled Hart. "When are you going to marry the girl, Jack!"

"As soon as this infernal business has blown over."

"You haven't asked her, I gather?"

"No."

"Tell me when you do, and I'll hie me to London town, though in torrid June. You're unbearable in love."

" The lash of your wit cuts deeply sometimes," said

Grant quietly.

"Dash it all, old chap, I was talking at random. Very well. I'll do penance in sackcloth and ashes by remaining here, and applauding your poetic efforts. I'll even help. I'm a dab at sonnets."

Meanwhile, Mr. Siddle had regained his poise.

"I meant nothing offensive to the donor of the beer," he said, tuning his voice to an apologetic note. "But I take it Robinson is conducting certain inquiries, and I imagine that his superiors demand a degree of circumspection in such conditions. That is all."

"Surely you do not rank with the stupid crowd in its suspicions of Mr. Grant?" said the girl.

"I'm pleased to think you refuse to class me with the gossip-mongers of Steynholme, Doris," was the guarded answer.

There had been no reference to the murder during tea, which was served as soon as the chemist came in. The visitor had tabled a copy of a current medical journal containing an article on the therapeutic qualities of honey, so the talk was lifted at once into an atmosphere far removed from crime. Doris was grateful for his tact. When her father went to the office she brought Mr. Siddle into the garden solely in pursuance of her promise to the detective, though convinced that there would be no outcome save a few labored compliments to herself. And now, by accident, as it were, the death of Adelaide Melhuish thrust itself into their conversation. Perhaps it was her fault.

"No," she said candidly. "No one who has known you for seven years, Mr. Siddle, could possibly accuse you of spreading scandal."

"Seven years! Is it so long since I came to Steynholme? Sometimes, it appears an age, but more often I fancy the calendar must be in error. Why, it seems only the other day that I saw you in a short frock, bowling a hoop."

"A tom-boy occupation," laughed Doris. "But dad encouraged that and skipping, as the best possible means of exercise."

"He was right. Look how straight and svelte you are! Few, if any, among our community can have watched your progress to womanhood as closely as I. You see, living opposite, as I do, I kept track of you more intimately than your other neighbors."

Siddle was trimming his sails cleverly. The concluding sentence robbed his earlier comments of their sentimental import.

"If we live long enough we may even see each other in the sere and yellow leaf," said Doris flippantly.

"I would ask no greater happiness," came the quiet reply, and Doris could have bitten her tongue for according him that unguarded opening. Suddenly availing herself of the advice which the detective, like Hamlet, had given to the players, she gazed musingly at the fair panorama of The Hollies and its gardens, with the two young men seated on the lawn. By this time Minnie was staging tea, and the picture looked idyllic enough. Doris saw, out of the tail of her eye, that her companion was watching her furtively, though apparently absorbed in the scene. He moistened his thin lips with his tongue.

"As a study in contrasts, that would be hard to beat," he said, after a long pause.

"Contrasts!" she echoed.

"Well, yes. Even an uncontentious man like myself can hardly fail to compare Sunday afternoon with Tuesday morning."

"Why not Monday night?" she flashed.

"Monday night, in part, remains a mystery yet to be unveiled. I blot Monday night from my mind. I have no alternative, being on the jury which has to arrive at a just verdict. Now, if Fred Elkin were here, he would foam at the mouth."

"Happily, Fred Elkin is *not* here."

"Ah, I am glad, glad, to hear you say that. You don't like him?"

"I detest him."

"He makes out, to put it mildly, that you are great friends."

" You will oblige me by contradicting the statement. Or - no. One treats that sort of man with contempt."

"I agree with you most heartily. I'm sorry I ever mentioned him."

Yet Doris was well aware that the chemist had dragged in Elkin by the scruff of the neck, probably for the sake of getting him disposed of thoroughly and for all time. Rather on the tiptoe of expectation, she awaited the next move. It was slow in coming, so again she looked wistfully at the distant tea-drinkers. She found slight difficulty in carrying out this portion of the stage directions. Truth to tell, she would gleefully have gone and joined them.

Siddle was not altogether at ease. The conversation was too spasmodic to suit his purpose. Though slow of speech he was nimble of brain, and, knowing Doris so well, he had anticipated a livelier duel of wits. In all likelihood, he cursed the tea-party on the lawn. He had not foreseen this drawback. But, being a masterful man, he tackled the situation boldly.

"I seized the opportunity of a friendly chat with you to-day, Doris," he went on, leaning over the fence to inhale the scent of a briar rose. "The story runs through the village that you and your father dined at The Hollies on Friday evening. Is that true?"

Now, Doris had it on reliable authority that Siddle himself had been the runner who spread that story, and the knowledge steeled her heart against him.

"Yes," she said composedly.

"It was kind and neighborly of you to accept the invitation, but a mistake."

She turned and faced him. His expression was baffling. She thought she saw in his sallow, clean-cut features the shadow of a confident smile.

"You mean that this horrid murder should make some difference in the friendship between ourselves and Mr. Grant?" she cried.

"Yes. To you, though to no one else would I speak so plainly, I have no hesitation in saying that Mr. Grant is far, very far, from being clear of responsibility in that matter. Three days from now you will understand what I mean. Evidence will be forthcoming which will put him in a most unenviable light. I am not alleging, or even hinting, that he may be deemed guilty of actual crime. That is for the law to determine. But I do tell you emphatically that his present heedless attitude will give place to anxiety and dejection. It cannot be otherwise. A somewhat sordid history will be revealed, and his pretense that relations between him and the dead woman ceased three years ago will vanish into thin air. Believe me, Doris, I am actuated by no motive in this matter other than a desire to further your welfare. I cannot bear even to think of your name being associated, in ever so small degree, with that of a man who must be hounded out of his own social circle, if no worse fate is in store for him."

"Good gracious!" cried Doris, genuinely amazed. "How do you come to know all this?"

"I listen to the words of those qualified to speak with knowledge and authority. I have mixed in varied company this past week, wholly on your account. Don't be led away by the mere formalities of the opening day of the inquest. The coroner deliberately shut off all real evidence except as to the cause of death. On Wednesday the situation will change, and you cannot fail to be shocked by what you hear, because you will be there."

"I am given to understand that, even if I am called, my testimony will be of no importance."

"Such may be the police view. Mr. Ingerman will press for a very different estimate."

"Has he told you that?"

"Yes."

"So, although foreman of the jury, you have not declined to hobnob with a man who is avowedly Mr. Grant's enemy?"

"I would hobnob with worse people if, by so doing, I might serve you."

Grant, "fed up," as he put it to Hart, with watching the *tête à tête* between Doris and the chemist, sprang to his feet and went through a pantomime easy enough to follow save for one or two signs. Doris held both hands aloft. Well knowing that anything in the nature of a pre-arranged code would be gall and wormwood to Siddle, she explained laughingly:

"Mr. Grant signals that he and Mr. Hart are going for a walk; he wants me to accompany them. But I can't, unfortunately. I promised dad to help with the accounts."

"If you really mean what you say, my warning would seem to have fallen on deaf ears."

Siddle's voice was well under control, but his eyes glinted dangerously. His state was that of a man torn by passion who nevertheless felt that any display of the rage possessing him would be fatal to his cause.

But, rather unexpectedly, Doris took fire. Siddle's innuendoes and protestations were sufficiently hard to bear without the added knowledge that a ridiculous convention denied her the companionship of a man whom she loved, and who, she was beginning to believe, loved her. She swept round on Siddle like a wrathful goddess.

"I have borne with you patiently because of the acquaintance of years, but I shall be glad if this tittle-tattle of malice and ignorance now ceases," she said proudly. "Mr. Grant is my friend, and my father's friend. In the first horror of the crime which has besmirched our dear little village, we both treated Mr. Grant rather badly. We know better to-day. Your Ingermans and your Elkins, and the rest of the busy-bodies gathered at the inn, may defame him as they choose, or as they dare. As for me, I am his loyal comrade, and shall remain so after next Wednesday, or a score of Wednesdays. I am going in now, Mr. Siddle, and shall be engaged during the remainder of the evening. Your shop opens at six, and I am sure you will find some more profitable means of spending the time than in telling me things I would rather not hear."

Siddle caught her arm.

"Doris," he said fiercely, "you must not leave me without, at least, learning my true motive. I -"

The girl wrested herself free from his grip. She realized what was coming, and forestalled it.

" I care nothing for your motive," she cried. " You

forget yourself! Please go!"

She literally ran into the house. The chemist, unless he elected to behave like a love-sick fool, had no option but to follow, and make his way to the street by the side door.

The only other happening of significance that Sunday was an unheralded visit by Winter to the policeman's residence.

He popped in after dusk, opening the door without knocking.

"You in, Robinson?" he inquired.

"Yes, sir. Will you - "

"Shan't detain you more than a minute. At the inquest you said that you personally untied the rope which bound Miss Melhuish's body. Here are a piece of string and a newspaper. Would you mind showing me what sort of knot was used?"

Robinson was nearly struck dumb, and his fingers fumbled badly, but he managed to exhibit two hitches.

"Ah, thanks," said Winter, and was off in a jiffy.

From the window of a darkened room Robinson watched the erect, burly figure of the detective until it was merged in the mists of night.

"Well, I'm -," he exclaimed bitterly.

"John, what are you swearing about?" demanded his

wife from the kitchen.

"Something I heard to-day," answered her husband. "There was a chap of my name, John P. Robinson, an' he said that down in Judee they didn't know everything. And, by gum, he was right. They knew mighty little about London 'tecs, I'm thinking. But, hold on. Surely -"

He bustled into his coat, and hastened to The Hollies. No, neither Mr. Grant nor Mr. Hart had spoken to a soul about the knot. Nor had Bates. Of course, Robinson did not venture to describe Winter. Finally, he put the incident aside as a clear case of thought-reading.

CHAPTER XV

A MATTER OF HEREDITY

Shortly before noon on Monday occurred two events destined to assume a paramount importance in the affair which was wringing the withers of Steynholme. As in the histories of both men and nations, these first steps in great developments began quietly enough. For one thing, Furneaux returned to the village. For another, the London telegraphist, who expected the day to prove practically a blank, was reading a newspaper when the telegraph instrument clicked the local call.

Doris was checking and distributing the stock of stamps which had arrived that morning; her father was counting mail-bags in a small annex to the main room, the Knoleworth office having acquired a habit of making up shortages by docking the country branches. No member of the public happened to be present. The girl could have heard what the Morse code was tapping forth had she chosen, but she had trained herself to disregard the telegraph when occupied on other work.

Suddenly, however, the telegraphist's pencil paused.

"Hello!" he said. "Theodore Siddle! That's the chemist opposite, isn't it!"

Louis Tracy

"Yes," said Doris, suspending her calculations at mention of the name.

"Well, his mother's dead."

"Dead?" she echoed vacantly. Somehow, it had never hitherto dawned on her that the chemist might possess relatives in some part of the country.

"That's what it says," went on the other. "'Regret inform you your mother died this morning. Superintendent, Horton Asylum.'"

"In an asylum, too," said the girl, speaking at random.

"Yes. Horton is the place for epileptic lunatics, near Epsom, you know."

"I didn't know. Does it mean that - that she was an epileptic lunatic?"

"So I should imagine, from the wording. If a nurse, or a matron, they'd surely describe her as such."

"I suppose we ought not to discuss Mr. Siddle's telegram," said Doris, after a pause.

"Well, no. But where's the harm? I wouldn't have yelled out the news if we three weren't alone. Where's that boy?"

"Gone to his dinner. Father will take it. By the way, say nothing to him as to the contents. Would you mind calling him?"

Doris hurried swiftly to the sitting-room, and thence

upstairs. The telegraphist explained the absence of a messenger, so Mr. Martin delivered the telegram in person.

Crossing the street, he detected a dead bee. He picked it up, horrified at the thought that the Isle of Wight disease might have reached Sussex. So it was an absent-minded postmaster who handed the telegram over Siddle's counter, inquiring laconically:

"Is there any answer?"

Siddle opened the buff envelope, and read. He glanced sharply at Martin.

"No," he said. "What's wrong with that bee?"

"I don't know. I have my doubts. When I have a moment to spare I'll put it under the microscope."

Siddle examined the telegram again. The handwriting was that beloved of Civil Service Commissioners. Unquestionably, it was not Doris's. No sooner had his friend gone off, still intent on the dead insect, than Siddle followed. He knew that the bee would undergo scientific scrutiny at once, so gave Martin just enough time to dive into the sitting-room before entering the post office.

"Did you receive this telegram a few minutes ago!" he inquired.

The young man became severely official.

"Which telegram?" he said stiffly.

Louis Tracy

"This one," and Siddle gave him the written message.

"Yes," was the answer.

"Excuse me, but - er - are its contents known to you only?"

"What do you mean, sir? It would cost me my berth if I divulged a word of it to anyone."

"I'm sorry. Pray don't take offense. I - I'm anxious that my friends, Mr. and Miss Martin, should not hear of it. That is what I really have in mind."

The telegraphist cooled down.

"You may be quite sure that neither they nor any other person in Steynholme will ever see the duplicate," he said confidentially. "I make up a package containing duplicates each evening, and it is sent to headquarters. If it will please you, I'll lock the copy now in my desk."

"That is exceedingly good of you," said Siddle gratefully. "You, as a Londoner, will understand that such a telegram from - er - Horton is not the sort of thing one would like to become known even in the most limited circle."

"You can depend on me, sir."

Siddle hastened back to his shop. The telegraphist looked after him.

"Queer! " he mused. "Miss Doris guessed him at once. Phi-ew, I must be careful! This village contains surprises."

Doris, watching from an upper room, saw the visitor, and timed him. She imagined he had dispatched an answer. Being a woman, she sought enlightenment a few minutes later.

"Mr. Siddle came in," she said tentatively.

"Yes," said the specialist, smiling. "And I agree with you, Miss Martin. We mustn't talk about telegrams, even among ourselves, unless it is necessary departmentally."

Doris was silenced, but she read the riddle correctly. The chemist was particularly anxious that no Steyn-holme resident should be made aware of his mother's death. She wondered why.

She was enlightened when Furneaux paid a call about tea-time. She took him into the garden. The lawn at The Hollies was empty.

"Well, you entertained an acquaintance yesterday?" he began.

"Yes. Am I to tell you what happened?"

"Not a great deal, I imagine," he said, with a puzzling laugh.

"No, but I annoyed him, as Mr. -"

"No names!" broke in the detective hastily. "Names, especially modern ones, destroy romance. Even the Georgian method of using initials, or leaving out vowels, lend an air of intrigue to the veriest balderdash."

"But no one can overhear us," was the somewhat surprised comment.

"How true!" said Furneaux. "Pardon me, Miss Martin. Tell the story in your own way."

Doris had a good memory. She was invariably letter-perfect in a play after a couple of rehearsals, and could prompt others if they faltered. The detective listened in silence while she repeated the conversation between Siddle and herself. He took no notes. In fact, he hardly ever did make any record in a case unless it was essential to prove the exact words of a suspected person.

"Good!" he said, when she had finished. "That sounds like the complete text."

"I don't think I have left out anything of importance - that is, if a single word of it *is* important."

"Oh, heaps," he assured her. "It's even better than I dared hope. Can you tell me if Siddle's mother is dead yet?"

The question found Doris so thoroughly unprepared that she blurted out:

"Have you had a telegram, too, then?"

"No. But Siddle has had one, eh? Don't be vexed. I'm not tricking you into revealing post office secrets. I knew she was dying, and, when I saw your father take a message to the chemist's shop I simply made an accurate guess.... Now, I'm going to scare you, purposely and of malice aforethought, because I want you to be a good little girl, and obey orders. Mrs. Siddle, senior, now happily deceased, was an epileptic lunatic of a peculiarly dangerous type. She suffered from what is classed by the doctors as *furor epilepticus*, a form of spasmodic insanity not inconsistent with a high degree of bodily vigor and long periods of apparently complete mental saneness. Now, if I were not speaking to one who has shared her father's studies in bee-life, I would not introduce the subject of heredity. But *you* know, Miss Martin, that such racial characteristics are transmitted, or transmissible, I should say, by sex opposites. Thus, an epileptic mother is more likely to give her taint to a son than to a daughter.... Yes, I mean all that, and more," he went on, seeing the look of horror, not unmixed with fear, in Doris's eyes. "There must be no more irritating of Siddle, or playing on his feelings - by you, at any rate. Treat him gently. If he insists on making love to you, be as firm as you like in a non-committal way. I mean, by that, an entire absence on your part of any suggestion that you are repulsing him because of a real or supposed preference for any other man."

"Do you want me to believe that he is liable to attack me?" demanded the girl, her naturally courageous spirit coming to her aid.

"I do," said Furneaux, speaking with marked earnestness.

"Yet you ask me to endure his company if he chooses to force himself on me?"

"For a few days."

"But it may be a few years?"

"No. That is not to be thought of. Leave it to me to devise a way. Besides, you need not allow him so many opportunities that the strain would become unbearable. You are busy, owing to the certain increase of work brought about by this murder. Your time will be greatly occupied. But, don't render him morbidly suspicious. For instance, no more dinners at The Hollies. No more gadding about by night, if you hear weird noises on the other side of the river. And you must absolutely deny yourself the pleasurable excitement of Mr. Grant's company."

"You are carrying a warning to its extreme limit."

"Exactly."

"And am I to keep this knowledge to myself?"

"In whom would you confide?"

"My father, of course."

"I know you better," and the detective's voice took on a profoundly serious note. "Your father would never admit that what he knows to be true of bees is equally true of humanity. You can trust the police to keep a pretty sharp eye on Siddle, of course, but the present is a strenuous period, both for us and for people with maniacal tendencies, so accidents may happen."

"You have distressed me immeasurably," said the girl, striving to pierce the mask of that inscrutable face.

"I meant to," answered Furneaux quietly. "No half measures for me. I've looked up the asylum record of Mrs. Siddle, senior, and it's not nice reading."

"There was a Mrs. Siddle, junior, then?"

"A Mrs. Theodore Siddle, if one adopts the conventional usage. Yes. She died last month."

"Last month!" gasped Doris, feeling vaguely that she was moving in a maze of deceit and subterfuge.

"On May 25th, to be precise. She lived apart from her husband. I have reason to believe she feared him."

"Yet -"

She hesitated, hardly able to put her jumbled thoughts into words.

"Yes. That's so," said the detective instantly. "Never mind. It's a fairly decent world, taken *en bloc*. I ought to speak with authority. I see enough of the seamy side of it, goodness knows. Now, forewarned is forearmed. Don't be nervous. Don't take risks. Everything will come right in time. Remember, I'm not far away in an emergency. Should I chance to be absent if you need advice, send for Mr. Franklin. You can easily devise some official excuse, a mislaid letter, or an error in a telegram."

"I think I shall feel confident if both of you are near," and the ghost of a smile lit Doris's wan features.

"We're a marvelous combination," grinned Furneaux, reverting at once to his normal impishness. "I am all brain; he is all muscle. Such an alliance prevails against the ungodly."

"Is Mr. Grant in any danger?' inquired Doris suddenly.

"No."

The two looked into each other's eyes. Doris was eager to ask a question, which Furneaux dared her to put. The detective won. She sighed.

"Very well," she said. "I'm to behave. Am I to regard myself as a decoy duck?"

"A duck, anyhow."

She laughed lightly. Furneaux would vouchsafe no further information, it would appear. For a girl of nineteen, Doris was uncommonly gifted with clear, analytical reasoning powers.

The detective returned to the Hare and Hounds, and went upstairs. He met Peters on the landing.

"The devil!" he cried.

"My *dear* pal!" retorted the journalist.

"Are you living here?"

"Why not?"

"Why not, indeed? Where the eagles are there is the carcase."

"Your misquotation is offensive."

"It was so intended."

"Come and have a drink."

"No."

"I say 'yes.' You'll thank me on your bended knees afterwards. The South American gent is having the time of his life. I've just been to my room for *Whitaker's Almanack*, wherewith a certain Don Walter Hart purposes flooring him."

Wally Hart had, indeed, succeeded in running to earth the Argentine magnate, and was giving Winter a most uncomfortable quarter of an hour.

"Ha!" shouted Hart, when Furneaux came in with Peters. "Here's the pocket marvel who'll answer any question straight off. What is the staple export of the Argentine!"

"How often have you been there?" demanded the detective dryly.

"Six times."

"And you've lived there?" This to Winter.

"Yes," glowered the big man, fearing the worst.

"Then the answer is 'fools,'" cackled Furneaux.

Wally laughed. He had remembered, just in time, that he had no right to claim acquaintance with the representative of Scotland Yard, and there were some farmers present, each of whom had a "likely animal" to offer the buyer of blood stock.

"Gad, I think you're right," he said.

"You wanted me to say 'sheep,' I suppose?"

"Got it, at once."

"As though one valuable horse wasn't worth a thousand sheep."

"Just what my friend, Don Manoel Alcorta, of Los Andes ranch, Catamarca, always held," put in Winter, drawing the bow at a venture.

Hart cocked an eye at him.

"Sir," he said, "I would take off my hat, if I wore one in Steynholme, to any man who claims the friendship of Don Manoel Alcorta, a sincere patriot. I suggest that we crack a bottle to his immortal memory."

"My doctor forbids me to touch wine," said Winter mournfully.

"But these bucolic breeders of browns and bays employ wiser medicos, I'll go bail. Landlord, a quart of the best, and six out, as they say in London."

Six glasses were duly filled with champagne. When it was consumed, Hart buttonholed Peters.

"A word with you, scribe," he said. "Good-day, gentlemen. I leave you to your nags. Treat Mr. Franklin fairly. The friend of Don Manoel Alcorta must be a true man."

Winter heaved a sigh of relief when the professional revolutionist had vanished.

"He's a funny 'un," commented one of the farmers.

"A bit touched, I reckon," said another. "Wot's 'e doin' now to the other one?"

They looked through the window. The two were standing in the middle of the road, and Wally was shaking Peters violently. The argument was not so fierce as it appeared to be. Peters had been commanded to bring both detectives to dinner that evening; when he demurred, trying to hedge on the question of Winter's identity, Hart grabbed him by the shoulder.

"Do as I tell you," he hissed. "Of course, I know now that the big fellow is the man Grant heard of a week ago. I was an idiot to take him seriously about the Argentine. Bring the pair of 'em, I tell you. We'll make a night of it."

"I'll try," said Peters faintly, "but if you stir up that wine so vigorously I won't answer for the consequences."

Winter, wishing devoutly that would-be sellers of horseflesh were not so numerous in the district, noted the names and addresses of the local men, and promised to write when he could make an appointment. Then he escaped upstairs, whither Furneaux soon followed. Winter had secured an extra bedroom, overlooking the river, which Tomlin had converted into a sitting-room. Thus, he held a secure observation post both in front and rear of the hotel.

"Well, how did she take it!" inquired the Chief Inspector, when he and his colleague were safe behind a closed door.

"Sensible girl," said Furneaux. "By the way, Siddle's mother is dead. Telegram came this morning. Things should happen now."

"I don't quite see why."

"No. You're still muddled after floundering in the mud of South America. What possessed you to let that cheerful idiot, Wally Hart, put you in the cart?"

"How could I help it? I was extracting some really helpful facts about Siddle and Elkin from Tomlin and the others when a shock-headed whirlwind blew in, and nearly embraced me because I claimed acquaintance with the El Dorado bar in Buenos Ayres. From that instant I was lost. Like St. Augustine on the gridiron, no sooner was I nicely toasted on one side than I was turned on to the other. That grinning penny-a-liner, Peters, too, helped as assistant torturer. Wait till he asks me for a 'pointer' in this or any other case. He sold me a pup to-day, but I'll land him with a full-sized mastiff."

"No, you won't. He's done you a lot of good. You were simply reeking with conceit when I met you this morning. It was 'Siddle this' and 'Siddle that' until you fairly sickened me. One would have thought I hadn't cleared the ground for you, left you with all lines open and yourself unknown to the enemy. Sometimes, you make me tired."

"Sorry, Charles," said Winter patronizingly. "I had a

bit of luck on Sunday, I admit. The chance turn taken by the conversation with Doris, with the result that I was able to occupy a strategic position on the cliff, and hear every word Siddle uttered, was really fortunate. But, isn't that just what men mean when they prate of success? Opportunity knocks once at every man's door, says the old saw. The clever man grabs hold instantly. The indolent one, often a mere gabbler, opens his eyes and his mouth weeks afterwards, and cries, 'Dear me! Was that the much-looked-for opportunity?' Of course, Robinson's by-play with the sack and rope was merely thrown in by the prodigal hand of Fate."

"Stop!" yelped Furneaux. "Another platitude, and I'll assault you with the tongs!"

It was the invariable habit of the Big 'Un and Little 'Un to quarrel like cat and dog when the toils were closing in around a suspect. Woe, then, to the malefactor! His was a parlous state.

"Let's cool down, Charles!" said Winter, opening a leather case, and selecting, with great care, one out of half a dozen precisely similar cigars. "We're pretty sure of our man, but we haven't a scrap of evidence against him. How, or where, to begin ringing him in I haven't the faintest notion. If only he'd kill Grant we'd get him at once."

"But he won't. He trusts to Ingerman playing that part of the game. He's as artful as a pet fox. I bought soap, and a pound of sal volatile, but he did up each parcel with sealing-wax."

"Sal volatile!" smiled Winter. "I, too, went in for soap, but my imagination would not soar beyond a packet of cotton-wool. It was the lumpiest thing I could think of."

"And perfectly useless!" sneered Furneaux. "I must say you do fling the taxpayers' money about. Now, *my* little lot will keep the electric bells in my flat in order for two years."

"You forget that constant association with you demands that I should frequently plug my two ears," retorted Winter.

Furneaux would surely have thrown back the jest had not a knock on the door interrupted him.

"Who's there? I'm busy," cried Winter.

"Me-ow!" whined Peters's voice.

"Oh, it's you, Tom. Come in!"

The journalist crept in on tiptoe.

"Hush! We are not observed," he said. "Wally Hart threatens to choke me if you two don't dine with him and Grant to-night."

There was silence for a little while. The detectives looked at each other.

"At what time?" said Winter, at last.

Peters was astonished, and showed it.

"Why, I assured him it was absolutely imposs.," he cried.

"Well, it isn't. In fact, it suits our plans. I want exercise, and shall walk back from Knoleworth. Furneaux will make his own arrangements. Tell Grant that I shall drop in without knocking."

"And tell him I shall arrive by parachute," added Furneaux.

"In case of accidents, and there is a shoot-up, with myself as the unresisting victim, my front name is James," said Peters.

"The only good point about you," scoffed Winter.

"You're strong on names to-day," tittered the journalist. "Don Manoel Alcorta was a superb effort as an authority on gee-gees. Wally tells me his donship is the recognized expert south of the line on seismic disturbances, and spends his days and nights watching a needle making scratches on a sensitive plate."

"He would be useful here in a day or two," said Winter.

"Ah, thanks! Is that a tip?"

"Not for publication. What you must say is that this affair looks like baffling the shrewdest wits in Scotland Yard."

"My very phrase - my own ewe lamb. Pardon. I shouldn't have alluded to sheep."

"The only known representative of the Yard in Steynholme is Furneaux," smiled the Chief Inspector.

Furneaux was drumming on a window-pane with his finger-tips.

"True," he cackled. "Just to prove it, he now informs you that Siddle, finding trade slow, has called on Mr. John Menzies Grant!"

CHAPTER XVI

FURNEAUX MAKES A SUCCESSFUL BID

The lawn front of The Hollies was not visible from the upper story of the Hare and Hounds owing to a clump of pines which had found foothold on the cliff, but, through the gap formed by the end of the post office garden, the entrance to the house from the Knoleworth road was discernible.

Furneaux's dramatic announcement brought the other two to the window. By this time Peters, gifted with a nose for news like a well-trained setter's for partridges, had begun to associate the quiet-mannered, gentle-spoken chemist with the inner circle of the crime, so waited and watched with the detectives for Siddle's reappearance.

At any rate the visitor must have been admitted, because a long quarter of an hour elapsed before he came in sight again. He walked out slowly into the roadway, thrust his hands into his trousers pockets, and glanced to right and left. Then, turning abruptly, he stared at the dwelling he had just quitted. What this slight but peculiar action signified was not hard to guess. Furneaux, indeed, put it into words.

"Having warned Grant off Miss Doris Martin , and

been cursed for his pains, the foreman of the jury does not trouble to await further evidence, but arrives at a true and lawful verdict straight off," announced the little man.

"We ought to hear things to-night," said Peters.

"We?" inquired Winter.

"Yes. Didn't I make it clear that I shared in the dinner invitation?"

"No, and I'm -"

"Don't say it!" pleaded the journalist. "If I fell from grace to-day, remember my unswerving loyalty since the hour we met on the platform at Knoleworth! Haven't I kept close as an oyster? And would any consideration on earth move me to publish an accurate and entertaining account of the roasting of Chief Inspector Winter by Wally Hart? Think what I'm sacrificing - a column of the best."

Winter bent a weighing look on the speaker. There was treason in the thought, as King James remarked to the barber who tried to prove his loyalty by pointing out how easily he might cut his majesty's throat any morning. But Peters maintained the expression of a sphinx, and the big man relaxed.

"The conditions are that not a word about this business appears in print, either now or in the future until we have a criminal in the dock," he said.

"Accepted," said Peters.

Furneaux laughed shrilly, even derisively, but him his colleague treated with majestic disdain. Then, the chemist having reentered the village, the group broke up, Peters to search his brains for "copy" which should be readable yet contain no hint of the new trail, Winter to take train to Knoleworth, and Furneaux to tackle Fred Elkin, who, he had ascertained earlier, would drive home from a neighboring hamlet about five o'clock.

Elkin had returned when the detective reached the house, a somewhat pretentious place, half farm, half villa, and altogether horsey. The entrance hall bristled with fox masks and brushes. A useful collection of burnished bits and snaffles hung on a side wall. A couple of stuffed badgers held two wicker stands for sticks and umbrellas, and whips and hunting-crops were ranged on hooks beneath a 12-bore and a rook rifle.

A pert maid-servant took Furneaux's card, blanched when she read it, and forgot to close the door of the dining-room. Hence, the detective heard Elkin's gruff comments:

"What? *That* chap? Wants to see me? Not more than I want to see him. Show him in."

Furneaux, looking very meek and mild, entered an apartment of the carpet-bag upholstery period. A set of six exceedingly good and rare sporting prints caught his eye.

"Good day," he said, finding Elkin drinking tea, and eating a boiled egg. "You're feeling better, I'm glad to see."

Now, no matter how ungracious a man may be, a courteous solicitude as to his health demands a certain note of civility in return.

"Yes," he said. "Sit down. Will you join me?"

"I'll have a cup of tea, with pleasure," said Furneaux.

"Right-o! Just touch that bell, will you?"

The other obeyed, and took a closer look at one of the prints. Yes, the date was right, 1841, and the stippling admirable.

"Nice lot of pictures, those," he said cheerfully, when the frightened maid, much to her relief, had been told to bring another cup and a fresh supply of toast.

"Are they?" Elkin had taken them and some kitchen furniture for a bad debt.

"Yes. Will you sell them?"

"Well, I haven't thought about it. What'll you give?"

Furneaux hesitated.

"I can't resist anything in the art line that takes my fancy," he said, after a pause of indecision. "What do you say to ten bob each?"

Elkin valued the lot at that figure, but Furneaux was a fool, and should be treated as such.

"Oh, come now!" he cried roguishly. "They're worth more than that."

Furneaux reflected again.

"Three pounds is a good deal for six prints," he murmured, "but, to get it off my mind, I'll spring to guineas."

"Make it three-ten and they're yours."

"Three guineas is my absolute limit," said Furneaux.

"Done!" cried Elkin. The original debt was under two pounds, so he had cleared more than fifty per cent. on the transaction, and was plus a number of chairs and a table.

Furneaux counted out the money, wrote a receipt on a leaf torn from his pocket-book, and stamped it.

"Sign that," he said, "pocket the cash, send the set to the Hare and Hounds for me in a dog-cart now, and the deal is through."

Leaving the table, he went and lifted down each picture carefully. Somewhat wonderingly, Elkin rang the bell once more, gave the necessary instructions, and the room was cleared of its art. He was quite sure now that Furneaux was, as he put it, "dotty." The latter, however, sat and enjoyed his tea as though well pleased with his bargain.

"And how are things going in the murder at The Hollies?" inquired the horse-dealer, by way of a polite leading up to the visitor's unexplained business.

"Fairly well," said the detective. "My chief difficulty was to convince certain important people that you didn't kill Miss Melhuish. Once I -"

"Me!" roared Elkin, his pale blue eyes assuming a fiery tint. "*Me!*"

"Once I established that fact," went on the other severely, "a real stumbling-block was removed. You see, Elkin, you have behaved throughout like a perfect fool, and thus lent a sort of credibility to an otherwise absurd notion. Your furious hatred of Mr. Grant, for instance, born of an equally fatuous - or, shall I say? fat-headed - belief that Miss Martin would marry you for the mere asking, led you into deep waters. It was a mistake, too, when you lied to P.C. Robinson as to the time you came home on that Monday night. You told him you walked straight here from the Hare and Hounds at ten o 'clock. You know you didn't - that it was nearer half past eleven when you reached this house. Consider what that discrepancy alone might have meant if Scotland Yard failed to take your measure correctly. Then add the fact that the murderer wore the hat, wig, and whiskers in which you made a guy of yourself while filling the rôle of Svengali last winter. Now, I ask you, Elkin, where would you have stood with the average British jury when the prosecution established those three things: Motive, your jealousy of Grant; time, your unaccounted-for disappearance during the hour when the crime was committed; and disguise, a clumsy suggestion of Owd Ben's ghost? Really, I have known men brought to the scaffold on circumstantial evidence little stronger than that. Instead of glaring at me like a cornered rat you ought to drop on your knees and thank providence, as manifested through the intelligence of the 'Yard,' that you are not now in a cell at Knoleworth, ruminating on your own stupidity , and in no small jeopardy of your life."

Many emotions chased each other across Fred Elkin's somewhat mean and cruel face while Furneaux rated him in this extraordinary manner. Surprise, wrath, even fear, had their phases. But, dominating all other sensations, was an overpowering indignation at the implied hopelessness of his pursuit of Doris Martin.

He literally howled an oath at his torturer. Furneaux was shocked.

"No, no," he protested in a horrified tone. "Don't swear at your best friend."

"Friend! By -, I'll make you pay for what you've said. There's a law to stop that sort of thing."

"But the law requires witnesses. A slander isn't a slander unless it's uttered to your detriment before a third party. How different would be Mr. Grant's action against you! Your well-wishers simply couldn't muzzle you. Whether before your pot-house cronies or mere strangers, you charged him openly with being a murderer. I'm sorry for you, Elkin, if ever you come before a judge. He'll rattle more than my three guineas out of you. Even now, you don't grasp the extent of your folly. Instead of telling me how you spent that hour and a half on the night of the crime you have the incredible audacity to threaten me, *me*, the man who has saved you from jail. One more word, you miserable swab, and I'll let Robinson arrest you. You'll be set free, of course, when I stage the actual villain, but a few remands of a week each in custody will thin your hot blood. You were with Peggy Smith after leaving the Hare and Hounds, making a fool of an honest girl who thinks you mean to wed her. Yet you blather about being 'practically engaged' to Doris Martin, a girl who wouldn't let you tie her shoe-lace. You're an impudent pup, Fred, and you know it. But you stock decent tea, so I'll take another cup. If you're wise, you'll take a second one yourself. It's better for you than whiskey."

Elkin, despite all his faults, was endowed with the shrewdness inseparable from his business, because no man devoid of brains ever yet throve as a horse-dealer. He smothered his rage, thinking he might learn more from this strange-mannered detective by seeming complaisance.

"You're a bit rough on a fellow," he growled sulkily, pouring out the tea.

"For your good, my boy, solely for your good. Now, own up about Peggy."

"Yes. That's right. She'd prove an alibi, so your torn-fool case breaks down when the flag falls."

"Does it? A girl may say anything to save her supposed lover. How will the twelve good men and true view Doris Martin's evidence on Wednesday? What did *you* mean, for instance, by your question to the coroner at the first hearing?"

"I thought Grant was guilty, and I think so still," came the savage retort.

"A nice juryman you are, I must say! May I trouble you to pass the sugar?"

"Look here! What are you gettin' at? Damme if I can see through your game. What is it?"

"I didn't want to worry poor Peggy. And her father might set about you if he knew the facts, so I'm probably saving you a hiding as well as a period in jail. The only reliable witness we had as to events in Tomlin's place was a commercial traveler, and he is positive that the house closed at ten o'clock. However, that's all right. How do you account for the marvelous improvement in your health? Dr. Foxton cannot understand your illness. He says you are wiry, and have a strong constitution."

"Dr. Foxton jolly near knocked me up," said Elkin. "I took his medicine till I was sick as a cat."

"But you took spirits, too."

"That's nothing fresh. Anyhow, I've dropped both, and am picking up every hour."

"Since when?"

"Since yesterday morning, if you want to know."

"I do. I'm most interested. Dr. Foxton doesn't compound his own prescriptions, does he?"

"No. I get 'em made up at Siddle's."

"Ah. These country chemists often keep drugs in stock till they deteriorate, or even set up chemical changes. Have you the bottles?"

"Yes. But what the -"

"Anything left in them?"

"The last two are half full. Still -"

"What a cross-grained chap you are? I buy your pictures, drink your tea, rescue you from a positively dangerous position, warn you against carrying any farther a most serious libel, yet you won't let me help you in a matter affecting your health!"

"Help me? How?"

"Even you, I suppose, realize that Scotland Yard employs skilled analysts. Give me your bottles, in strict confidence, of course, and I'll tell you what they really contain. Then you can compare the analyses with the doctor's prescriptions. The knowledge should be useful, to say the least. Siddle's reputation needn't suffer, but, unless I am greatly mistaken, you will have the whip hand of him in future."

The prospect was alluring. Elkin would enjoy showing up the chemist, who had treated him rather as a precocious infant of late.

"By jing!" he cried, "I'm on that. Bet you a quid - But, no. You'd hardly lay against your own opinion. Just wait a tick. I'll bring 'em."

Furneaux stared fixedly at the table while his host was absent. His conscience was not pricking him with regard to an unmerited slur on the country chemists of Great Britain. All is fair in love and the detection of crime, and he simply had to get hold of those bottles by some daring yet plausible ruse.

"Now - I wonder!" he muttered, as Elkin's step sounded on the stairs.

"There you are!" grinned the horse-dealer. "Take a dose of the last one. It'll stir your liver to some tune."

Furneaux drew the corks out of both bottles, and sniffed the contents. Then he tasted, with much tongue-smacking.

"Um!" he said. "Stale laudanum, for a start. I expected as much. Bought by the gallon and sold by the drop. Is that the dogcart with my pictures?"

"Yes."

"Hail your man. He can give me a lift."

"But there's lots of things I want to ask you -"

"Probably. I'm here to put questions, not to give information. I've gone a long way beyond the official tether already. If you've a grain of sense, and I think you're not altogether lacking in that respect, you'll keep a close tongue, and act on the tips thrown out. You'll find pearls of price among the rubbish-heap of my remarks generally. Good-by. See you on Wednesday."

And Furneaux climbed into the cart, holding the pictures so that they would not rattle, and perhaps loosen the old gilded frames.

"Drive me to the chemist's" he said to the groom; within five minutes, he was explaining his purchase to Siddle, and requesting, as a favor, that the latter should wrap the set of prints in brown paper, making two parcels, and tying each securely, so that they might be dispatched by train.

Siddle examined one, the first of the series, which depicted the Aylesbury Steeplechase.

"Rather good," he said. "Where did you pick them up?"

"At Elkin's."

"Indeed. What an unexpected place!"

"That's the only way a poor man can get hold of a decent thing nowadays. The dealers grab everything, and sell them as collections."

"Art is not in my line, though anyone can see that these are excellent."

"Yes. But you're looking at 'The Start.' Have a peep at this one, 'The Finish.' The artist *would* have his joke. You see that the dark horse wins."

"How did you persuade Elkin to part with them?"

"By paying him a tempting price, of course. I'm a weak-minded ass in such matters."

The chemist busied himself to oblige the detective, wrapping and tying the packages neatly. Furneaux insisted on paying sixpence for the paper, string, and labor. There was quite a friendly argument, but he carried his point.

The dog-cart then brought him to the station, where he

tipped and dismissed the man; a little later, he caught a London-bound train.

At half past seven precisely, Winter turned in through the Knoleworth-side gate of The Hollies (there were two, the approach to the house being semi-circular) and pushed the door open, as it was standing ajar.

Grant was waiting in the hall, and greeted him pleasantly.

"Here's a telegram which is meant for you, I fancy," he said.

Winter read:

"Sorry to spoil your party. Compelled to travel to London. Returning early to-morrow. F."

"That's pretty Fanny's way," smiled the Chief Inspector. "But there's something in the wind, or he would never have hurried off in this fashion. He tells me that the only pleasant evening he spent in Steynholme was under your roof, Mr. Grant."

"Come along in, Don Jaime!" drawled Hart's voice from the "den," which had been cleared of its litter, the lawn being deemed somewhat unsuitable for the purposes of a drawing-room on that occasion. It was overlooked from too many quarters.

"Ah, we meet now under less uneven conditions, Mr. Hart," said Winter. "Do you know that Enrico Suarez is in London?"

Hart, startled for once in his life, gazed at the

detective fixedly.

"Since when?" he cried.

"He crossed from Lisbon last week."

Hart took a revolver from his hip pocket, and opened it, apparently making sure that it was properly loaded.

"What's the law in England?" he inquired. "Can I shoot first, or must I wait till the other fellow has had a pop?"

Winter laughed.

"It's all right," he said. 'Suarez is in Holloway, awaiting extradition. But I owed you one for the rise you took out of me to-day."

A bell sounded, and Peters came in. He glanced around.

"Where's Furneaux?" he demanded.

"Gone to London. Why this keen interest?" said Winter.

"There's something up. Elkin dropped in at the Hare and Hounds. He was simply bursting with curiosity, and had to talk to somebody. So he chose me."

"He would," was the dry comment.

"Fact, 'pon me honor. I didn't lead him on an inch. It seems that Furneaux bought some prints which caught his eye in Elkin's house, and Tomlin says that that hexplains hit."

"Explains what?"

"Furneaux's visit to Siddle, and certain bulky parcels brought in and brought out again."

"Queer little duck, Furneaux," said Hart. "Now that my mind is at ease about the immediate future of the biggest rascal in Venezuela I can take an active part in Steynholme affairs once more. When it's all through I'll make a novel of it, dashed if I don't, with the postmaster's daughter in the three-color process as a frontispiece."

"But who will be the villain?" said Peters.

Hart waved the negro-head pipe at the other three.

"Draw lots. I am indifferent," he said.

CHAPTER XVII

AN OFFICIAL HOUSEBREAKER

No word bearing on the main topic in these men's minds was said during dinner. Grant was attentive to his guests, but markedly silent, almost distrait. Two such talkers as Hart and Peters, however, covered any gaps in this respect. Cigars and pipes were in evidence, and, horrible though it may sound in the ears of a *gourmet*, the port was circulating, when Winter turned and gazed at the small window.

"Is that where the ghost appears!" he inquired.

"Yes," said Grant. "You know the whole story, of course?"

"Furneaux misses nothing, I assure you."

"He missed a daylight apparition this afternoon, at any rate. I have no secrets from my friends, so I may as well tell you -"

"That Siddle called, and implored you to consider Doris Martin's future by avoiding her at present," put in the Chief Inspector.

Such shocks were losing some of their effect, on the

principle that a man hears the burst of the thousandth high-explosive shell with a good deal less trepidation than attended the efforts of the first dozen. Still, Grant gazed at the speaker in profound astonishment.

"You Scotland Yard men seem to know everything," he said.

"A mere pretense. Try him on sheep-raising in the Argentine, Jack," murmured Hart.

"Wally, this business is developing a very serious side," protested Grant. Hart stretched a long arm for the port decanter.

"Come, friend!" he addressed it gravely. "Let us commune! You and I together shall mingle joyous memories of

> "A draught of the Warm South,
> The true, the blushful Hippocrene."

"We read Siddle's visit aright, it would appear," said Winter quietly.

"Yes. That was his mission, put in a nutshell."

"And what did you say?"

"I told him that, after Wednesday, I would ask Doris Martin to marry me, which is the best answer I can give him and all the world."

"Why 'after Wednesday'?"

" Because I shall know then the full extent of the

annoyance which Ingerman can inflict."

"Did you give Siddle that reason?"

"Yes."

Winter frowned.

"You literary gentlemen are all alike," he said vexedly. "You become such adepts in analyzing human duplicity in your books that you never dream of trying to be wise as a serpent in your own affairs. The author who will split legal hairs by way of brightening his work will sign a contract with a publisher that draws tears from his lawyer when a dispute arises. Why be so candid with a rank outsider, like Siddle?"

"I distrust the man. Doris distrusts him, too."

"So you take him into your confidence."

"No. I merely give him chapter and verse to prove that his interference is useless."

"Have you engaged a lawyer for Wednesday"

"No. Why should I? My hands are clean."

"But your clothes may suffer if enough mud is slung at you. Wire to this man in the morning, and mention my name - Winter, of course, not Franklin."

"Codlin's your friend, not Short," said Hart. "Sorry. It's a time-worn jape, but it fitted in admirably."

The detective scribbled a name and address on a card.

"I don't think you need worry about Ingerman," he went on, "though it's well to be prepared. A smart solicitor can stop irrelevant statements, especially if ready for them. But there must be no more of this heart-opening to all and sundry, Mr. Grant. Siddle is your rival. He, too, wants to marry Miss Martin, and regards you now as the only stumbling-block."

"Siddle! That stick!" gasped Grant.

"Ridiculous, indeed monstrous," agreed Winter, rather heatedly, "but nevertheless a candidate for the lady's hand."

Then he laughed. Peters's keen eyes were watching him, and Wally Hart was giving more heed to the conversation than was revealed by a fixed stare at the negro's head in meerschaum.

"You've bothered me," he went on. "I thought you had more sense. Don't you understand that all these bits of gossip reach Ingerman through the filter of the snug at the Hare and Hounds?"

"The man's visit was unexpected, and his mission even more so. I just blurted out the facts."

"Well, you've rendered the services of a solicitor absolutely indispensable now."

Grant, by no means so clear-headed these days as was his wont, followed the scent of Winter's red herring like the youngest hound in a pack; but Wally Hart and Peters, lookers-on in this chase, harked back to the right line.

"May I -" they both broke in simultaneously.

"Place to the fourth estate," bowed Hart solemnly.

"Thanks," said the journalist. "May I put a question, Winter?"

"A score, if you like."

"Totting up the average of the murder cases in which Furneaux and you have been engaged, in how many days do you count on spotting your man?"

"Sometimes we never get him."

"Oh, come a bit closer than that."

"Generally, given a clear run, with an established motive, we know who he is within eight days."

"Wednesday, in effect?"

"Can't say, this time?"

"Suppose, as a hypothesis, you are convinced of a man's guilt, but can obtain little or no evidence?"

"He goes through life a free and independent citizen of this or any other country. Arrests on suspicion are not my long suit."

"How does one get evidence?" purred Hart. "It isn't scattered broadcast by a clever criminal. And you fellows seem to object to my method, which has been the only effectual one so far in this affair."

"If you had shot that specter the other night there would have been the deuce to pay."

"But you would now be sure of the murderer?"

"Why do you assume that?"

"Like Eugene Aram, he can't keep away from the scene of his crime."

Winter felt he was skating on thin ice, so hastened to escape.

"Detective work is nearly all guessing," he said sententiously, "yet one must beware of what I may term obvious guessing. If cause and effect were so closely allied in certain classes of crime my department would cease to exist, and the protection of life and property might be left safely to the ordinary police. By the way, P. C. Robinson has been rather inactive during two whole days. That makes me suspicious. What's he up to? Can you throw a light on him, Peters?"

The journalist knew that he was being told peremptorily to cease prying. He kicked Hart under the table.

"Hi!" yelled Wally. "What's the matter? Strike your matches on your own shin, not mine."

"Peters is announcing that the discussion is now closed," said Winter firmly.

"Very well. He needn't emphasize the warning by a hob-nailed boot. When my injured feelings have recovered I'll discourse to you of strange folk and stranger doings on the banks of the Rio de la Plata, and your stock as an Argentine plutocrat will rise one hundred per cent, next time you're badgered by a man who knows the country."

"Meanwhile, Robinson is hot-foot on the Elkin trail," laughed Peters. "His face was a study to-day when the groom supplied details of the picture-buying."

"Furneaux wanted that transaction to be widely known," said Winter. "He gave every publicity to it."

"Did he secure a bargain, I wonder?" said Grant.

"Oh, I expect so. He doesn't waste his hard-earned money, even for official purposes."

But Winter was well aware of, and kept to himself one phase of the art deal, at any rate. Furneaux had persuaded Siddle to fasten two bulky packages with string!

He was shaving next morning when his colleague entered, spruce as ever in attire, but looking rather weary. The little man flung himself at full length on Winter's bed.

"Been up all night," he explained. "Chemical analysis is fascinating but slow work - like watching a moth evolve from a grub. Had a fearful job, too, to get an analyst to chuck a theater and attend to business. The blighter talked of office hours. *Cré nom!* Ten till four, and an hour and a half for lunch! Why can't we run *our* show on those lines, James!"

Winter finished carefully the left side of his broad

expanse of face.

"You came down by the mail, I suppose?" he said casually.

"What a genius you are!" sighed Furneaux. "If *I* were trembling with expectation I could no more put a banal question like that than swallow the razor after I was done with it. You might at least have the common decency to thank me for leaving you to gorge on rare meats and vintage wines while I dallied with the deadly railway sandwich."

Winter scraped the other cheek, his chin, and upper lip.

"Shall I go to the bathroom first, or listen?" he inquired.

"Ah, well, I'm tired, and hiking these frail bones to bed till twelve, so I'll give you a condensed version," snapped Furneaux. "Elkin 's illness, begun by whiskey and over-excitement, developed into steady poisoning by Siddle. The chemist used a rare agent, too - pure nicotine - easy, in a sense, to detect, but capable of a dozen reasonable explanations when revealed by the post-mortem. But Elkin wasn't to be killed outright, I gather. The idea was to upset stomach and brain till he was half crazy. As you can read print when it's before your eyes, I needn't go into the matter of motive; Elkin's behavior supplies all details."

"How about the knots? Hurry! I hate the feeling of soap drying on my skin."

"One running noose and twice two half hitches on each package."

"Good! Charles, we're going to pull off a real twister."

"*We!* Well, that tikes it, as the girl said when her hat blew off with the fluffy transformation pinned to it."

Winter rushed to the bathroom, and Furneaux crept languidly to bed.

Before going to Knoleworth, Mr. Franklin consulted with Tomlin as to a suitable dinner, to which the other guests staying in the inn, namely, Mr. Peters and the Scotland Yard gentleman - the little man with the French name - might be invited. This important point settled, Mr. Franklin caught an early train, and was absent all day, being, in fact, closeted with Superintendent Fowler and a Treasury solicitor.

Furneaux was sound asleep long after twelve o'clock, and swore at Tomlin in French when the landlord ventured to arouse him. Tomlin went downstairs scratching his head.

"Least said soonest mended," he communed, "but we may all be murdered in our beds if them's the sort of 'tecs we 'ave to look arter us."

However, he cheered up towards night. Ingerman, a lawyer, and some pressmen, arriving for the inquest, filled every available room, and the kitchen was redolent of good fare. All parties gathered in the dining-room, of course, and Ingerman had an eye for Mr. Franklin's party. The scraps of talk he overheard were nothing more exciting than the prospects of a certain horse for the Stewards' Cup. Peters had the tip straight from the stables. A racing certainty, with a stone in hand.

After dinner the financier was surprised when Furneaux approached, and tapped him professionally on the shoulder.

"A word with you outside," he said.

Ingerman was irritated - perhaps slightly alarmed.

"Can't we talk here?" he said, in that singularly melodious voice of his.

"Better not, but I shan't detain you more than five minutes."

"Anything my legal adviser might wish to hear?"

"Not from me. Tell him yourself afterwards, if you like."

In the quiet street the detective suddenly linked arms with his companion. Probably he smiled sardonically when he felt a telltale quiver run through Ingerman's lanky frame.

"You've brought down Norris, I see?" he began.

"Yes."

"Meaning to make things hot for Grant tomorrow?"

"Meaning to give justice the materials -"

"Cut the cackle, Isidor. I know you, and it's high time you knew me. Grant has retained Belcher. Ah! that gets you, does it? You haven't forgotten Belcher. Now, be reasonable! Or, rather, don't run your head into a noose. Grant had no more to do with the murder of your wife than you had. Call off Norris, and Grant withdraws Belcher. Twig? It's dead easy, because the Treasury solicitor will simply ask for another week's adjournment, as the police are not ready to go on. In the meantime, you pay off Norris, and save your face. Is it a deal?"

"Am I to understand -"

"Don't wriggle! The key of the situation is held by Belcher. Name of a pipe! What prompting does Belcher need from me or anybody else after the Bokfontein Lands case?"

"But -"

"Isidor, this is the last word. I was at the funeral on Saturday, and met your wife's mother and sister. They do love you, don't they?"

Ingerman died game.

"If I have your assurance that Mr. Grant is really innocent of Adelaide's death, that is sufficient," he said slowly.

"Well, if it pleases you to put it that way, I'm agreeable. Which is your road? Back to the hotel? I'm for a short stroll. Mind you, no wobbling! Go straight, and I'll attend to Belcher. But, good Lord! How his eyes will sparkle when they light on you to-morrow!"

Neither the redoubtable Belcher, nor the Bokfontein Lands, nor poor Adelaide Melhuish's mother and sister may figure further in this chronicle. The inquest opened at the appointed hour next day, and was closed down again for a week with a celerity that was most disappointing both to the jury and the general public. Of three legal luminaries present only one, the Treasury man, uttered a few bald words. Belcher and Norris did not even announce the names of their clients. Norris noticed that Belcher surveyed Ingerman with a grim smile, but thought nothing of it until he received a check later in the week. Then he made some inquiries, and smiled himself.

The foreman of the jury looked a trifle pinched, though his cheeks bore two spots of hectic color. Mr. Franklin, drawn to the court by curiosity, happened to glance at him once, and found him gazing at Furneaux in a peculiarly thoughtful manner.

Elkin, thriving on a diet of tea and eggs, was also interested in the representative of Scotland Yard. He seemed to ignore Grant entirely. Doris Martin was not in court. Superintendent Fowler had called about half, past nine to tell her she would not be asked to attend that day.

Near Mr. Franklin sat a few village notabilities, who, since they had not the remotest connection with anyone concerned in the tragedy, have been left hitherto in their Olympian solitude. He listened to their comments.

"As usual, the police are utterly at sea," said one.

"Yes, 'following up important clews,' the newspapers say," scoffed another.

"It's a disgraceful thing if a crime like this goes

undetected and unpunished."

"Which is the Scotland Yard man!"

"The small chap, in the blue suit."

"What? *That* little rat!"

"Oh, he's sharp. I met a man in the train and he told me -"

Mr. Franklin grinned amiably; Hobbs, the butcher, intercepting his eye, grinned back. It is not difficult to imagine what portion of the foregoing small talk reached Furneaux subsequently.

Oddly enough, both detectives had missed a brief but illuminating incident which took place in the Hare and Hounds the previous night, while Winter was finishing a cigar with Peters, and Furneaux was bludgeoning Ingerinan into compliance with his wishes.

Elkin's remarkable improvement in health was commented on by Hobbs, and Siddle took the credit.

"That last mixture has proved beneficial, then?" he said, eying the horse-dealer closely.

"Top-hole," smirked Elkin. "But it's only fair to say that I've chucked whiskey, too."

"Did you finish the bottle?"

"Which bottle?"

"Mine, of course."

"Nearly."

"Don't take any more. It was decidedly strong. I'll send a boy early to-morrow morning with a first-rate tonic, and you might give him any old medicine bottles you possess. I'm running short."

Elkin hesitated a second or two.

"I'll tell my housekeeper to look 'em up," he said. After the inquest he communicated this episode to Furneaux as a great joke.

"Queer, isn't it?" he guffawed. "A couple of dozen bottles went back, as I'm always getting stuff for the gees, but those two weren't among 'em. You took care of that, eh? When will you have the analysis?"

"It'll be fully a week yet," said the detective. "Government offices are not run like express trains, and this is a free job, you know. But, be advised by me. Stick to plain food, and throw physic to the dogs."

Another singular fact, unobserved by the public at large, was that a policeman, either Robinson or a stranger, patrolled the high-street all day and all night, while no one outside official circles was aware that other members of the force watched The Hollies, or were secreted among the trees on the cliffside, from dusk to dawn.

Next morning, however, there was real cause for talk. Siddle's shop was closed. Over the letter-box, neatly printed, was gummed a notice:

"Called away on business. Will open for one hour after

arrival of 7 p. m. train. T. S."

Everyone who passed stopped to read. Even Mr.
Franklin joined Furneaux and Peters in a stroll across
the road to have a look.

"I want you a minute," said the big man suddenly to
Furneaux. There was that in his tone which forbade
questioning, so Peters sheered off, well content with
the share permitted him in the inquiry thus far.

"That fellow, Hart, is no fool," went on Winter rapidly.
"He said last night 'How does one get evidence?' It was
not easy to answer. Siddle has gone to his mother's
funeral. What do you think!"

"You'd turn me into a housebreaker, would you?"
whined Furneaux bitterly. "I must do the job, of
course, just because I'm a little one. Well, well! After a
long and honorable career I have to become a sneak
thief. It may cost me my pension."

"There's no real difficulty. An orchard -"

"Bet you a new hat I went over the ground before
you did."

"Get over it quickly now, and get something out of it,
and I'll *give* you a new hat. Got any tools?"

"I fetched 'em from town Tuesday morning," chortled
Furneaux. "So now who's the brainy one?"

He skipped into the hotel, while Winter went to the
station to make sure of Siddle's departure and destination. Yes, the chemist had taken a return ticket to

Epsom, where a strip of dank meadow-land on the road to Esher marks the last resting-place of many of London's epileptics. On returning to the high-street, Winter lighted a cigar, a somewhat common occurrence in his everyday life, where-upon Furneaux walked swiftly up the hill. A farmer, living near the center of the village, owned a rather showy cob. Winter found the man, and persuaded him to trot the animal to and fro in front of the hotel. There was a good deal of noise and hoof-clattering, and people came to their doors to see what was going on. Obviously, if they were watching the antics of a skittish two-year-old in the high-street, their eyes were blind to proceedings in the back premises. Even the postmaster and his daughter were interested onlookers, and a policeman, who might have put a summary end to the display, vanished as though by magic.

Luckily, Winter was a good judge of a horse. When the cob was stabled, and the farmer came to the inn to have a drink, he was forced to admit a tendency to cow hocks, which, it would seem, is held a fatal blemish in the Argentine.

Meanwhile, Furneaux had dodged into a lane and thence to a bridle-path which emerged near Bob Smith's forge. When he had traversed, roughly speaking, one-half of a rectangle in which the Hare and Hounds occupied the center of one of the longer sides, he climbed a gate and followed a hedge. Though not losing a second, he took every precaution to remain unseen, and, to the best of his belief, gained an inclosed yard at the back of Siddle's premises without having attracted attention. He slipped the catch of a kitchen window only to discover that the sash was fastened by screws also. The lock of the kitchen door yielded to persuasion, but there were bolts above and below. A wire screen in a larder window was impregnable. Short of cutting out a pane of glass, he could not effect an entry on the ground floor.

Nimble as a squirrel, and risking everything, he climbed to the roof of an outhouse, and tried a bedroom window. Here he succeeded. When the catch was forced, there were no further obstacles. In he went, pausing only to look around and see if any curious or alarmed eye was watching him. He wondered why every back yard on that side of the high-street was empty, not even a maid-servant or woman washing clothes being in sight, but understood and grinned when the commotion Winter was creating came in view from a front room.

Then he undertook a methodical search, working with a rapid yet painstaking thoroughness which missed nothing. From a wardrobe he selected an overcoat and pair of trousers which reeked with turpentine. They were old and soiled garments, very different from the well-cut black coat and waistcoat, with striped cloth trousers, worn daily by the chemist. He drew a blank in the remainder of the upstairs rooms, which included a sitting-room, though he devoted fully quarter of an hour to reading the titles of Siddle's books.

A safe in the little dispensing closet at the back of the shop promised sheer defiance until Furneaux saw a bunch of keys resting beside a methylated spirit lamp.

"'Twas ever thus!" he cackled, lighting the lamp. "Heaven help us poor detectives if it wasn't!"

In a word, since murder will out, Siddle had forgotten

his keys! Probably, he had gone to the safe for money, and, while writing the notice as to his absence, had laid down the keys and omitted to pick them up again.

Furneaux disregarded ledgers and account books. He examined a bank pass-book and a check-book. In a drawer which contained these and a quantity of gold he found a small, leather-bound book with a lock, which no key on the bunch was tiny enough to fit. A bit of twisted wire soon overcame this difficulty, and Furneaux began to read.

There were quaint diagrams, and surveyor's sketches, both in plan and section, with curious notes, and occasional records of what appeared to be passages from letters or conversations. The detective read, and read, referring back and forth, absorbed in his task, no doubt, but evidently puzzled.

At last, he stuffed the book into a pocket, completed his scrutiny of the safe, examined the bottles on the shelf labeled "poisons," and took a sample of the colorless contents of one bottle marked "$C10H14N2$."

Then he went to the kitchen, replaced all catches and the lock of the door, and let himself out by the way he had come.

Winter saw him from afar, and hastened upstairs to the private sitting-room. Furneaux appeared there soon.

"Well?" said the Chief Inspector eagerly.

"Got him, I think," said Furneaux.

Not much might be gathered from that monosyllabic

question and its answer, but its significance in Siddle's ears, could he have heard, would have been that of the passing bell tolling for the dead.

CHAPTER XVIII

THE TRUTH AT LAST

Not often did Furneaux qualify an opinion by that dubious phrase, "I think," which, in its colloquial sense, implies that the thought contains a reservation as to possible error.

Winter looked anxious. Both he and his colleague knew well when to drop the good-natured banter they delighted in. They were face to face now with issues of life and death, dark and sinister conditions which had already destroyed one life, threatened another, and might envisage further horrors. Small wonder, then, if the Chief Inspector's usually cheerful face was clouded, or that his hopes should be somewhat dashed when Furneaux seemed to lack the abounding confidence which was his most marked characteristic.

"You've got something, I see," he said, trying to speak encouragingly, and glancing at the bundle of clothing which Furneaux had wrapped in a newspaper before dropping from the bedroom window of Siddle's house.

"Yes, a lot. What to make of it is the puzzle. We either go ahead on the flimsiest of evidence or I carry out another housebreaking job this afternoon and restore things in status quo. First , the bundle - an old

Louis Tracy

covert-coating overcoat and a pair of frayed trousers which probably draped Owd Ben's ghost. They've been soaked in turpentine, which, chemist or no chemist, is still the best agent for removing stains. We'll put 'em under the glass after we've examined the book. Siddle keeps a sort of diary, a series of jumbled memoranda. If we can extract nutriment out of that we may have something tangible to go upon. Let's begin at the end."

Opening the leather-bound note-book, Furneaux stood with his back to the window. Winter, owing to his superior height, could look over the lesser man's shoulder. Many an occult document affecting the famous crimes and social or dynastic intrigues of the previous decade had these two examined in that way, the main advantage of scrutiny in common being that they could compare readings or suggested readings without loss of time, and with the original manuscript before both pairs of eyes.

In the first instance, there were no dates - only scraps of sentences, or comments. The concluding entry in the book was:

"A tactical error? Perhaps. Immovable."

Then, taking the order backward:

"Scout the very notion of such an infamy. You and every scandal-monger in S. may do your worst."

"Free to confess that events have opened my eyes to the truth, so, not for the first time, out of evil comes good."

"A prig."

"Visit for such a purpose a piece of unheard-of impudence."

These were all on one page.

"Quite clearly a *précis* of Grant's remarks when Siddle called on Monday," said Winter.

At any other time, Furneaux would have waxed sarcastic. Now he merely nodded.

"Stops in a queer way," he muttered. "Not a word about the inquest or the missing bottles."

The preceding page held even more disjointed entries, which, nevertheless, provided a fair synopsis of Doris's spirited words on the Sunday afternoon.

"Malice and ignorance."

"Patient because of years."

"Loyal comrade. Shall remain."

"Code."

"No difference in friendship."

"E. hopeless. Contempt."

"Skipping - good."

On the next page:

"Isidor G. Ingerman. Useful. Inquire."

"E.'s boasts? Nonsensical, surely!"

"Why has D. gone?"

Both men paused at that line.

"Detective?" suggested Winter.

"That's how I take it," agreed Furneaux.

Then came a sign: "+10%."

"Elkin's mixture was not 'as before.' It was fortified," grinned Furneaux. "That's the exact increase of nicotine. By the way, I have a sample. We can take care of him on that charge, without a shadow of doubt."

Winter blew softly on the back of his friend's head.

"You're thorough, Charles, thorough!" he murmured. "It's a treat to work with you when you get really busy."

Furneaux ran his thumb across the end of several leaves.

"I can tell you now," he said, "that there's nothing of real value in the earlier notes. So far as I can judge, they refer either to a sort of settlement with his wife or chance phrases used by Doris Martin which might imply that she was heart whole and fancy free. There's not a bally word dealing with the murder, or that can be twisted into the vaguest allusion to it. But here's a plan and section which have a sort of significance. I've seen the place, so recognized it, or thought I did. We must check it, of course. Here you are! You know the footbridge across the river from Bush Walk?"

"Yes."

"The eastern end is supported on a hollow pier of masonry, in which one might tog up unseen. These drawings would be useful as an *Aide Memoire* on a dark night. A false step, with the river in flood, might be awkward."

"What's that on the opposite page?"

"I give it up - at present."

This somewhat rare display of modesty on Furneaux's part was readily understandable. A series of straight lines and angles conveyed very little hint of their purport; but Winter smiled behind his friend's back.

"I've been prowling about this wretched inn longer than you," he said. "Look outside, to the left."

"Don't need to, now," cackled Furneaux. "It's the profile of a wall, gate, and outhouse along which one could reach the window of the club-room. Would you mind stopping grinning like a Cheshire cat?"

"Anything else?"

"Yes. This one: 'S.M.? 1820.' That beats you, eh?"

"Dished completely."

"Doris Martin, as usual, supplies the answer. An old volume of the *Sussex Miscellany*, probably that for

1820, contains the full story of Owd Ben. I might have mentioned it to you, but focussed on current events. Siddle has it among his books, which, by the way, are made up largely of scientific and popular criminal records."

"Is that the lot?"

"I'm afraid so. Have a look."

"Just a minute. I want to think."

Winter turned and gazed through the open window. Seldom had a more gracious June decked England with garlands. The hour was then high noon, and a pastoral landscape was drowned in sunshine. The Chief Inspector cut the end off a cigar dreamily but with care.

"Broadmoor - perhaps," he muttered. "But we can't hang him yet, Charles. A couple of knots and a theory won't do for the Assizes. We haven't a solitary witness. Hardly a night but he goes home at 9.30. If only he had killed Grant! But - Adelaide Melhuish!"

In sheer despair he struck a match.

"Well, let's overhaul these duds," said Furneaux savagely. "I'll chance the dinner hour for the return visit. Steynholme folk eat at half past twelve to the tick, and you can hardly get up another horse show."

There was a knock at the door.

"Let me in, quick!" came Peters's voice, and the handle was tried forcibly.

"Go away! I'm busy!" cried Winter.

"This is urgent, devilish urgent," said Peters.

Furneaux snatched up the note-book, and Winter tore off his coat, throwing it over the package which reposed in an armchair. Then the Chief Inspector unlocked the door, blocking the way aggressively.

"Now, I must say - " he began.

But Peters clutched his shoulder with a nervous hand.

"Siddle has just hurried up the street and entered his shop," he hissed.

The journalist had not only kept his eyes open, but excelled in the art of putting two and two together, an arithmetical calculation which, as applied to the affairs of life, is not so readily arrived at as many people imagine.

"Buncoed! He's missed his keys!" shrilled Furneaux.

"Confound the man! He might at least have attended his mother's funeral!" stormed Winter, retrieving his coat.

Thus it happened that Furneaux was the first down the stairs, though the three emerged from the door of the inn on each other's heels. A stout man, in all likelihood a farmer with horses for sale, was mounting the two steps which led to the entrance. His head was down, and his weight forward, so he successfully resisted Furneaux's impact, but Peters and Winter were irresistible, and he tumbled over with a muffled yell.

At that instant Siddle quitted his shop, and headed straight for the post office. In his right hand he carried an automatic pistol. The street was wide. Furneaux, absolutely fearless in the performance of his duty, ran in a curve so as to bar the chemist's path, and it was then that Siddle saw him. The man's face was terrible to behold. His eyes were rolling, his teeth gnashing; he had bitten his tongue and cheeks, and his stertorous breathing ejected from his mouth foam tinged with blood.

"Ha!" he screamed in a falsetto of fury, "not yet, little man, not yet!"

With that he raised the pistol, and fired point-blank at the detective. Furneaux ducked, and seized a small stone, being otherwise quite unarmed. He threw it with unerring aim, and, as was determined subsequently, struck the hand holding the weapon. Possibly, almost by a miracle, the blow caused a faulty pressure, because the action jammed, though the pistol itself was most accurate and deadly in its properties.

By this time Winter, sweeping Peters aside, was within ten feet of the maniac, who turned and ran into the shop. The door, a solid one, fitted with a spring lock, slammed in the Chief Inspector's face, and resisted a mighty effort to burst it open. A few yards away stood an empty, two-wheeled cart, uptilted, and Winter demanded the help of a few men who had gathered on seeing or hearing the hubbub.

"I call on you in the King's name!" he shouted. "We must force that door! Then stand clear, all of you!"

He raced to the cart, and, when his object was

perceived, willing hands assisted in converting the heavy vehicle into a battering-ram. The gradient of the hill favored the attack, which was made at an acute angle, and the first assault smashed the lock. There were a couple of seconds' delay while the cart was backed out, and the detectives rushed in, Furneaux leading, because Winter gave his great physical strength to the shafts. But the Chief Inspector grabbed his tiny friend by the collar as the latter darted around the counter and into the dispensary in the rear.

"Two of us can't go abreast, and you'll only get hurt," he said, speaking with a calmness that was majestic in the circumstances.

"The nicotine is gone!" yelped Furneaux; both saw that the safe stood open.

Behind the dispensary was a small passage, whence the stairs mounted, and a door led to the kitchen. That door was closed now, though it was open when Furneaux ransacked the house. Therefore, they made that way at once. No ordinary lock could resist Winter's shoulder, and he soon mastered this barrier. But the kitchen was empty - the outer door locked but unbolted. Since it is practically impossible for the strongest man to pull a door open, the two made for the window, and tore at screws and catch with eager fingers. Furneaux, light and nimble-footed, scrambled through first, so it was he who found Siddle lying in the orchard beyond the wall of the yard. The unhappy wretch had swallowed nearly the whole remaining contents of the bottle of nicotine, or enough to poison a score of robust men. He presented a lamentable and distressing spectacle. Some of the more venturesome passers-by, who had crowded after the detectives and Peters, could not bear

Louis Tracy

to look on, and slunk away in horror.

Furneaux soon brought an emetic, which failed to act. Siddle breathed his last while the glass was at his lips.

In that moment of crisis only three men did not lose their heads. Winter cleared away the gapers, while Furneaux remained with the body. P.C. Robinson came up the hill at a run, and was sent for a stretcher, bringing from Hobbs's shop the very one on which the ill-fated Adelaide Melhuish was carried from the river bank.

But where was Peters? In the post office, writing the first of a series of thrilling dispatches to a London evening newspaper. What journalist ever had a more sensational murder-case to supply "copy"? And when was "special correspondent" ever better primed for the task? He wrote on, and on, till the telegraphist cried halt. Then he hied him to London by train, and began the more ambitious "story" for next morning. What he did not know he guessed correctly. A fagged but triumphant man was Jimmie Peters when he "blew in" to the Savage Club at 1 A.M. to seek sustenance and a whiskey and soda before going home.

Furneaux was white and shaken when Winter escorted the stretcher-bearers to the orchard.

"Poor devil!" he said, as the men lifted the body. "Foredoomed from birth! We can eradicate these diseases from cattle. Why not from men!"

The villagers could not understand him. Already, in some mysterious way, the word had gone around that Siddle had murdered the actress, and taken his own life to avoid arrest, after shooting at the detective who was hot on his trail.

Not until Peters's articles came back to Steynholme did the public at large realize that the chemist undoubtedly meant to kill Doris Martin. He was going straight to the post office when the way was barred by Furneaux. The bullet which missed the latter actually pierced the zinc plate of the letter-box, and scored a furrow, inches long, in an oak counter which it struck laterally.

The village did not recover its poise for hours. Grant and Hart, to whom Bates brought the news about one o'clock, rose from an untasted luncheon and hurried to the high-street. Knots of people stared at Grant, some sheepishly, others with frank relief, because all who knew him liked him. One man, a retired ironmonger and an impulsive fellow, came forward and wrung his hand heartily. A few prominent residents followed suit. Grant was greatly embarrassed, but managed to endure these awkward if well-meant congratulations. There could be no mistaking their intent. He had been tried for murder at the bar of public opinion, and was now formally acquitted.

Even Fred Elkin, ignorant as yet of his own peril, yielded to the influences of the moment and bustled through the crowd.

"Mr. Grant," he cried outspokenly, "I ask your pardon. I seem to have made a d - d fool of myself!"

"Easier done than said," chimed in Hart. "But, among all this bell-ringing, can anyone tell what has actually happened? Where's Peters?"

"In the post office."

The two went in, and found the journalist scribbling against time. Hart coolly grabbed a few slips of manuscript, and commenced reading. Grant looked about for Doris. She was not visible, but Mr. Martin, pallid and nervous, nodded toward the sitting-room. The younger man, taking the gesture as a tacit invitation, entered the room.

Doris was sitting there, crying bitterly. Poor girl! She had seen that portion of the drama which was enacted in the street, and the shock of it was still poignant. She looked up and met her lover's eyes. Neither uttered a word, but Grant did a very wise thing. He caught her by the shoulders, raised her to her feet, and, after kissing her squarely on the lips, gave her a comforting hug.

"It will be all right now, Doris," he whispered tenderly. "Such thunderstorms clear the air."

An eminent novelist might have found many more ornate ways of avowing his sentiments, but never a more satisfactory one. At any rate, it served, so what more need be said?

Certain rills of evidence accumulated into a fair-sized stream before night fell. P.C. Robinson, for instance, scored a point by ascertaining that Peggy Smith had seen Furneaux dropping from the bedroom window of the chemist's shop. She was some hundreds of yards away, and could not be positive that some man, perhaps a glazier, had not been there legitimately effecting repairs. Still, when she met Siddle hurrying from the station, she told him of the incident.

"He never even thanked me," she said, "but broke into a run. The look in his eyes was awful."

The girl had, in fact, confirmed his worst fears, and her neighborly solicitude had merely hastened the end.

Again, the railway officials showed that Siddle had returned from Victoria instead of taking train to the asylum. Furneaux had guessed aright. The discovery that his keys had been left behind drove the man into a panic of fright.

It took nearly three weeks before the unhappy business was finally disposed of. A Treasury solicitor was given the chance of his career by the medico-legal disquisition which cleared up an extraordinary record. The annals of the disease which predisposed Theodore Siddle to crime went back many years. He was a fairly wealthy man by inheritance, and adopted the profession of chemistry as a hobby. One fact stood out boldly. He was aware of his hereditary taint, and had settled down in Steynholme believing that a quiet life, free from care or the distractions of a town, would enable him to overcome it. Probably, the lawyer held, the man owned two distinct individualities, and the baser instincts gradually overpowered the humane ones.

Of course, the whole history of those trying days had to come out in open court, and the postmaster's daughter was given a descriptive and pictorial boom which many an actress envied. Peters was restored to grace when he showed plainly that his articles had kept the fickle barometer of public opinion at "set fair," in so far as Grant and Doris were concerned.

"But," as Hart drawled during a dinner of reconciliation, "you needn't have been so infernally personal about my hat."

Grant and Doris were married before the year was out. Mr. Martin retired on a pension, and the young couple decided that they could never dissociate The Hollies from the tragic memories bound up with its ghost-window and lawn. So the place was sold, and Steynholme knows "the postmaster's daughter" no more. Winter and Furneaux week-ended with them recently at a pretty little nook in Dorset. Hart, just home from the Balkans, traveled from town with the detectives, and Doris, a radiant young matron, was as flippant as the best of them.

One evening, when the men were sitting late in the smoking-room, the talk turned on the now half-forgotten drama in which the hapless Adelaide Melhuish played her last rôle.

"I met Peters in the Savage Club the other night," said Hart, filling the negro-head pipe with care while he talked, "and he was chortling about his 'psychological study,' as he called it, of that unfortunate chemist. He still clings to the theory that your wife was the intended victim, Grant. Do you agree with him?"

"Rubbish!" cried Furneaux, before his host could answer. "At best, Peters is only a clever ass. Siddle never had the remotest notion of killing Miss Doris Martin, as Mrs. Grant was then. We shall never know for certain just what happened, but there are elements in the affair which give ground for reasonable guesswork. The first thing that impressed Winter and me - at least, I suppose I really evolved the idea, though my bulky friend elaborated it" (whereat Winter smiled forgivingly, and beheaded a fresh Havana) "was the complete noiselessness of the crime. Here we had Mr. Grant startled by the face at the window, and actually searching outside the house for the ghostly visitant, while Miss Doris was gazing at The Hollies from the other side of the river, and not a sound was heard, though it was a summer's night, without a breath of wind, and at an hour when the splash of a fish leaping in the stream would have created a commotion. Now, Miss Melhuish was an active and well-built young woman, an actress, too, and therefore likely to meet an emergency without instant collapse. Yet she allows herself to be struck dead or insensible without cry or struggle! How do you account for it?"

"Go on, Charles; don't be theatrical," jeered Winter. "You've got the story pat. Even that simile of the jumping fish is mine."

"True," agreed Furneaux. "I only brought it in as a sop. But, to continue, as the tub-thumper says. Isn't it permissible to assume that Siddle accompanied the lady, either by prior arrangement or by contriving a meeting which looked like mere chance? We know that she went to his shop. We know, too, that he was clever and unscrupulous, and any allusion to Grant would stir his wits to the uttermost. He would see instantly how interested Miss Melhuish was in the owner of The Hollies, while she, a smart Londoner, would recognize in Siddle an informant worth all the rest of the babblers in Steynholme. At any rate, no matter how the thing was brought about, it is self-evident that Siddle brought his intended victim into the grounds, and told her of the small uncovered window through which she could peer at Grant after Miss Doris had gone. He showed her which path to use, and undoubtedly waited for her, and stayed her flight when Grant rose from his chair. She was close to him, and wholly unafraid, finding in him an ally. They were purposely hidden, in the gloom of dense foliage, and remained there until Grant had closed the window again. Then, and not till then, did the murderer strike, probably stifling her with his free hand. He had the implement in his pocket. The rope was secreted among the bushes. He could carry through the whole wretched crime in little more than a minute. And his psychology went far deeper than Peters gave him credit for. He had weighed up the situation to a nicety. No matter who found the body, Mr. Grant was saddled with a responsibility which might well prove disastrous, and was almost sure to affect his relations with the Martin household. For instance, nothing short of a miracle could have stopped Robinson from arresting him on a charge of murder."

"You, then, are a miracle?' put in Hart, pointing the pipe at the little man.

"To the person of ordinary intelligence - yes."

"After that," said Winter, "there is nothing more to be said. Let's see who secures the pocket marvel as a partner at auction."

* * * * *

As a fitting end to the strange story of wayward love and maniacal frenzy which found an unusual habitat in a secluded hamlet like Steynholme, a small vignette of its normal life may be etched in. The trope is germane to the scene.

On a wet afternoon in October Hobbs and Elkin had adjourned to the Hare and Hounds. Tomlin was reading a newspaper spread on the bar counter. He was alone. The day was Friday, and the last "commercial" of the week had departed by the mid-day train.

"Wot's yer tonic?" demanded the butcher.

"A glass of beer," threw Elkin over his shoulder. He had walked to the window, and was gazing moodily at the sign of the "plumber and decorator" who had taken Siddle's shop. The village could not really support an out-and-out chemist, so a local grocer had elected to stock patent medicines as a side line.

Tomlin made play with a beer-pump.

"Where's yer own?" inquired Hobbs hospitably.

Elkin came and drank. After an interlude, Tomlin ran a finger down a column of the newspaper.

"By the way, Fred, didn't you tell me about that funny little chap, Furno, the 'tec, buyin' some pictures of yours?" he said.

"I did. Had him there, anyhow," chuckled Elkin.

"How much did you stick 'im for?"

"Three guineas."

"They can't ha' bin this lot, then, though I've a notion it wur the same name, 'Aylesbury Steeplechase.'"

"What are you talking about?"

Louis Tracy

"This."

Tomlin turned the paper, and Elkin read:

At their monthly art sale on Wednesday Messrs. Brown, Jenkins and Brown disposed of an almost unique set of colored prints, by F. Smyth, dated 1841. The series of six represented various phases of the long defunct Aylesbury Steeplechase, "The Start," "The Brook," "The In-and-Out," and so on to "The Finish." It is understood that this notable series, produced during the best period of the art, and at the very zenith of Smyth's fame, were acquired recently by a Sussex amateur at a low price. Bidding began at fifty guineas, and rose quickly to one hundred and twenty, at which figure Messrs. Carnioli and Bruschi became the owners.

Elkin read the paragraph twice, until the words burnt into his brain.

"No," he said thickly. "They're not mine. No such luck!"

Choose from Thousands of 1stWorldLibrary Classics By

Adolphus William Ward
Aesop
Agatha Christie
Alexander Aaronsohn
Alexander Kielland
Alexandre Dumas
Alfred Gatty
Alfred Ollivant
Alice Duer Miller
Alice Turner Curtis
Alice Dunbar
Ambrose Bierce
Amelia E. Barr
Andrew Lang
Andrew McFarland Davis
Anna Sewell
Annie Besant
Annie Hamilton Donnell
Annie Payson Call
Anton Chekhov
Arnold Bennett
Arthur Conan Doyle
Arthur Ransome
Atticus
B. M. Bower
Basil King
Bayard Taylor
Ben Macomber
Booth Tarkington
Bram Stoker
C. Collodi
C. E. Orr
C. M. Ingleby
Carolyn Wells
Catherine Parr Traill
Charles A. Eastman
Charles Dickens
Charles Dudley Warner
Charles Farrar Browne
Charles Ives
Charles Kingsley
Charles Lathrop Pack
Charles Whibley
Charles Willing Beale
Charlotte M. Braeme
Charlotte M.Yonge
Clair W. Hayes
Clarence Day Jr.
Clarence E. Mulford

Clemence Housman
Confucius
Cornelis DeWitt Wilcox
Cyril Burleigh
D. H. Lawrence
Daniel Defoe
David Garnett
Don Carlos Janes
Donald Keyhole
Dorothy Kilner
Dougan Clark
E. Nesbit
E.P.Roe
E. Phillips Oppenheim
Edgar Allan Poe
Edgar Rice Burroughs
Edith Wharton
Edward J. O'Biren
John Cournos
Edwin L. Arnold
Eleanor Atkins
Elizabeth Cleghorn
Gaskell
Elizabeth Von Arnim
Ellem Key
Emily Dickinson
Erasmus W. Jones
Ernie Howard Pie
Ethel Turner
Ethel Watts Mumford
Eugenie Foa
Eugene Wood
Evelyn Everett-Green
Everard Cotes
F. J. Cross
Federick Austin Ogg
Ferdinand Ossendowski
Francis Bacon
Francis Darwin
Frances Hodgson Burnett
Frank Gee Patchin
Frank Harris
Frank Jewett Mather
Frank L. Packard
Frederick Trevor Hill
Frederick Winslow Taylor
Friedrich Kerst
Friedrich Nietzsche
Fyodor Dostoyevsky

Gabrielle E. Jackson
Garrett P. Serviss
Gaston Leroux
George Ade
Geroge Bernard Shaw
George Ebers
George Eliot
George MacDonald
George Orwell
George Tucker
George W. Cable
George Wharton James
Gertrude Atherton
Grace E. King
Grant Allen
Guillermo A. Sherwell
Gulielma Zollinger
Gustav Flaubert
H. A. Cody
H. B. Irving
H. G. Wells
H. H. Munro
H. Irving Hancock
H. Rider Haggard
H. W. C. Davis
Hamilton Wright Mabie
Hans Christian Andersen
Harold Avery
Harold McGrath
Harriet Beecher Stowe
Harry Houidini
Helent Hunt Jackson
Helen Nicolay
Hendy David Thoreau
Henrik Ibsen
Henry Adams
Henry Ford
Henry Frost
Henry James
Henry Jones Ford
Henry Seton Merriman
Henry Wadsworth
Longfellow
Henry W Longfellow
Herbert A. Giles
Herbert N. Casson
Herman Hesse
Homer
Honore De Balzac

Horace Walpole
Horatio Alger, Jr.
Howard Pyle
Howard R. Garis
Hugh Lofting
Hugh Walpole
Humphry Ward
Ian Maclaren
Israel Abrahams
J.G.Austin
J. Henri Fabre
J. M. Barrie
J. Macdonald Oxley
J. S. Knowles
J. Storer Clouston
Jack London
Jacob Abbott
James Allen
James Lane Allen
James Andrews
James Baldwin
James DeMille
James Joyce
James Oliver Curwood
James Oppenheim
James Otis
Jane Austen
Jens Peter Jacobsen
Jerome K. Jerome
John Burroughs
John F. Kennedy
John Gay
John Glasworthy
John Habberton
John Joy Bell
John Milton
John Philip Sousa
Jonathan Swift
Joseph Carey
Joseph Conrad
Joseph Jacobs
Julian Hawthrone
Julies Vernes
Justin Huntly McCarthy
Kakuzo Okakura
Kenneth Grahame
Kate Langley Bosher
L. A. Abbot
L. T. Meade
L. Frank Baum
Laura Lee Hope

Laurence Housman
Leo Tolstoy
Leonid Andreyev
Lewis Carroll
Lilian Bell
Lloyd Osbourne
Louis Tracy
Louisa May Alcott
Lucy Fitch Perkins
Lucy Maud Montgomery
Lydia Miller Middleton
Lyndon Orr
M. H. Adams
Margaret E. Sangster
Margaret Vandercook
Maria Edgeworth
Maria Thompson Daviess
Mariano Azuela
Marion Polk Angellotti
Mark Overton
Mark Twain
Mary Austin
Mary Cole
Mary Rowlandson
Mary Wollstonecraft
Shelley
Max Beerbohm
Myra Kelly
Nathaniel Hawthrone
O. F. Walton
Oscar Wilde
Owen Johnson
P.G.Wodehouse
Paul and Maple Thorn
Paul G. Tomlinson
Paul Severing
Peter B. Kyne
Plato
R. Derby Holmes
R. L. Stevenson
Rabindranath Tagore
Rahul Alvares
Ralph Waldo Emmerson
Rene Descartes
Rex E. Beach
Richard Harding Davis
Richard Jefferies
Robert Barr
Robert Frost
Robert Gordon Anderson
Robert L. Drake

Robert Lansing
Robert Michael Ballantyne
Robert W. Chambers
Rosa Nouchette Carey
Ross Kay
Rudyard Kipling
Samuel B. Allison
Samuel Hopkins Adams
Sarah Bernhardt
Selma Lagerlof
Sherwood Anderson
Sigmund Freud
Standish O'Grady
Stanley Weyman
Stella Benson
Stephen Crane
Stewart Edward White
Stijn Streuvels
Swami Abhedananda
Swami Parmananda
T. S. Ackland
The Princess Der Ling
Thomas A. Janvier
Thomas A Kempis
Thomas Anderton
Thomas Bailey Aldrich
Thomas Bulfinch
Thomas De Quincey
Thomas H. Huxley
Thomas Hardy
Thomas More
Thornton W. Burgess
U. S. Grant
Valentine Williams
Victor Appleton
Virginia Woolf
Walter Scott
Washington Irving
Wilbur Lawton
Wilkie Collins
Willa Cather
Willard F. Baker
William Makepeace
Thackeray
William W. Walter
Winston Churchill
Yei Theodora Ozaki
Young E. Allison
Zane Grey